Caitlyn broke the silence first and spoke with what little of her patience remained. "I'm going to say this once, and I'll say it slow so that you get it the first time around." She walked over to the door and placed her hand on the knob. "I'm not one of your pastime passions. There is no we, no us, no nothing." Unlocking the door, she snatched it open. "Now get that through that thick skull of yours and leave."

In two powerful strides, Marcel was in front of her. "That's where you're wrong, kitten. Despite what you think about me or your perception of who I am, you can't deny there's something between us."

She inched up her eyebrow. "You wanna bet?"

A confident smile touched his lips. "I'll bet every dime I've got on it." He caressed her cheek with the pad of his thumb. "And the feelings between us tell me I'll win this bet, lady, hands down."

Without waiting for her response, he walked out.

WHEN I'M WITH YOU

LACONNIE TAYLOR-JONES

Genesis Press, Inc.

Indigo

An imprint of Genesis Press, Inc.
Publishing Company

Genesis Press, Inc.
P.O. Box 101
Columbus, MS 39703

ISBN-13: 978-1-58571-250-2
ISBN-10: 1-58571-250-7
Manufactured in the United States of America

First Edition

Visit us at www.genesis-press.com or call at 1-888-Indigo-1

DEDICATION

*To the matriarchs of African-American romance
whose shoulders I stand on and who opened the doors
for so many to follow.*

ACKNOWLEDGEMENTS

So many people have shared in this wonderful three-year journey on my path to becoming a published writer that I hardly know where to begin in expressing my heartfelt thanks.

First and foremost, I thank God for all He has given. Through Him, I received the patience, wisdom, creativity, and endurance needed to help make the dream of becoming a published romance author a reality.

To my soul mate and best friend, my husband Colin, I thank you. Thank you for your words of encouragement when I wanted to quit. I especially thank you for all the times you gathered our children and quietly took them to the park, so I could squeeze in another hour or two of uninterrupted writing.

To my children, Christian, Caelin, Colin, and Caryn who share with me everyday how proud they are of their mom, Honey, writer or not.

To Susan Malone, Karlyn Thayer, and Chandra Sparks-Taylor who helped guide me in shaping this story.

To my friend and author, Beverly Jenkins, who unselfishly gave me her time and the benefit of her experience as a published writer.

To the members of the San Francisco and Black Diamond Romance Writers chapters, thanks ladies.

PROLOGUE

Marcel Baptiste rested his head against the shower wall, his eyes drifting shut. Relaxation washed over him as the hot water from the massaging showerhead sprayed across his face. He felt as if twenty years had been added to his life in the last forty-eight hours.

The past two days had been nonstop. He had delivered the keynote address at the annual conference for the National Automobile Association held in Atlanta. Countless meetings in stuffy conference rooms, late-night strategy sessions that, coupled with the three-hour time change, had taken their toll on his thirty-eight-year-old body. He was grateful to finally be headed home to Oakland to wrap up the bid for his newest automobile dealership.

After the soothing shower and an hour-long workout, Marcel donned a pair of jeans, a cap, T-shirt and tennis shoes. With soaring adrenaline and razor sharp concentration, he leisurely strode back to the main cabin of his Execuliner jet.

"Mr. Baptiste, we're cruising at an altitude of thirty-seven thousand feet over the Rockies. If our tailwind holds, we should land about twenty minutes ahead of schedule." The words from his long-time pilot, Russ Jenkins, were welcome news. Marcel decided to squeeze in more work before he landed.

Sitting down in a plush-leather seat next to the window, he grabbed the lone item atop his cherrywood desk: the proposal to fund a youth center in East Oakland. He'd read it umpteen times over the last three weeks. His desire to help the underprivileged, especially youth, had him spending every available moment he could spare considering the East Oakland Youth Center's request. As he flipped through the dog-eared pages, he easily found the key points he'd circled. Each of them stirred his philanthropic commitment to worthy causes.

His vow to share his wealth with others was as steadfast as his commitment to accomplish his goals. His astute business ability had made his family's business, BF Automotive Enterprises, the top-ranked Black-owned dealership in the country. Under his leadership, the company had maintained several years of steady growth and enjoyed skyrocketing profits. Three years ago, he'd launched a mammoth expansion plan throughout the nine Bay Area counties in California, expanding the BMW dealership from three to eleven. Company revenues would easily exceed the billion-dollar mark by year's end, three months ahead of schedule.

A wrinkle etched along Marcel's forehead as he tried to figure out how the grant writer knew he was a philanthropist. He'd always believed that generosity and publicity didn't mix, so he'd insisted on complete anonymity in the various causes he'd funded over the years, and had gone to great lengths to ensure he couldn't be connected to his sizeable donations.

Trailing his finger along the proposal's edge, he closed it and placed it back on his desk. In the past five years, he had received scores of proposals, and he'd personally read them all. This one had a uniqueness he couldn't explain. Whoever had written the proposal had lived the words they'd written. Over the years, Marcel made many decisions based on instinct alone and his sixth sense was telling him to relinquish his steadfast rule of anonymity. He wanted to put a face to the grant writer's name.

He wanted to meet Caitlyn Thompson.

CHAPTER 1

Two days later – Oakland, California

"What the hell do you mean, we have a problem securing the dealership?" Seated inside his corporate office in downtown San Francisco, Marcel's baritone voice was sharp enough to split a single strand of hair.

Ken Terrell shook his head in frustration and sighed. "Marcel, I'm just as dumfounded as you are, but someone upped our bid for the dealership."

"Why?" Marcel shot to his feet and angrily paced the length of his glass-topped desk as he listened to the explanation from his vice president of operations and second in command.

In the business world, Marcel had garnered a reputation for scrupulous fairness and unmatched ruthlessness, especially when someone told him no. His usual controlled and tempered nature was teetering on the brink of eruption at the news he was hearing. He had no reason to doubt Ken who had been with the company from day one when his father, Alcee Baptiste, started the business with one dealership. He stopped pacing and glanced over at Ken who appeared to be as frustrated as he was. But nothing Ken had said so far made any sense. How could something as simple as acquiring a twelfth car dealership create such a problem?

Marcel flung his head back and pinched the bridge of his nose. He'd heard enough bad news and sat heavily. "Listen, find out what the problem is and get back to me as soon as you can."

"Will do." Ken slid a folder inside his briefcase and stood. "Marcel, do me a favor and get your mind off this bid for a while, okay? Why don't you stop by the Oakland dealership before going home?"

Marcel's smile was flinty. "Is that an order?"

Ken stood near the door and chuckled. "No, but it's a suggestion you would do well to heed."

Marcel watched as Ken left and quietly closed the door. Releasing a loud groan, he swung his arm up and glanced at his gold watch. "Dammit." It was already two o'clock, and there was no way he'd be able to keep his three o'clock meeting with the grant writer of the proposal for the youth center, Caitlyn Thompson, when he still had more than an hour's drive ahead of him.

He pressed the intercom on his phone with more force than intended and spoke with forced patience. "Marilyn." Marilyn Jenkins, the wife of his pilot Russ, had been his executive assistant for the past five years and ran his office with the precision of a synchronized swim team.

"Yes, sir." Marilyn replied in a calm, strong alto voice.

"Cancel my three o'clock."

"You sure about that?"

Generally, Marilyn's opposition to his directives didn't faze him. She was one of the few people who had the balls to challenge him and win. But after the news Ken just delivered, he wasn't in the mood to listen to logic, even if it was in his best interest. "Just cancel it."

Marilyn cleared her throat. "I'm sorry, I didn't catch your last request, sir."

He inhaled deeply and slowly released his breath. His tone softened to a sweet plea once he realized he hadn't uttered Marilyn's favorite word. "Please."

"All right. A reschedule date?"

"Let me get back to you on that one."

"Aren't you the one who scheduled the meeting in the first place?"

She had him there. He picked up his Palm Pilot and carefully studied his calendar. He did want to reschedule his meeting with Caitlyn, sooner rather than later. Marilyn knew how he loathed having to cancel meetings, especially those he initiated. "How about Monday, say ten o'clock. Happy now?"

She answered in her best I-thought-you'd-see-it my-way tone. "I am now."

All he could do was shake his head and smile. The woman had the innate ability to read him with her eyes closed. He grabbed the inventory report from the center of his desk. Tension rode his shoulders like a freight train. Rotating his neck provided some relief, but fifteen minutes later, he realized it had settled even deeper. Plus, he was still on page one and didn't recall a thing he'd read. Sighing, he conceded his day was shot to hell. He tossed the report onto the desk and stood. Grabbing his suit coat off the back of his chair, he slipped it on. The more he thought about it, he realized Ken was right. Perhaps a visit to his Oakland-based dealership wasn't a bad idea.

"Not now, dear God, not now," Caitlyn Thompson anxiously cried out when her late-model BMW jerked as she approached the westbound entrance to the Caldecott Tunnel just outside the Oakland city limits. She didn't need to spend a lot of time analyzing this dilemma. She wasn't going to make it through.

With less than twenty feet to go before she entered the mile-long span, her car released another not-so-friendly mutter and a swirl of blue-gray smoke drifted over the front windshield. Seconds later, she smelled fumes from her tailpipe. She had about as much faith her car would make it through the tunnel as she did in men. Both registered a zero on her scale.

The car hesitated when she shifted from first to second in the bumper-to-bumper traffic, but there was little she could do about it. She couldn't even move to the shoulder. She gripped the steering wheel with determination, pulled her bottom lip between her teeth as she got to the tunnel's entrance, and prayed. "Oh, dear God, just let me make it through." The car slowed and California drivers, infamous for their lack of patience, blasted their horns behind her.

On this hot Thursday afternoon, the temperature had hit triple digits. She regretted the decision to put the top up on her merlot-red convertible before starting home and would've made a deal with the devil himself at that moment to turn on the car's air conditioner. Despite being mechanically inept, even she knew that turning on the air would cause the car to flat line. Perspiration plastered her shoulder-length hair to the back of her neck like Saran Wrap. She fumbled in her purse and found her mother-of-pearl comb. In between gear changes, she piled the mass of wavy, black curls on top of her head and pushed the comb through.

Her afternoon had ended in a futile attempt to secure the funding needed to keep the doors open at the East Oakland Youth Center. As the center's executive director, part of her responsibilities included fundraising and grant writing. She did it well by relying on the skills she'd obtained working as the CEO at a corporate philanthropy foundation overseeing hundreds of grants each year. It was the first day of July, and short of a miracle, the center would close by year's end. After receiving a call from the associate of a wealthy philanthropist who'd expressed interest in funding the center, she'd traveled to Concord for their meeting, only to learn after arriving that the meeting had been cancelled.

To say she was annoyed was an understatement. She'd driven out to no-man's-land for what? she mused. A cancelled meeting due to an emergency? An argument with an overly secretive receptionist named Sherry who wouldn't reveal the philanthropist's identity? Plus, she'd skipped lunch. Her slender fingers drummed against the steering wheel.

"Yeah, I just bet you had an emergency."

With just a few feet to go before she was out of the tunnel, the car backfired and her frustration escalated. "Darn it. What else can go wrong?"

She wasn't sure how, but as she did in all the other difficult times in her life, she made it through. Pulling off at the first exit, she spotted a gas station a few feet away. No sooner had she turned into the station's entrance than the engine died and the car coasted to a halt.

Caitlyn took a deep breath and peered out the front windshield to determine where the heck she was. Even with her sunglasses on, she shielded her eyes against the sun to make out the street sign above. Piedmont Avenue. The name was unfamiliar and she chewed the nail of her right index finger. "Oh, God, where am I?"

She was originally from New Jersey and had lived in Oakland for six months. The only area with which she was even remotely familiar was the two-mile stretch between her one-bedroom apartment in East Oakland and the youth center. Putting in thirteen-hour days to scrape up every dime she could for the center left little time for much else. Saturdays were spent volunteering at the center and on Sundays, she hung out with her best friend since college, Victoria Bennett.

Caitlyn saw a shadow approaching her car from behind. Instantly, her heart began to pound and her palms became clammy. Snatching her purse off the passenger seat, she frantically dumped everything out looking for a can of mace. As the shadow came closer, she locked the doors and prayed her ex-boyfriend, Cole Mazzei, hadn't found her. Moments later, she breathed a sigh of relief

9

when she realized the shadow was an elderly lady walking her dog.

Once her heart settled, Caitlyn picked up her wallet and counted. Two twenties and some change weren't much if major repairs were needed. She sighed and bitterly thought about the fact she'd been forced to stop using her credit and ATM cards. Every transaction she'd made for almost three years had been cash only, another painful reminder of Cole. She didn't even own a cell phone because she feared it would be another way for him to track her whereabouts.

"Come on, Caitlyn, think, think."

With her head against the headrest, she released a weary sigh. She was sweaty, tired and hungry. Spotting a pay phone, she got out, went to it, and thumbed through the yellow pages. She called the first tow company she found and waited.

When the tow truck pulled up to the BMW dealership in Oakland forty-five minutes later, Caitlyn glanced at her watch, figuring the service department would close in fifteen minutes. The last thing she wanted to do was leave her car on the back of a tow truck overnight. What if someone stole it? She knew if she stuck to her budget, she had enough money to live comfortably on for a couple of years, at least. But her budget had not been designed to take on a car note.

Grateful for the cool air circulating in the empty service room, Caitlyn stood at the door swiping at the tiny beads of sweat at her temple.

"Hello." Her greeting bounced off the walls, and her second attempt didn't fare much better. Since the doors weren't locked, she knew someone had to be inside, so she walked behind the service desk and headed toward an opening. Two steps later, the heel of her right shoe caught on the floor mat. As she tried to avoid falling, a pair of hands grabbed her at the waist. Straightening, she realized that her rescuer topped her by more than a foot. He had to be six-three, if not more, because she was a half inch shorter than five feet. She was close enough to detect the citrus scent of his aftershave, but had to tilt her head back to see his face. And when she did, her mouth dropped. He was drop-dead, make-you-want-to-scream gorgeous.

"T-Thank you." Her breath hitched from the fire of his touch and she tried to think of something else to say, but her mind went completely blank.

Beautiful eyes, Marcel's brain registered. "How can I help you today, ma'am?"

She never took her gaze away from his smooth café-au-lait face and aimed her finger toward the door. "My car died and since you were the nearest BMW dealership, the towing company brought it here."

He nodded. "All right. Where is it?"

Together, they headed to the door where she pointed to the tow truck and glanced up at his profile. "I know you're about to close, but do you think you could take a look at it?"

"Not a problem."

Marcel had made the drive across the Bay Bridge from San Francisco to Oakland in record time. Business was brisk, and once he'd settled in, he learned his service technician, Sean Richards, had taken ill around noon and left. Marcel had quickly changed out of his black linen suit and collarless raw silk shirt and put on Sean's uniform to lend a hand. Around half past four, things had calmed down and he decided to change and head out. He'd just placed his watch on his wrist when he heard the front door open. At the sound of the soft, melodious voice that called out, he'd gravitated toward the lobby.

It wasn't until she pushed her sunglasses on top of her head that he got an unobstructed view of the woman's oval face. Oh, yeah, he liked everything he saw. He'd bet his year-end bonus she didn't weigh more than a hundred pounds. She was stunning in a red silk dress that draped below a slender waistline and fell just short of her knees. The straps on her pumps wrapped around slim ankles that connected to a pair of shapely legs. But it was those eyes he'd first noticed. Dark brown and slanted, they were mesmerizing, and he was spellbound.

"Tell you what, let me go and take a look at your car." He motioned to the space behind her. "Have a seat in the customer waiting area. Shouldn't take me more than a few moments to see what's going on."

Ten minutes passed, and Caitlyn surged to her feet when she saw him open the door. But the sudden jolt made her lightheaded, and a wave of nausea hit her. She slumped back to the chair and rested her head on top of her knees.

Marcel squatted in front of her, his voice filled with concern. "Ma'am, are you okay?"

"I'm sorry." Caitlyn managed to say the words a few moments later, embarrassed. She flashed a weak smile. "Guess that's what happens when you don't eat all day."

Marcel stood. "Here, let me get you some water."

She shook her head. "No, please. I'm fine. Just moved a little too fast, that's all." God, she'd taken up enough of his time. The woeful look in his gray-green eyes concerned her, and she sensed it was bad news concerning her car. "Can you fix it?"

"I can, but not tonight."

Caitlyn looked away, then back at him again as she pulled her bottom lip between her teeth. "Any idea of what it'll cost to fix it?"

He shook his head and answered truthfully. "I won't know that until tomorrow."

Worried the expenses would be astronomical, Caitlyn was almost too afraid to ask the question, but she did anyway. "Are we talking a…lot?"

"Well, that depends on what you consider a lot."

"A thousand?" She held her breath and waited.

"Hmm, not that much. You've got a problem with your fuel line and a couple of sensors. My best estimate right now is around five hundred."

Caitlyn swallowed the urge to scream. Tension seeped along the space between her neck and shoulders, and the sharp, prickling sensation felt like stickpins. She needed her car, period. But five hundred dollars? At that moment, she was so tired, she couldn't think straight. She figured the best thing to do was head home, get a good night's sleep, and worry about the car expenses the next morning.

"I see." She stood and extended her hand. "Well, thank you for your help anyway. I'm sorry I bothered you." She placed the strap of the purse on her shoulder and headed for the door.

The cloud of distress that pierced her eyes didn't go unnoticed, and Marcel certainly didn't want to add to her frustration. From behind, he called out. "Wait. How are you getting home?"

She stopped and turned around. "I'll call a taxi."

Marcel walked toward her. "Tell you what, let me give you a loaner car for tonight, Mrs.—"

"I'm not married, and I prefer to call a cab." She glanced around the room. "Perhaps there's a phone I could use?"

"Ma'am, you don't need to call a cab. The loaner is part of our service."

Marcel quickly turned and made his way toward the service desk, subtly making the sign of the cross to whatever fate that had landed this Nairobian beauty at his doorstep. Grabbing the necessary paperwork, he placed the key to the loaner in his pocket and took the seat next to her. "We can settle up your bill tomorrow when your car's ready, and I'll do my best to stay within the five-hundred-dollar range."

He looked over the information she handed back to him and frowned slightly. C. R. Thompson. That couldn't be her full name, he thought. And even if by some off chance it was, it didn't tell him a whole lot. He wanted vital statistics, like her address, telephone number, and whether she was single, and not necessarily in that order. His thick, black eyebrows bunched as he reviewed several sections of the form she'd left blank. "You didn't put down all your information."

Confused, she stared at him. "Like what?"

Turning to face her, he tilted his head and gave her a quizzical stare. "Address, phone number, you know, the things people give to other people so they can be contacted."

With a pointed look, Caitlyn jerked around in her seat to face him. "You have my car, so there's nothing to worry about. I'm not a thief, and I'm not going to steal your loaner."

"Listen, lady, you're not getting my loaner if I don't get your contact information."

"Fine." She huffed and pointed her nose in the air. "I'll call a cab then."

"Are you always this elusive?"

With a trembling hand, Caitlyn swiped a strand of hair back that had fallen across her face. "No…no. It's nothing like that." At that moment, she was in no position to be ungrateful. He no doubt had a car in working order; she didn't. She took the clipboard, added the information and handed it back. "I'm sorry I was curt and I'm really not trying to be evasive."

You could have fooled me, Marcel thought, dropping the clipboard in the seat next to him without bothering to glance over what she had added. He stood and reached inside his pocket.

Caitlyn focused on the key dangling from a spiral ring on his left index finger. "Uh, listen, thank you for all your help." She grabbed the key and rushed out without a backward glance.

The next day, Marcel abruptly ended a conversation with one of his service managers the moment he looked across the room and noticed Caitlyn standing quietly by the door. "Hi, buddy, give me a sec, okay?" He moved past several customers straight toward her with the grace and agility of a panther ready to pounce.

"I told you I'd be—"

"Come with me." He placed his hand under her elbow and walked them down a hallway.

"Wait. W-Where are you taking me?" Caitlyn's voice was strained and she tried to back away from his hold, not sure what he had in mind.

He didn't bother to answer. Instead, he opened the door to a small conference room, ushered her inside and whirled around. "Why did you run off from me last night?"

"I didn't run from you. I told you I'd be back." Her voice trembled, along with her hand, as she reached inside her purse and pulled out a brown envelope. "How much are the repairs?"

"Five hundred."

She placed the envelope in his hands. "It's all there. You can count it, if you'd like."

He took the envelope and placed it on the table without looking inside. "Listen, we got your car up and running for now at least, but I'm not sure how much longer your engine will hold up."

"I see."

"Have you considered getting a new car?"

"No!" She fumbled with the zipper on her purse before she looked up at him again. "Besides, I can't afford it right now, even if I wanted to. At least this one's paid for."

Marcel urged her to sit in one of the two chairs at the table while he took the other. "Listen, I'm no genius, but it doesn't take one to know that you're awfully edgy."

She nervously chuckled. "Why would you think that?"

"For one thing, you jump every time someone comes near you. And second, getting any information from you requires the skill of a surgeon, which obviously I'm not." He relaxed his long frame and touched his left index finger to his head. "Now tell me, if you were me, what would you think?"

Long, black lashes swept across her high cheekbones. "It has nothing to do with you, honestly." After a pregnant pause, she stared at the carpeted floor, her voice a mere whisper. "I-I just try to keep a low profile, that's all."

"You don't have anything to fear from me, okay? If I can help you, I will." He pulled a business card from his shirt pocket, picked up a Cross pen and wrote on the back. He slid it to her. "Just in case."

Picking up the card, she smiled. "All your digits, huh?" He'd even given her his home address. She slipped the card inside her purse. "Thanks, but I'm okay."

It took a bit of persuasion, but Marcel finally convinced Caitlyn to grab a bite to eat with him at the restaurant across the street. It looked like a hole-in-the-wall, but they served the best burgers and fries in town. Marcel noticed during lunch that the uneasiness and nervousness she'd shown earlier had disappeared. Afterward, they enjoyed a couple of café mochas.

He placed his cup on the table and looked across at her. "Do I detect a slight East Coast accent?"

Her smile was soft, warm. "Darn it, I thought I'd lost it."

Shaking his head, he smiled back. "No such luck. So, where're you from?"

"Newark."

"Certainly not Newark, California."

She arched her brow. "There's a Newark, California?"

"You got it. About twenty miles or so from Oakland."

"Really? Well, my Newark is in New Jersey."

"So, what brings you to California?"

She shrugged. "A lot of things."

"I see." There was that evasiveness again. He decided to try a different approach. "So, what do you do?"

"I run a youth center."

"Here in Oakland?"

She nodded.

"Which one?"

"The East Oakland Youth Center."

Startled, Marcel felt his chest collide with the table edge. "The one on Webster Street?" He needed to confirm it was the same one he'd received the funding request from three weeks ago.

"Yes. Do you know about us?"

He nodded. "In a manner of speaking, I do."

Inclining her head sideways, her brow rose. "How?"

His response was temporarily trapped in his throat as he observed her striking beauty. Her gorgeous ebony skin without a single blemish and the same shade as dark chocolate was alluring. It was so striking she looked like a priceless piece of onyx. His gaze drifted to her pointed nose and the lushness of her mouth. Forget attractive. She was absolutely exquisite.

"I've worked with a lot of community programs over the years." He propped his elbows on the table. "So, tell me more about the center." Not only did he hope to find out firsthand about the center's programs, hopefully he'd learn more about the beauty seated across from him.

Placing her cup down, Caitlyn's passion for her job burst forth, along with a smile as bright as the lights in Times Square. "We have a reading and literacy club for our elementary and middle school kids. Oh, and our investment club has taught the kids a lot about how to manage their money." She clapped, threw her head back and laughed. "I think I'll hire a couple of the kids as my personal investors soon. Anyway, we offer conflict resolution, and I'd love to add a mentoring program."

"What's stopping you?"

"Funding—or lack of, I should say."

"You enjoy what you do, don't you?"

She smiled. "Yeah, I really do."

"How did you get into this?"

"I grew up in the inner city and spent a lot of time at the local youth center in my neighborhood. I saw firsthand the struggles that come from a lack of economic development in poor communities."

"So you decided to do something about it, huh?"

"I didn't initially start out doing this, but I'm happy with it."

"So, what did you do before this?"

"Corporate philanthropy."

"Really? Why did you quit?"

She sucked in a deep breath and released it. "Personal reasons." Glancing at her watch, she reached for her purse. "I really do need to get back to the center."

Marcel didn't want the time they had shared to end so soon, and his mind raced to think of a way to prevent it from happening. He inconspicuously inched his hand across the table until the glass of water in front of her tumbled over. "Oh, God—" He grabbed a handful of napkins from the holder. "I'm sorry about that. I guess I'm showing off my clumsiness today."

"It's okay." Caitlyn quickly rose to her feet and scooped her purse off the table to avoid the spreading pool of liquid. She glanced down at the water dripping on the floor. "Here, let me have a few of those."

"There you go." Marcel placed several napkins in her hand and nodded at her purse. "Here, let's put your purse over here so it doesn't get wet." He placed it in his seat as she bent to mop the floor. While Caitlyn's attention was diverted, he stopped long enough to unzip her bag and tuck the envelope of money she'd given him earlier inside. He straightened quickly as she stood.

Once they settled down again, he smiled. "We've known each other for almost twenty-four hours, and I still don't know your first name."

She chuckled. "I'm sorry. It's Caitlyn." She extended her hand across the table. "Caitlyn Thompson."

Well, well, well. This was the Caitlyn Thompson who'd written the funding proposal and the one he'd known only by name for the last three weeks. He made a mental note to be sure to get to mass early on Sunday and light a candle for this blessing. Marcel took back what he'd told himself three days earlier about wanting to meet the grant writer. Meeting her wasn't enough. Now he wanted to get to know Caitlyn on a personal level.

"Marcel Baptiste." He slipped his hand from hers. "Any luck with that funding?"

"No. I was supposed to meet with a potential funder yesterday, but the meeting was cancelled." She lifted her chin high with determination. "But don't worry, I'll get another meeting."

Marcel gazed her intently. The confidence in her eyes was just as impressive as the challenge in her voice. "Have dinner with me, Caitlyn."

"I don't think—"

"I'll meet you wherever you say. Just say yes."

"It's not that simple."

"It is that simple. Say yes."

"No."

He hitched his brow. "No?"

She chuckled. "Must be an echo in here, huh?"

"Why not?"

"Because I don't know you."

He smiled again. "Well, that's the whole purpose for dinner, so we can get to know each other." Driven by the need to know this woman better, he leaned forward slightly, his words a hushed whisper. "Say yes, Caitlyn."

"I appreciate the invitation, but I think I'll pass."

He mockingly clutched his hands to his heart. "I'm mortally wounded by your words."

A grin worked at her jaw. "Are you always this persistent?"

With his face void of any expression, he answered easily. "Yes."

"Why?"

"Because I don't accept the word *no*."

"My instincts tell me very few people say that word to you."

His compelling gaze bore into her hesitant one. "Always trust your instincts."

With her bottom lip pulled between her teeth, she contemplated the offer. "Anywhere I say, right?"

He nodded. "Anywhere you say."

"And you promise—"

"To be on my best behavior." He finished off her sentence and lifted his left hand, flashing the Boy Scout salute.

She conceded with a nod. "All right, I'll meet you at the dealership around seven."

CHAPTER 2

Caitlyn adamantly shook her head when Marcel reached over to grab the dinner check the waitress had placed in the center of their table. She slipped several bills inside the leather folder.

"It's the least I can do, since I just mysteriously found an envelope of money in my purse."

He chuckled. "All right, I'm busted. Your car is on the house."

"Listen, Marcel, I really do appreciate the gesture." She released a long sigh and shook her head at the same time. "But I can't accept it."

"Why not?"

"Let's just say I learned a hard lesson about accepting a person's generosity a while ago."

He cocked his head. "I'm not following you."

"My last relationship…" Her voice trembled and she dropped her head. Finally, she glanced up at Marcel and saw his puzzled expression, the kind marked, "Explain this to me." How did she reveal she had been on the run for almost three years from an ex-boyfriend who had flat out stalked her? And how could she tell Marcel, or any man for that matter, what Cole had done to her the last time he found her? She briefly shut her eyes, trying to block out the pain. Revealing that hurt to him was out of the question. Her trust in the male species had disappeared three years earlier. She quickly shifted gears to another topic. "So, tell me about you."

He settled himself comfortably in his chair, but wasn't at all oblivious to the fact that she hadn't finished her statement about her past. "There's really not a lot to tell. I have a twin sister, and we have two brothers and two sisters who are younger." He smiled. "And then there's Mama Z. She's my maternal grandmother and helped my dad raise our rowdy crew after my mother died."

She smiled sadly. "I always wanted a big family."

He paused and lifted his glass to his lips. "Do you have family back in New Jersey?"

"No. I'm an only child. I lost my mother a long time ago, and I never knew my father."

"I'm sorry." Marcel spoke sincerely. He leaned forward and cleared his throat. "You need to know something."

"What's that?"

"I'm not him."

She stared, stunned at the boldness of his statement, but decided asking what he meant would make her look like a complete idiot since in her heart she knew exactly what he was referring to. "I never said you were."

"But you're determined to keep your distance from me, right?"

"At this point in my life, from anyone, so don't feel like the Lone Ranger here."

"Remember, Caitlyn, I don't accept the word *no* very well."

She looked down and toyed with the edge of a napkin. "There's a first time for everything, Marcel." Her breathing almost stopped at his assessing gaze. "Is something stuck on my face?"

His eyes never left hers. "It wouldn't matter if it was. They're beautiful."

"What?" She'd never considered herself to be a stunning beauty when she was younger, and at thirty-seven, she didn't stand a chance. She looked at the enamel gems on her antique gold charm bracelet. "My bracelet?"

"No. Your eyes. They're beautiful."

She placed her hands in her lap and slowly lifted her head. "Thank you." She glanced around at the back of her chair and grabbed her purse. "I better head home."

"Have dinner with me tomorrow night?"

"No."

He gave her a sexy smile. "You're saying the "n" word again."

She chuckled this time. "Since you don't like hearing the word, how's this?" She pointed her right thumb downward.

"Was everything to your satisfaction?" Their waitress walked up and asked the question when she picked up the leather folder containing the money.

They both nodded.

The waitress smiled. "That's good. You two have a great evening."

After the waitress left, Marcel's devastatingly sexy grin returned. "I don't give up easily."

Caitlyn braced both hands beneath her chin. "Somehow, I get the feeling you're telling the truth, the whole truth, and nothing but the truth."

Marcel saw Caitlyn safely to her car. After she drove off, he stood in the parking lot at a total loss to explain the feelings bombarding him. What was it about this woman that had him tied up in knots? She'd captivated him from the moment he'd laid eyes on her.

It wasn't until her taillights disappeared that Marcel released the pent-up emotions he'd held in check most of the evening. He wasn't sure what he was feeling, but whatever it was, it was too strong to ignore. He had to find a way to maneuver around Caitlyn's reluctance to get to know him, and at the same time, convince her he was nothing like the man who'd obviously caused her pain. He also had to find a way to tell her he'd known about her and her center for the past three weeks.

He needed a plan, and he needed one fast because he had only one mission now: getting to know Caitlyn Thompson a lot better.

Caitlyn hurriedly unlocked the front door to her apartment, closing it behind her almost before she got inside, and scrambled to find the nearby light switch. Maybe one day her fear of Cole would disappear. But until then, she'd do what she'd done every night for almost three years: search her apartment from top to bottom.

With mace in hand, she looked under the bed, peeked inside every closet and checked all the windows to be sure they were locked. Only then did she drop her purse on a small table in the living room and shrug out of her navy blue suit jacket. Releasing a long sigh of contentment, she walked through the brightly lit, sparsely furnished space.

The six-hundred-square-foot apartment was a far cry from the two-bedroom penthouse she'd fled from in New Jersey, but it was definitely a step above the out-of-the-way motels she'd stayed in as she zigzagged her way to Oakland. With the horror of her relationship behind her now, the only thing that mattered at the moment was that she was safe.

Finally, she noticed the blinking light on her answering machine in the bedroom. At least she didn't have to worry that Cole had gotten her telephone number since the number was listed in the name of the youth center, and he didn't have a clue where she worked. She knew exactly who'd left the message. Before she could check the caller ID to be sure, the phone rang.

"Yes."

Her best friend, Victoria, roared into the conversation full speed ahead. "Uh-uh. Don't 'yes' me. Girl, where the hell have you been all evening? I called at our usual time and there was no answer. I was worried sick and just short of calling the police."

Chuckling, Caitlyn sat on the side of the bed and kicked her shoes toward the closet. Once she removed her pantyhose, she slowly massaged the soles of her feet, and decided to say something she knew would ruffle her best friend's feathers even more.

"And a very pleasant evening to you, too, Victoria."

"Stop. You know I hate it when you call me Victoria. What's going on, girl? Give up the tapes. Remember, this is me, your friend—your best friend, I might add."

Caitlyn knew once Vic started in on something, she wasn't going to stop until she got what she wanted. "Vic, I'm okay." She stood and reached behind to unzip her skirt and wiggled her hips until it pooled at her feet.

"You sure?" Vic paused. "You're always home and in bed before the highlights of the ten o'clock news finish."

Caitlyn had placed the phone on the nightstand to pull her blouse over her head and missed Vic's last statement. She picked up the phone again.

"Caitlyn?"

"Hmmm?"

"Did you hear what I just said?"

"Uh…"

"I said…oh, never mind. I didn't know if he—"

"No, Vic, Cole hasn't found me."

"That's good." Vic blew out a sigh of relief. "But where have you been?"

Stretched out on the double bed, clad in a pair of silk navy blue panties and a matching bra, Caitlyn lay on her back with the receiver cradled between her neck and shoulder. With a schoolgirl's enthusiasm, she proceeded to share the activities of the past two days, including her lunch and dinner with Marcel. "Vic, there's something about him that I like—a lot."

Vic's voice went up at least two octaves. "Child, status report on the man."

Caitlyn sat up and tucked her legs beneath her. "There's only one word to describe him."

"What's that?"

"Fine." Caitlyn was so excited she gurgled. "Oh, listen, he wears his hair in a low-cut fade."

"Girl…"

"I know. He has a beard, but it's trimmed close enough, you know, that you can see a really deep dimple, but only on the left side though."

"Shut up."

With her arms wrapped around her waist, Caitlyn chuckled. "I know."

"So, when am I going to get to meet this fine brother?"

Caitlyn frowned and her enthusiasm faded as quickly as it came. "Vic, don't go there. I just met the man. He was kind enough to help me out. He took me to lunch, and we had dinner tonight. That's it."

"Okay, okay, but I'm telling you, you snooze, you lose."

"Good night, Vic. Love you."

"Love you, too."

Overcome with exhaustion, Caitlyn slipped between the cool, crisp sheets and pulled the comforter to her chin. She knew she needed to go to sleep, but every time she shut her eyes, she saw Marcel's face. For almost three years, she'd been forced to live underground, afraid to lead a normal existence. But since arriving in Oakland six months earlier, she had started to feel safer. And much of the security she felt came from the love and protection Vic and Vic's family had provided. Twenty-four hours ago, though, her serene life had taken an unexpected twist because she'd never been attracted to any man as she was to Marcel.

Before she knew what had hit her, she threw back the comforter and found herself in the middle of her living room. Retrieving Marcel's business card from her purse, she scanned the neat penmanship on the back. Maybe Vic was right about snoozing and losing. Although she was attracted to Marcel, she wondered whether she had the capacity to ever trust a man again. Tears blurred her vision as she returned the card to her purse. Snuggling back under the covers again, Caitlyn had her answer.

She needed to forget about Marcel Baptiste.

Two weeks later, Caitlyn removed her reading glasses and pushed aside the proposal she'd worked on most of the morning when she heard the soft knock at her office door. "Come in."

Marcel stuck his head in. "Caitlyn, sorry I'm late. The traffic coming over the Bay Bridge was a nightmare."

"Hi, Marcel." Caitlyn waved him in and motioned to the chair in front of her desk while admiring his tailor-made navy-blue suit, striped French-cuff shirt and matching silk tie.

Unbuttoning his coat, he sat. "Catch you at a bad time?"

"Not at all. Just let me wrap this up, and I'll be ready to go."

After two weeks, Caitlyn had finally run out of excuses to give Marcel for not going out with him. She'd at last relented and accepted his lunch date.

She rounded the desk and stood in front of him dressed in a floral-print skirt with an asymmetrical hemline, drape-neck top and open-toed sling back sandals, and braced her hip on the desk. "Thanks for inviting me to lunch."

"No, thank you. I thought I was going to starve to death waiting for you to say yes."

"Listen, Marcel, I know I didn't make a good first impression the first two times we met." Pulling her bottom lip between her teeth, she focused on the concrete floor then continued. "I've given you a lot of lame excuses the last couple of weeks. I didn't think you'd want to—"

"Have lunch with you?" Marcel released a soft chuckle. "You're kidding, right?"

She lifted her head and smiled. "No, I'm not kidding. I know my behavior has been a bit strange. I-I just don't want you to think I'm a nutcase, because I'm not."

"Trust me, I don't think that. I'm just glad you've finally released me from my fast." He patted his stomach and smiled. "I lost a few pounds, you know." Peering around her slender frame, he pointed to her desk. "What are you working on over there?"

She looked at the neatly stacked pile and sighed. "Another proposal."

"Don't you have an assistant for that?"

She chuckled and bobbed her head. "Umm-umm. You're looking at her. Our budget can't afford an assistant right now."

"So, who's the proposal to?"

"Anyone and everyone who'd give us money to purchase this building and fund our existing programs."

Marcel frowned. "Why money for the building?"

"Simple. The city owns it, and they've gotten a bid to sell it. We don't have the money to purchase it, and if we don't buy it, we're out the door." Caitlyn's voice was strained. "This center means the world to this community. I've got to find a way to keep it here."

She'd wanted to tell somebody about her frustrations with the building all morning, and getting it off her chest was a relief. She waved her hand in mid-air. "Come on, let's do lunch. I'm starved." She started to move, but stopped. "Oh, wait." She grabbed a small gift-wrapped box from the opposite side.

She'd brought it for Marcel a couple of days after he helped her with her car. Since then, she hadn't had a chance to drop it in the mail, and since he was here, it was a good time to give it to him. "For you. It's not much, but I wanted you to know how much I appreciated everything you did to help me out with my car."

Marcel opened the box and lifted out a small, car-shaped gold charm and smiled. "Thank you."

They had a quick lunch at a nearby Chinese restaurant and afterward, Caitlyn accepted Marcel's offer for an afternoon stroll around Lake Merritt in downtown Oakland. The summer afternoon was perfect; not a cloud marred the sky. Traffic breezed along the street surrounding the lake, and the footpath around the lake's perimeter was filled with bicyclists and joggers.

It seemed that it had been forever since she'd felt a sense of peace and tranquility, and Caitlyn inwardly marveled at how comfortable she was in Marcel's presence. They communicated without words and slowly began their stroll around the two-mile lake. She didn't feel the slightest bit of awkwardness when halfway around, he slipped his hand around hers.

"I've enjoyed the afternoon." Marcel stood next to a bench and swept his hand in front of him.

Caitlyn sat down. "Me, too." She bunched her brows together. "You said earlier you drove over from San Francisco."

"I did." Marcel propped one foot on the bench and rested an elbow on his knee.

"But I thought you worked in Oakland."

"My office is in San Francisco. I work for BF Automotive, and they have eleven dealerships in the Bay Area. The Oakland dealership is one of them."

"Oh, I see." She was silent for a few moments. "So what do you do for them?"

He shrugged. "A little bit of everything."

She tilted her head. "Meaning?"

He chuckled. "Pretty much run all the dealerships."

"So, you're the general manager then?"

"Well, not exactly."

"Okay, then exactly what are you?"

"CEO."

"Oh."

Finally, Marcel sat next to Caitlyn and stretched his arm along the back of the bench. "You never told me how you ended up in Oakland."

"Long story. Trust me."

"I've got time. Trust me."

Her eyes bore into his before shifting to a group of joggers in the distance. She took a deep breath and slowly released it. "I ended up here six months ago after I left Dallas. My best friend, Vic, lives here, and at the time I needed to be around a friend."

Marcel tensed and a frown etched across his forehead. "Uh…this friend, Vic. Are you and he close?"

The comment actually made her laugh out loud. "Yes and no. Yes, we're extremely close. But *he* is a *she*. Vic is short for Victoria."

He smiled and relaxed.

"Vic and I met at Columbia University during our freshman year, and we've been friends ever since." Caitlyn held up her hand. "Let me forewarn you: If you ever meet her and call her Victoria, you'll be minus a head."

He chuckled even though he was confused. "Why?"

"Vic's the youngest of three children, and the only girl. She felt her brothers got to do things she couldn't do simply because she was a girl. So, by the time she was four, she demanded everyone call her Vic. I think the name made her feel like she was one of the boys."

"Got it." He scooted on the bench until he was next to her. "So, how did you end up at the youth center?"

"A stroke of luck, I guess. I met the center's board president, Fran, about four years ago at a conference. A couple of weeks after I settled here, we ran into each other at the grocery store, of all places. She told me about the center and the problems it was having."

Marcel lifted a brow. "Problems?"

"Umm-hmm. Among other things, they don't have the funds to pay me a salary."

"What?" Marcel jumped to his feet and shouted so loud, he attracted the attention of several joggers nearby.

Caitlyn held up her hands in defense. "I know, I know. But it works out for me. For now, in exchange for my salary, they cover my rent, utilities and phone."

"Wait a minute." Marcel shook his head in disbelief. "You don't get a salary?"

"No. But it won't always be like this and its fine for now. I have some money saved, and I won't starve. Listen, I need to get back and finish that proposal. I try to get home before dark." Caitlyn stood and looked up at him. "I really did enjoy lunch. Thank you."

It was around three that afternoon before Marcel arrived back at his office in San Francisco's financial district. On the drive back, he'd thought of nothing but Caitlyn and was flabbergasted she didn't earn a salary. He stopped at the desk of his assistant, Marilyn, before heading to his office.

"Do me a favor."

Marilyn grabbed a pencil and pad. "Shoot."

"Buy the building at 1707 Webster Street in Oakland and have the deed put in the name of the youth center."

"All right." Marilyn looked up. "Anything else?"

"Yeah. Have a contractor go over and estimate the cost of renovations." Marcel gave his instructions without lifting his head while glancing over the messages he'd grabbed off Marilyn's desk. "Inside and out."

"Anything else?"

"I want a check to them by the end of the week." Walking toward his office, he snapped his finger as if suddenly remembering something and spoke over his shoulder. "Wait. Look over their budget again. I didn't see a line item for an administrative assistant, so put it in. Salary needs to be competitive to attract someone with nonprofit experience. Also, call Ken and have him put in a special order for a Z4 that was needed like yesterday."

"Color?"

Marcel smiled lazily at the thought of Caitlyn's sexy feet strapped inside her sandals and shiny painted toenails. "Red."

"Wow." Marilyn stopped writing to work a cramp out her finger. "Finished?"

"No. Add a line item for the director's salary up to say…mid-six figures. The car is for the director."

Marilyn laughed out loud. "Heck, I'll quit here if you hire me over there."

He smiled. "Fat chance."

WHEN I'M WITH YOU

Marilyn pulled the youth center's file from her drawer and frowned once she glanced over the budget. "They don't have a line item for a director's salary."

"Add it." Marcel sat on the edge of Marilyn's desk again. "Make sure their operating expenses are covered at least for the next five years with a five percent salary and cost-of-living increase for staff included." He stood and once more started for his office only to stop in mid-stride. "Condition of funding is that everything be accepted in totality or the grant's denied. Got it?"

"Oh, yes." Marilyn glanced over everything she'd written and did a mental calculation. "You know this will run into the millions, don't you?"

He gave her a nonchalant shrug. "And your point is?"

CHAPTER 3

Two weeks later, Marcel sat with his feet propped on the long cherry wood table in the huge conference room at BF Automotive and carefully reviewed the monthly sales report that his vice president of operations, Ken, had dropped off earlier in the afternoon. Deep in concentration, it took a few seconds for him to register the light tap at the door.

"Looks like you're working hard." The jab came from his father, Alcee Baptiste, who stood in the doorway.

Marcel smiled and stood. "Well, well, glad you could finally join me."

Alcee smiled back. "The benefits of retirement, Son."

Marcel sat and propped his feet up again. "Pop, I need to bring you up to speed. Ken told me a few days ago that we seem to have a little competition for the new dealership. He said that after we placed our initial bid, another dealership from back East raised it. Ken countered, of course, but the other company upped the ante. We all know that financing isn't a problem, but what I don't understand is why someone would shell out more money." He shook his head and frowned. "Something doesn't feel right."

With his hands laced behind his head, Alcee tossed out a possibility. "Perhaps they're getting more money out of the deal on the back end."

Briefly considering the possibility, Marcel rubbed his chin. "But it doesn't make any sense."

"You've got two options, Son. Go for the dealership, but find out what's going on behind the scene, or forget about it."

Marcel nodded and conceded to the wisdom of the man who had almost forty years of experience in the industry. "Tell you what. Let's see what happens with the new bid. If there's still a problem, I'll contact Alex and have him make a few discreet inquiries. It'll be interesting to see what he comes up with."

Marcel's best friend, Alex Robinson, was a top-notched private investigator, and if anyone could get to the bottom of a mystery, Alex could.

Later in the evening around six, Marcel and Alcee were still reviewing sales reports when suddenly Marcel lifted his head. "What's that?"

Alcee listened intently. "Sounds like someone's knocking on your office door."

Marcel got up and walked down the hallway from the conference room to his office and found Caitlyn standing patiently outside.

Caitlyn titled her head back and smiled. "Hi."

"Hi yourself." Marcel placed a soft kiss against her cheek. Glancing at his watch, he sighed, frustrated with himself because he'd lost track of time and the fact they had dinner reservations at Farallon's in San Francisco's Union Square. "I'm sorry. I didn't realize it was so close to seven."

"Don't worry about it."

Marcel and Caitlyn headed back toward the conference room, but before they entered, she stopped abruptly when she realized someone else was there. Placing her hand over her mouth, she slowly backed away. "Oh, Marcel, I'm so sorry. I didn't mean to interrupt your meeting."

"You didn't interrupt anything."

Caitlyn pointed over her shoulder to the waiting room. "Listen, I can wait there until you're finished."

"No way. Come on. You need to meet someone anyway." Marcel placed his hand under her elbow, and they walked inside. "Pop, I'd like you to meet Caitlyn Thompson."

"Ms. Thompson…" Alcee, who was seated with his back to the door, stood and turned. His voice vanished the moment he came face-to-face with Caitlyn.

Caitlyn smiled and extended her hand to Alcee. "Mr. Baptiste, I'm pleased to meet you."

Wide-eyed, Alcee managed to hold his hand out, but stammered over his words. "Uh…I-I'm pleased to meet you."

Marcel turned to Caitlyn. "Let me grab my briefcase. Be right back."

"Marcel's told me a lot about you." With an arched brow, Caitlyn tried to discreetly remove her hand from Alcee's firm grip. "Excuse me. Is everything all right?"

Alcee's hazel eyes were riveted to the antique fourteen-karat gold slide bracelet on Caitlyn's wrist. He jammed his hand inside his pants pocket. "Uh, yes…yes, of course. Everything's fine." He glanced at the bracelet again, recognizing the intricate design scrolled on it. Sweat beaded on his forehead. "I-I'm sorry, I didn't mean to stare. Your bracelet—I was just admiring it."

Caitlyn looked at her wrist and smiled. "Thank you. It was my mother's."

"Your, uh…mother's…" Alcee's words were faint, his voice unsteady.

Caitlyn nodded. "Yes."

"If you don't mind me asking…what is your mother's name?"

"Her name was Della Thompson."

Alcee managed to change the choke rumbling in his throat into a quiet cough. "You said was…"

"My mother passed away several years ago."

Alcee could only stare.

Marcel returned with his briefcase. "Pop, let's call it a night." He moved next to Caitlyn. "We need to get going if we're going to make our reservation."

Alcee nodded and stared at Caitlyn's bracelet again. "Listen, you two enjoy the evening. Uh…I think I'll stay another hour or so before heading out."

Marcel flashed a lopsided grin. "Don't tell me this is coming from the man who brags about retirement?"

Everyone laughed. Alcee left and closed the door behind him. Once they were alone, Marcel turned to Caitlyn who was smiling brightly. "So what has you so happy tonight?" He winked. "Seeing me?"

She giggled softly. "That could be one reason, but really it's because we got the deed to the building and funding for the next five years." Caitlyn's words zoomed out as fast a racecar whizzing around the track at the Daytona 500.

Marcel reached to give her a brief hug, and before he knew it, he had his face burrowed against her scented neck, inhaling her soft, floral fragrance. "And that makes you happy?"

"Oh, yes. Not so much for me, but for the kids. They need it so much." With her arms still looped at his neck, she leaned back, her eyes twinkling with delight. "Know what else?"

"What?"

"The grant offered a salary and car to the director. Can you believe that?"

Marcel didn't acknowledge the question. What gave him joy was seeing the sparkle in her eyes.

"You deserve it, Caitlyn." He grabbed her hand and walked them to the door. He was just about to shut off the lights when he heard a knock and opened the door.

"Hi, Ken. Come on in. Want you to meet someone." Once Ken entered the conference room, Marcel called out to Caitlyn from behind. "Caitlyn, this is Ken Terrell, the man who really runs things around here." He glanced back at Ken. "Ken, I'd like to introduce you to Caitlyn Thompson."

Startled, Ken dropped the folder in his hand the moment Caitlyn faced him. "I-I'm pleased to meet you, C-Caitlyn." He stooped to gather the papers and regain his composure. Then he straightened and glanced at Marcel. "I-I'm sorry. I didn't mean to interrupt anything. I can come back later."

Marcel waved off the apology. "No problem. Listen, Pop is still here if you want to see him." He grabbed

Caitlyn's hand. "Come on. Let's get out of here before we lose our reservation."

Caitlyn tightly clutched her small handbag to her chest. "Thanks again for dinner. It's been a wonderful evening."

Marcel drove Caitlyn back to her apartment after dinner since she'd taken BART to San Francisco to meet him. Seated inside his plush, black BMW, Caitlyn glanced over to find he'd turned his back against the door. From the moment he'd put the car in park, he hadn't said a word, but his penetrating gaze spoke volumes. As far as she was concerned, he didn't need to speak because what she saw in his eyes said it all. She saw unabashed desire and it burned her to a crisp. She knew if they ever got together, they would set off a five-alarm blaze.

Caitlyn tore her gaze away and stared out the front windshield. Fear from the past reared its ugly head. At this point in her life, she didn't want to feel an attraction for any man, and she certainly didn't want to feel it this soon for the one sitting next to her. She'd experienced one disastrous relationship all because she'd foolishly placed her confidence in someone she thought she could trust. That error had nearly destroyed her, and it was one she'd vowed to never make again.

She sucked in a deep breath. "Marcel, I-I don't think we should see each other anymore." The words came out hoarse and choked, despite her best effort to maintain a rock-steady tone.

Marcel frowned. "Why?"

"I-I'm not the right person for you to get involved with."

He shook his head. "You're wrong on that one, Caitlyn." He grabbed her left hand. "Can you honestly sit here and tell me I'm solo in what I'm feeling?"

It was a long while before she could say anything. She could no more deny the attraction she felt for Marcel than not take her next breath. "No, and if I knew how to stop my emotions right now, I would."

He lifted her hand to his mouth and placed a gentle kiss on the back of it. "Tell me what you feel."

She turned to him, staring with a soft gaze. "When?"

"Right now." He kissed the inside of her palm. "Tell me what you're feeling."

"When I'm with you, I feel safe…like nothing in the world can ever hurt me."

"Then hold on to that." Releasing her hand, he inched over and braced his arm along the passenger seat.

Caitlyn glanced over at him. "What do you feel?"

He trailed his finger along her cheek and focused on her lips. "I feel like I'll lose my mind if I don't kiss you." Despite the darkness, he tried to search her eyes for permission. He wouldn't rush her. She'd been hurt once and he vowed no one would ever do it again. He waited patiently for her answer. The moment she looped her arm around his neck and parted her lips, it was all the acknowledgment he needed.

The kiss started out gentle, but grew hotter, more urgent, and she moaned under the assault of his mouth. Marcel deepened the kiss, and she clutched the lapels of his jacket as though they were a life preserver that would protect her against the carnal storm threatening to sweep her out into the Pacific Ocean.

When they parted, Caitlyn fought to breathe, fought to control her heart, which was beating as if she'd run a twenty-mile marathon. With her head bowed, she placed her hand at the center of her chest. "There's something you should know."

Marcel released a long sigh of satisfaction. "Talk to me."

"I-I'm…"

Marcel gently lifted her chin and met her gaze. "Come on, Caitlyn. Talk to me." He stroked his finger along her brow. "You can trust me."

Tears shimmered in her eyes. "He hurt me."

"What did he do?"

The words lodged in her throat. The pain was still too raw, the hurt too deep. Caitlyn shook her head, an indication she wasn't ready to discuss it.

Marcel nodded his acceptance of her stance. "Listen, whenever you're ready, all right?"

With a solemn look, Caitlyn turned her face to hide the fear in her eyes. "I've been running from him for three years."

"Is that why you've been so reluctant to share information about yourself?"

"Yes."

Without uttering another word, Marcel got out and walked around to the other side of the car. He opened the passenger door and helped Caitlyn out.

Caitlyn looked up at him. "Marcel, I'll understand if you don't want my baggage at your doorstep."

He didn't bother to shut the door and kept his gaze steady with hers. "When can I see you again?"

"Why haven't you made any headway with BF Automotive?" Seated behind a huge marble-topped desk, Louis Hennings, president of New York City's largest car dealership, held the phone from his ear and stared at it, unable to believe what he'd just heard.

When he jammed the receiver back to his ear, he shouted, "You incompetent fool. This should never have gone on this long. The meeting for the new dealership is in a few weeks, and BF Automotive is still in the picture."

Leaning back, he whispered in a low, cold tone. "I don't want to hear about problems. Frankly, I don't care about problems." With a death grip on the receiver, his voice inched up a notch with every word. "Fix the damn problems."

"Incompetent bastard." Louis mumbled another string of oaths right before he slammed down the phone. A light tap at his door made him momentarily hold back another outburst. "What?"

"Wow. What's your beef?" Antonio, the company's chief financial officer sauntered inside and stood in front of Louis's desk.

Louis frowned, his brown eyes almost black from fury. He rose from his chair so abruptly it toppled over. "What do you want?"

Antonio looked stunned and tossed a manila folder in the center of Louis's desk. "I want to know why you're tossing money down the drain going after a dealership in California. That's what."

Louis stalked over to the floor-to-ceiling windows overlooking downtown Manhattan. "BF Automotive is making things difficult for me." He spaced each word evenly. "I hate complications."

"Tell me something I don't already know."

Louis whirled around. "I want the dealership they bid on."

Antonio shook his head in confusion. "Back up. First of all, who the hell is BF Automotive?"

Louis faced the window again without answering.

"We have more business here than we can handle right now." Antonio propped his right hip on the edge of the desk. "Besides, this is another business deal, right?"

Louis turned around slowly, a wry smile at the corner of his lips. "For your information, it's not."

"Then what is it?"

"Listen, your job around here is to handle the finances." Louis jabbed a finger at the center of his chest. "I'm the CEO, and I decide what dealerships we go after. Clear?"

After their first lunch date, Caitlyn and Marcel saw each other every day. She eagerly accepted his invitation to attend a banquet at the Marriott City Center in downtown Oakland. Merritt Corporation, an Oakland-based communications company, hosted the annual black-tie affair, and

Caitlyn was thrilled that Marcel was being honored with an award for his outstanding achievements in community service.

After the two-hour event ended, Caitlyn made a quick trip to the ladies' room. She looked stunning in a black-and-white off-the-shoulder gown with a bias-split front that clung to her petite frame and showed a hint of cleavage.

On her way back, she spotted Marcel in the hallway outside the ballroom. She stopped, her eyes moving admiringly over the man dressed in a black tailored tuxedo accented with a brilliant red-and-silver brocade vest and a black silk ascot. Not wanting to disturb his conversation, she walked closer, but remained silent behind him.

"Marilyn, thank you for coming." Marcel leaned down and placed a soft kiss against her cheek.

Marilyn offered a genuine smile. "I wouldn't have missed it for the world." She looked up and softly cleared her throat. "I believe your lovely date has returned."

Marcel turned and slowly bobbed his head up and down. Caitlyn was a deadly combination any man would be a fool not to appreciate. She was classy and sexy at the same time.

Caitlyn smiled. "I didn't mean to interrupt." She walked up to Marilyn. "Hello. I'm Caitlyn Thompson."

Marilyn nodded graciously. "I'm Marilyn. I'm pleased to meet you."

Caitlyn figured this was one of Marcel's business associates and tossed her thumb in a joking gesture in his direction. "So, do you work with this character?"

"Uh…yes, I do."

Caitlyn studied the soft golden features of the woman in front of her until her brow arched. "God, your voice sounds very familiar." The sweet, husky utterance was unmistakable. She stared a few seconds longer, her mind rewinding in the process. "I'm sorry, but I'd swear on a stack of bibles that I've talked to you before."

Marilyn glanced nervously at Marcel, but didn't comment.

Without warning, Caitlyn's stomach flipped, and she stepped back with her arms hugging her small waist. "I have spoken to you." She swallowed back the lump lodged in her throat. "You're the person I spoke to a few weeks ago to arrange a meeting with a philanthropist to discuss funding my youth center, aren't you?"

Caitlyn studied the agitated glance between Marcel and Marilyn. "If I remember correctly, you said your name was Marilyn Jenkins, right?"

Marilyn nodded slowly. "That's correct."

"Y-You said the philanthropist you represented received my proposal. Isn't that right?"

Marilyn quickly glanced over at Marcel then to Caitlyn before she lowered her head. "Yes."

"And…" Caitlyn sensed something wasn't right and immediately turned to Marcel. "What's going on here?"

He grabbed her hand. "Caitlyn, listen, let's go some-where—"

"Marcel, do you know anything about all of this?" She pulled her hand free.

He released a long sigh. "Yes."

Caitlyn stood rigid. "Well, are you going to tell me?"

After a pregnant pause, Marcel softly uttered his admission. "Caitlyn, I'm the philanthropist Marilyn represents."

Caitlyn took a step back, her dark brown eyes flashing and jaw clenched. "So, you're telling me you've known about me and the youth center all along?"

Marcel jammed his hands in his pockets, took a deep breath and planted his feet apart. "Yes."

Caitlyn started to laugh, but the solemn look on Marcel's face made her think otherwise. "This is a joke, right?"

When Marcel didn't say anything, she silently prayed he would tell her her imagination had gotten the best of her. "Marcel—"

"Caitlyn, listen…"

"How long have you known about me and the center?" Before he could answer, she hit him with another question. "Don't tell me from the day we first met."

With his eyes focused on the floor, and without lifting his head, he admitted the truth. "No. Long before that."

Caitlyn's slanted eyes grew to the size of quarters. "What do you mean, long before that?"

He released a hard breath and his left hand landed at the base of his neck. "I-I received your proposal three weeks before I met you."

Caitlyn felt insulted as the impact of his admission settled in. He had merrily gone along for five weeks now, not once bothering to reveal the truth to her. She'd done it again, she inwardly chided. She'd trusted another man who'd betrayed her, and at that moment, she felt like the biggest fool who had ever walked the face of the earth. Without so much as another word, she turned and strode toward the lobby door.

Marcel's attempt to catch up with Caitlyn was halted by business associates and friends who surrounded him to offer their congratulations. His only goal as he half listened to what they were saying was to reach her before she made it out the door.

He issued a number of apologies, brushing against people in the crowded hallway as he swiftly pushed forward. He wasn't as close as he wanted to be, but it was near enough for her to hear. "Caitlyn."

When his hand touched her shoulder, she spun and landed a punch on him. "You no-good slime ball son-of-a-bitch."

He raked his hand across the top of his wavy black hair. "This isn't the way I wanted you to find out."

A group of attendees walked by, and she pursed her lips together. Once they passed, she connected with a left hook. "Well, guess what, you didn't try hard enough."

"Caitlyn, please—"

"Don't." She shook her head and took a couple of steps away from his outstretched hand. "You knew and didn't tell me." Pointing to the center of her chest, her voice quivered. "God, I was such a fool to trust you." Despite glossy eyes and a rigid back, she regained her composure. Not for anything would she let him see her fall apart. "You know what? It's not a problem. You didn't matter to me anyway."

He shook his head furiously. "Don't go there, Caitlyn. We matter."

"Well, if we matter so much, w-why didn't you tell me?"

He didn't answer right away, and for the first time in his life, he didn't want to be Marcel Baptiste the philanthropist. "I didn't want what I have to get in the way of who I am." He moved closer to her. "Not where you're concerned."

"I'm not following you."

Inching even closer, he blew out a hard breath. "When I became a philanthropist five years ago, it was under the condition I remain anonymous."

Realizing their conversation was taking place in the middle of the lobby she turned and walked down a hallway. "Okay, let's say I believe you. It still doesn't explain why you didn't tell me, especially since we've gotten to know each other."

Marcel's words lodged at the back of his throat and prevented him from doing what he'd never done with any woman: share the desires of his heart. "I'm sorry."

"*I'm sorry.*" She planted her hands at her waist and arched her brow. "*I'm sorry*? That's it? That's all you can stand here and say?" Her brow rose coolly. "What kind of game are you playing here with me, Marcel? Do you truly think you can waltz into my life, turn on your charm, flash your wealth behind the scenes and I'll fall down at your feet? Is that it?"

"No, Caitlyn. It's not like that at all. I admit I made a mistake." He scanned the hallway where they stood. "Please, let's go inside one of these rooms and talk about this. Can we do that?"

"No…we…can't…The time for you to talk was five weeks ago." A perfectly manicured red nail waggled in front

53

of his face. "Look, I don't know how you're used to dealing with women, and I don't plan to stay around to find out, understand?" She stepped to her left to move past him.

He quickly followed, gently grabbing her wrist. His tone was contrite. "Sweetheart, I'm sorry."

She ignored the endearment and mimicked his baritone voice. "Talk to me, Caitlyn. You can trust me, Caitlyn." A single tear rolled down her cheek. "Well, you know what? You can go to hell."

He winced. Her words stung more sharply than any physical blow. "Caitlyn—"

"Don't Caitlyn me."

Marcel glanced down the hallway again, wanting to locate a place they could talk alone. He would've begged for a spot in a broom closet at the moment. "Okay. Let's just leave here and go somewhere to talk this over. Anywhere you say. Your place, my place…anywhere." He placed his hand on her arm and pleaded. "I want to try and make this right."

"Well, I don't want you to make it right." She looked down at his hand and slowly let her gaze trail back to his face without uttering a word, silently warning that his hand and arm were perilously close to detachment.

"Caitlyn, please—"

"Didn't you hear what I just said?"

He dropped his hand. "All right. I'll take you home."

"No."

"What do you mean, no?"

She whacked the side of her head. "Oh, I forgot. You don't understand *that* word, do you? Well, let me see if I can make it a little plainer for you here." She crooked her finger, urging him closer until his face was near hers. "Go straight to hell." She turned and walked away.

Marcel caught up with her outside near the valet station. "Caitlyn, you don't need to take a cab. I brought you here, and I plan to take you home."

She folded her arms across her chest and didn't bother to look in his direction. "I prefer it this way."

He turned her so they faced each other. "Caitlyn, I'm sorry."

"Save it for the next sucker who comes along."

"I'm not giving up on us."

She ignored his comment and waved at the approaching cab. When it stopped, she reached out to open the door.

He loosely grabbed her wrist. "My woman doesn't ride in the back of a cab."

Although her heart melted at his declaration of ownership, Caitlyn glared back with a look as pointed as a switchblade. "Be sure to tell her that when you find her."

"I've already found her."

She shrugged, snatched her wrist free and climbed in the backseat.

He held the door open and squatted. "You know and I know we can work through this."

"The only thing I know is that this discussion is over. I want you to take your testosterone-induced ego and leave me alone." She grabbed the door handle and pulled, causing the door's edge to hit his knee.

"Ouch." He groaned and quickly moved out of the door's path before it slammed shut. Reaching down, he rubbed at the throbbing spot. "Oh, dammit, Caitlyn!" He knew she didn't hear his last remark because the cab had sped off into traffic, its taillights disappearing into the darkness of the night.

If Marcel could have reached his own behind, he'd have kicked it because he'd hurt her deeply, something he never meant to do. There was nothing he could figure out or say that would make a difference tonight. With the night's cool breeze swirling around him, he silently vowed Caitlyn would come to understand he didn't get to where he was by giving up. He was a master when it came to designing a plan, and his next one included her in his life. He wasn't going to give up on her.

Not by a long shot.

"What in the world?"

Caitlyn entered her office Monday morning and dropped her briefcase to the floor. Her gaze roamed over the floral arrangements covering every square inch.

She made her way to her desk and discovered a single rose with a card on her chair. She opened it and read:

I'm sorry.
M.B.

"Yeah, right. You should've thought of that before you decided to play Robin Hood." She sniffed the fragrant flower. Finally, she tossed it in the trashcan, plopped down hard in her chair and scooted closer to the desk.

She rubbed the aching throb at her temple. She was more frustrated with herself than she was angry with Marcel. It took a lot for her to curse, and in the past forty-eight hours, she'd invented and uttered words that didn't exist. "He's lost his damn fricking-ass mind," she mumbled, kicking the trashcan.

Around ten o'clock, Marcel, dressed in a tan suit with a French-cuff shirt adorned with solid gold cufflinks, knocked on Caitlyn's office door and walked in without waiting for a response.

Caitlyn didn't move. The same thunderclouds from Friday night shadowed her eyes as her heart slammed into her chest. "Do you mind explaining why all of these flowers are in my office?"

He walked over and stood on the opposite side of her desk. "It was the only way I could think to let you know how sorry I am."

"Yeah, right."

"After you left, I realized I should have been completely honest with you, especially after we started seeing each other."

"My, my, that's the first honest thing that's come out of your mouth since I've known you."

He blew out a hard breath. "Caitlyn, I'm really sorry."

"You said that already."

"Will you accept my apology?"

She glared at him.

"Well, will you at least try to forgive me?"

"Yes…I mean no…I mean—" She threw her hands up in the air. "Hell, right now, I'm not sure what I mean."

WHEN I'M WITH YOU

With her head down, she closed her eyes, and massaged the back of her neck.

Marcel rounded her desk and squatted beside her chair. "Caitlyn, if I could take back the other night, I would." He rotated her chair so she faced him. "I never meant to hurt you" he whispered, his mouth mere inches from hers.

She turned her head away, praying he didn't see in her eyes that she believed every word he said.

Marcel stood, bringing her with him, and placed a soft, feathery kiss at both corners of her mouth.

"Marcel…no."

His response was low and husky. "Yes."

"All right, you're sorry." She pushed on his chest. "But your apology chances nothing. Our relationship isn't going to work."

His brows bunched in confusion. "Why not?"

"Because of who you are."

"Hold it right there." A harsh frown distorted his features, and he stepped back. The button of his suit coat slipped free, and with both hands at his waist, he assumed a wide-legged stance. "Let me see if I'm understanding this. You were okay with our relationship before you knew I was a philanthropist, right?"

"That's not—"

"No, let me finish here. Before you found out, everything seemed to be going along fine between us, right?"

She threw her hands in the air out of frustration. "But you lied to me."

"I never lied to you, Caitlyn."

"That's right, you didn't lie. You just conveniently decided to omit the truth about some things." She sucked in a deep breath and released it. "Marcel, it's just that—"

"Talk to me, Caitlyn!"

"Don't you shout at me," she warned.

Marcel raked his hand over his hair and his tone softened. "All right, I'm sorry. Come on, cat eyes, just what?" When she didn't answer immediately, he coaxed her again in a gentle but forced tone. "Caitlyn?"

"It won't work out."

"Why?"

"We're from two different worlds."

He closed the space between them and placed both hands on her arms. "I can't help the fact that I've got money. And just for the record, I'm not ashamed of it." He paused, searching for the right words. "Money doesn't make a person, okay? I didn't steal, kill, or sell drugs to get it. I worked hard…damn hard…for it, and I'm not going to apologize for that." His voice softened to a whisper. "Nor will I apologize for what I decide to do with it." He ran his strong hands up and down her slender arms. "There's something between us, and you know it."

At the moment, she wasn't buying his argument and mentally counted to ten, hoping it would keep her from going ballistic at the nerve of him thinking he could barge into her office, say a few sweet words and things would be like they were before. He had some balls.

"There can be no *us* because there's no trust." She stepped back and went to her desk to retrieve the letter she'd drafted and held it out to him.

His brows knitted together. "What's this?"

"I can't accept the salary or the car."

"They come with the grant."

"*They* may come with the grant." She pointed to herself. "I don't." She glared at him through narrow eyes when he stared back speechless. "And don't you dare take that grant away from my kids."

"Trust me, I'd never do that."

She nodded.

He took the letter, crumpled it and threw it somewhere near her desk. "We'll get back to that in a minute." With his focus dead on her, he closed the gap between them. "First, we need to discuss us, this thing between you and me."

Before she could mouth a protest, he walked around her to the door, and in one swift motion closed it and turned the lock.

Caitlyn stood in the middle of her office fuming. "You can't just come into my office and take over."

"I'm not taking over," he advised calmly. "I'm taking care of some serious business. There's a difference."

Her hands landed on her hip. "You're the most arrogant man I've ever met."

He inched closer and assumed the same position as she did. "And you're the most stubborn woman I've ever wanted."

Caitlyn broke the silence first and spoke with what little of her patience remained. "I'm going to say this once, and I'll say it slow so that you get it the first time around." She walked over to the door and placed her hand on the knob.

"I'm not one of your pastime passions. There is no we, no us, no nothing." Unlocking the door, she snatched it open. "Now get that through that thick skull of yours and leave."

In two powerful strides, Marcel was in front of her. "That's where you're wrong, kitten. Despite what you think about me or your perception of who I am, you can't deny there's something between us."

She inched up her eyebrow. "You wanna bet?"

A confident smile touched his lips. "I'll bet every dime I've got on it." He caressed her cheek with the pad of his thumb. "And the feelings between us tell me I'll win this bet, lady, hands down."

Without waiting for her response, he walked out.

CHAPTER 4

"Vic, haven't you heard anything I've been telling you?" Caitlyn asked her best friend over lunch at Kincaid's.

Vic took a bite from her celery stick and gave Caitlyn a nonchalant nod. "Yeah, I heard you."

"Well?" Caitlyn coaxed.

Vic slung her auburn dreads over her shoulders and shrugged. "Well, what?"

"Come on, Vic. Whose side are you on?"

A soft curve touched the corner of Vic's lips. "Based on what you've just told me? Marcel's."

Caitlyn's mouth dropped. "What?"

She'd been miserable for two weeks, ever since Marcel walked out of her office. Her concentration had flat lined two seconds after he'd left, and since then, Caitlyn had felt like a member of the walking dead. She was more frustrated now than she was angry because her heart was overruling every objection her mind could think of to remain mad at Marcel. Her heart said to trust him. She'd called Vic and hoped lunch and some one-on-one girl time would lift her out of her funk. Never in a million years had she expected Vic to take Marcel's side, and suddenly she was right back at square one. She was mad as hell.

Vic chuckled and chomped on her celery stick. "Close your mouth. It's summer and a fly might land in there."

"But, Vic—"

"Look, you asked the question, not me."

"But—"

"Caitlyn, you owe the man an apology. Plain and simple."

Stunned, Caitlyn stared at her best friend. "How do you figure?"

Vic wiggled her broad hips in her seat until she found a comfortable spot. With both elbows on the table, she laced her hands in front of her. "Let me see if I've got this right. You're mad at him because he didn't tell you he was a philanthropist, right?"

"Right."

"Went postal on the brother when you found out, right?"

Caitlyn nodded.

"Can't...or won't...can't figure out which, accept the man's apology after he admitted he made a mistake, right?"

Caitlyn stared off in the distance.

"Did I get it all, sweetie?"

"Vic—"

"Nope, not finished yet. Let me ask you this. Did you tell him everything you've gone through for the last three years?"

Caitlyn lowered her head and shook it from side to side.

"Why not?"

Caitlyn's head snapped up. "Because that's not something you tell a person when you're just getting to know them!"

Vic slapped the table. "Bingo." She grasped Caitlyn's hand. "Sweetie, not every man is like that no-good bastard, Cole."

Caitlyn stared down at their hands. "Vic, I'm scared. I'm just at the point where I'm getting my life back on track—"

"*Sssh*. Listen, I know what you're going to say. It's been almost three years since you've heard from him, right?"

"Right."

"All right then. Stop trying to analyze everything and figure out where all the pieces will fit. Sometimes you have to step out on nothing but faith. At some point, you've got to learn how to trust again. Understand what I'm saying?" Vic pushed the tray of appetizers to the side. "You really like him, don't you?"

"Vic, I swear I've never felt this way about any man in my life."

"That boy got you dripping like a faucet between the legs, huh?"

Caitlyn looked mortified. "Vic."

"Child, please" Vic waved a silencing hand in front of her. "Girl, we've been through too much together to get prim and proper now." With a sly wink, she asked again, "Well, does he?"

Caitlyn appeared chagrined. "Yes. Satisfied now?"

Vic smiled. "It's not about me. It's about you, and I say go for what you know."

"He's so arrogant and makes me so mad, I can't see straight at times."

Vic sighed. "Get over it. You ain't exactly Mother Teresa yourself, you know?"

"Do you know he had the nerve to tell me I was stubborn?"

Victoria chuckled. "Hell, I've been telling you that for years. So both of us can't be wrong, right?"

"That's not funny, Vic."

"Didn't intend for it to be."

Several minutes later, Caitlyn smiled. "Vic, what would I do without you?"

"I've been asking myself that for almost seventeen years."

Caitlyn grabbed her purse. Where to next?"

Vic signed her credit card slip to pay for lunch and grinned. "Trust me, all right? Don't you know by now I know how to shop until I drop?"

Marcel rifled through the well-stocked liquor cabinet behind his father's bar like a stray dog trying to find food in a back-alley trash bin. He glanced at the neatly stacked bottles and wondered which beverage would take the edge off his nerves the fastest. It had been the longest two weeks of his life, and he was about to lose his mind. Caitlyn had managed to do two things no one else had done since he'd entered adulthood: ignore him and flat-out tell him no. She wouldn't take his calls at her office and didn't answer them at home. Seven weeks ago, he'd had only one priority: secure a new car dealership. Then he'd met Caitlyn. Since then, his life hadn't been the same. God, she was wonder-

WHEN I'M WITH YOU

fully exasperating, stubborn as a mule, and had caused him more than one sleepless night.

Enough. He needed to see her smile, needed to hear the softness in her voice again. That wouldn't happen if he didn't see her, talk to her. He needed her. Marcel shook his head in disbelief. How could someone so tiny cause the mammoth chaos she'd managed to create in his life in such a short amount of time?

He was giving her another twenty-four hours to get over being mad at him. After that, he vowed to go over to her apartment and hold her hostage, if he had to, until he could talk some sense into her.

"Whiskey, neat," Alcee said, followed by a weary sigh.

Marcel looked over his shoulder and found his father standing next to him. "You, too, huh?" Marcel handed Alcee's drink to him, then fixed himself a snifter of Grand Marnier.

"Yeah." Alcee accepted the drink, clinked his glass with Marcel's and shook his head. "Women...Son, I'm telling you, they'll drive a man to drink."

"Hmph, tell me about it." Taking a sip, Marcel lifted his brow. "So who ruffled your feathers?"

"Your sister."

Marcel chuckled. "Which one?"

"Aimee."

Marcel shook his head and smiled. "Say no more." The twenty-four-year-old Stanford graduate was the youngest member of the family and spoiled rotten.

Alcee took a seat in the leather recliner. "Decided to pay your old man a visit, huh?"

LACONNIE TAYLOR-JONES

Marcel sat on the couch across from Alcee. "Come on, Pop. It hasn't been that long."

"Well, it's been two weeks."

"Can't a man visit with his family without everyone keeping a time log?" Marcel leaned over, absently swirling the Grand Marnier until it sloshed over the rim.

"So, what woman has your feathers ruffled? Caitlyn?"

"Yeah."

"Happened the night of the banquet, huh?"

Marcel's head snapped up. "How did you know?"

Looking over his half-rimmed glasses, Alcee smiled. "Moni told Brie, and Brie told me." Monique, whom everyone called Moni, was the only married sibling of the clan, and Gabrielle, Marcel's fraternal twin, was nicknamed Brie.

"What?"

"Listen, Son, you know that nothing's sacred in this family, even the stuff that's between you and Jesus." Alcee took another sip. "Apparently Moni saw you and Caitlyn, uh…discussing a few things in the lobby after the awards ceremony."

Marcel shook his head in disgust. The last person in the world he would have wanted to see that exchange was Moni. At twenty-eight, he knew she felt it was her God-given right to transport information from one family member to the other, and her primary cargo vessel was Brie. He'd thought since Moni was due to give birth in early December, her mind would be preoccupied with the baby, not gossiping.

"Don't think I've ever seen you this taken by a woman before."

"I haven't been."

"You really like her, don't you?"

"Yeah, Pop, I really do."

"Is this something more than a date here or there?"

"Hell, she's not even talking to me now, so I'm not sure what we have."

"What happened?"

Marcel told Alcee everything that happened the night of the banquet.

Alcee nodded. "Stubborn, huh?"

Marcel snorted. "As a century-old mule."

"She's pretty, you know."

"Exquisite," Marcel corrected.

"Not impressed by material things, I bet."

"Couldn't care less."

Alcee nodded. "Umm-hmm. She's just like your mother." He placed his empty glass on the table next to him. Leaning over with his elbows on his knees, he studied Marcel. "Son, you need to brand your woman."

Marcel snapped his head up. "What did you just say?"

"You heard me the first time." Alcee's tone was serious, yet gentle. "Listen, any man can wine and dine a woman, buy her the world. But you've got to put your brand on her. Not with material things...that doesn't count anyway. What I'm talking about is branding her here." He placed his hand next to his heart. "Brand her with the things you hold there. Allow her to come into the inside of you, so she knows who you really are. It's not until you share the secrets of your heart with her that you'll have a chance at a true relationship. Trust me on this one, Son."

Alcee settled back in the recliner and crossed one long leg over the other. "You know, Baptiste men have a tradition. Goes back at least four generations that I know of."

"And that is?"

"We go after our women. Not just any woman, mind you, but the right one."

"How the hell do I go after her when she won't even talk to me?"

Alcee made a tsking sound, threw back his head and laughed. "You run a billion-dollar corporation, and you're asking me that question?"

Marcel shot straight off the couch and began to pace. "I've spared no expense with this woman."

"Maybe that's the problem. She trusted you before she knew about your money, right?"

"Yeah."

"Son, don't you see? Caitlyn's not impressed with Marcel Baptiste, the philanthropist. That's not what attracted her to you in the first place."

Marcel halted mid-stride and whirled to face his father. "Well, what am I supposed to do then?"

"Go back to doing the things you did before she found out. If you can get back to that, the rest will fall in place. You want her to trust you here…" He touched his heart again. "…with her very life."

Marcel stared at Alcee and shook his head in amazement. "Never thought I'd live to see the day that I would be getting advice from my old man on how to get a woman."

They both laughed.

"Got a plan in mind?"

"Oh, hell yeah."

Alcee stood and patted Marcel on the shoulder. "That's good. I knew you would." He moved toward the door. "Work your plan, then reel her in. A good woman is hard to find."

Marcel nodded with confidence. "Believe me I plan to do just that."

"Caitlyn…" Marcel tapped once on the partially open office door and walked in.

Caitlyn jerked her head up from the mound of paperwork on her desk. She angrily narrowed her eyes even though her heart accelerated to a frantic pace at the sight of him. Her tone was curt. "Why are you here?"

He stood in front of her desk. "To ask you one question."

She placed her reading glasses on top of her head. "Listen, I don't appreciate you barging into my office."

"Get over it. I'm here."

"But I don't want you to be here." Over the past two weeks, her anger had diminished, but Marcel's arrogance had her so mad she saw stars.

"Touché."

She stood and braced her hands on the edge of the desk. With her head inclined, she narrowed her eyes to slits. "You know, I don't like you very much right about now."

He bunched his brows together and assumed her position. "Well, guess what? You don't exactly bring greetings from the welcome wagon yourself."

They stood silently glaring at each other.

She opened her mouth to speak, but abandoned her words when he held up his left hand.

"Hear me out, all right?" He straightened, walked around the desk and stood in front of her. "What's the one thing you want most for your center?"

She hitched her brow. "You really want to know?"

"Yes."

She pushed back her chair, moved over to the small wired window behind her and pointed to the activity outside. "Tell me what you see."

Standing next to her, Marcel stared at the scene. "A group of teenagers hanging around."

She looked up at his profile. "What are they doing?"

He shrugged. "Nothing."

"That's right. Nothing. They're doing nothing, Marcel. You want to know why they're doing nothing? Because there's nothing for them to do." She turned back to face the window and sadly stared at the group. "There's so much potential standing out there, but no one has given them a chance to find it." She turned and looked up at the side of his face again. "So, if you really want to know what I want, it's this." She held up one finger at a time as she named her wishes. "I want something that will pull them away from the corner they're standing on. I want something that will build their confidence and shape them for the challenges they'll face in life. I want to open the door of potential I know is inside of them. That's what I want."

He turned his attention away from the window and looked at her. "Okay."

She glanced up and tossed him a puzzled look. "What exactly does okay mean?"

"You'll see."

Without another word, he turned and walked out.

"I don't believe I heard you correctly. Come again."

Caitlyn knew it wasn't the most professional response, but before her brain had a chance to consult with her mouth, the words tumbled out. It was a week later at the youth center's monthly board of directors meeting, and she'd almost fallen out of her chair at the announcement Fran Jenkins, the board president, had just made.

Fran beamed with delight as she glanced over at Caitlyn and the other board members seated around the table. "Oh, Caitlyn, Mr. Baptiste was very impressed with the idea you presented to him about establishing a cooperative program for the kids."

Fran turned to the other board members. "The program would offer the youth part-time jobs at local businesses throughout Oakland as a way to earn money and learn job skills.

"It would?" Caitlyn stuttered.

"Oh, yes," Fran exclaimed. "Mr. Baptiste has even offered to fund the program. That was such an ingenious idea, Caitlyn. Thank you."

"Uh…well…thanks."

Fran patted her chest. "Oh, dear, in my excitement I forgot to mention that Mr. Baptiste has agreed to volunteer one afternoon a week to mentor our young men."

"He has?" Caitlyn managed to say when she finally found her voice.

Fran touched Caitlyn's hand. "Isn't that wonderful?"

Caitlyn sighed. "Oh, it's wonderful all right."

"And Caitlyn, I don't need to tell you how much it would mean to have Mr. Baptiste serve on our board of directors." Fran looked at the affirmative nods given by the other board members around the table. "Do I, dear?"

"O-Our board of directors?" Caitlyn nearly choked on her words.

"He'd be a valuable asset." Fran beamed.

Caitlyn silently conceded to Fran's statement with a slight nod.

Fran patted Caitlyn's hands, which now were tightly laced together on top of the table. "I'm sure you'll see to that happening, won't you, dear?"

Caitlyn pointed to herself, her eyes taking on the shape of half dollars. "Who? Me?"

"Why of course, dear. You're the most logical person since you're the one who's established a relationship with him."

"But Fran—"

"Is there a problem, dear?" A frown marred Fran's forehead.

Caitlyn shook her head. "No. There's no problem at all."

73

Fran clapped her hands together in delight. "Well, ladies and gentlemen, I believe we have a win-win situation for everyone involved." Again, she patted Caitlyn's hands that had now balled into tiny fists. "Wouldn't you agree, Caitlyn?"

Caitlyn muttered under her breath. "Oh, it's a win-win all right."

CHAPTER 5

Caitlyn sat quietly behind the wheel of her old BMW, staring out the windshield at her surroundings. She popped two Tums in her mouth, hoping they would settle her stomach.

It was just past seven o'clock in the evening, the day after the board meeting. Exiting the car, she walked around, braced herself against the hood and stared down on the city below. Even though she'd slipped on her shades, the rays from the setting sun danced off the waters of San Francisco Bay where ships slowly docked at the Port of Oakland. In the distance, the Bay Bridge hovered over the Pacific Ocean.

She'd debated all day whether to go to Marcel's home. After their heated exchange when he had come to her office and asked her what she wanted most for the center, she wasn't sure if he'd even agree to see her. It'd taken her most of the day to calm her nerves and get this far. Deciding not to put off what she knew she needed to do, she squared her shoulders, walked to the front door and pushed in the small pearl button of the doorbell.

"Hi." Her voice was shaky.

"Hi, yourself." Marcel answered just as nervously. He was casually dressed in faded jeans and tennis shoes. His tank top showed off powerful shoulders and a broad chest covered with thick, curly black hair.

She chewed on her bottom lip. "I-I don't mean to intrude, and I'm sorry I didn't call to let you know—"

"You're always welcome here." He reached for her hand and pulled her inside.

The Mediterranean-style estate had a fabulous grand foyer and featured a Travertine dual staircase. A fifty-inch crystal chandelier hung from a circular sky dome over a gorgeous water fountain, providing an enormous amount of light in the spacious entryway.

"Marcel…"

"Caitlyn…"

They both attempted to speak at the same time. Marcel gestured for her to go first.

"I came for two reasons." She felt that she would collapse from her buckling knees and bouncing stomach and looked toward the living room for a place to sit. From where she stood, the living room was breathtaking. The hand-carved wood-and-marble fireplace accented the open space and multiple windows offered an unimpeded view of the Oakland Hills.

"Do you mind if I sit down?"

"Not at all." Marcel touched the small of her back and ushered her inside.

Caitlyn took a seat on one end of a long snow-white couch and placed her hand right at the top of her midsection, hoping it would calm the roller coaster in her stomach. She glanced around the room. "Your home is beautiful."

"Thanks." On the other end of the couch, Marcel bent forward and hooked his fingers together. "Has your car given you any more trouble?"

It took two attempts, but she eventually answered in a hoarse voice. "No. It's running fine."

"That's good." He rubbed sweaty palms up and down the sides of his thighs.

Caitlyn cleared her throat. "Well, you certainly made quite an impression on Fran."

"How?"

"She wants you to serve on our board of directors."

"I think that could be arranged." He relaxed a bit and sat back with a muscled arm stretched across the back of the couch. His potent gaze was as gentle as a caress.

"Thank you for the offer to establish the co-op project."

"Fran told you?"

"Yes." She looked down at her hands, which shook like a leaf in the middle of a windstorm. "I found out at last night's board meeting." She glanced at him with a soft look in her eyes. "Thank you so much."

"No. Thank you. If it hadn't been for you, I never would have known about the youth center."

Caitlyn nodded.

Marcel cleared his throat. "You said there were two reasons for your visit."

She swallowed and opened her mouth to speak. Whatever she was about to say died on her lips the moment she spotted the car-shaped charm she'd given him hanging from a gold chain around his neck. "You kept it?"

He looked down at the charm and smiled. "Absolutely. Did you think I'd get rid of it?"

She shrugged. "I figured since we—"

"I've worn it since the day you gave it to me, and I don't ever plan to take it off."

She released an anxious chuckle. "It was a silly gift."

"It's the most precious gift anyone has ever given to me."

She bowed her head at his words. "Marcel, I owe you an apology." Slowly lifting her head, she looked over at him. "I took my inability to trust out on you, and for that I'm so, so sorry." The tears she'd willed to stay hidden suddenly made their appearance. "It took the tongue-lashing of a good friend to help me understand that I'm just as guilty of the crime I accused you of. I was wrong, and I'm sorry."

He scooted down the couch until he was next to her and laced their fingers together. "We're both to blame, all right?" He lifted their hands to kiss the back of hers. "I'm willing to trust. What about you?"

"I'm willing to try."

With his finger, he lifted her chin, brushing his lips across hers. "I'm sorry, kitten. And on my mother's grave, I swear I'll never do anything to hurt you again, and I'll do whatever it takes to gain your trust." With the pad of his thumb, he gently wiped away the wetness that still clung to her cheek. Between a kiss at each corner of her mouth, he whispered a request. "Will you let me earn your trust?"

She tilted her head back to look into his eyes.

"Will you at least try? That's all I'm asking."

"Yes," she replied breathlessly.

He gathered her close. "Missed you, hellion."

"Missed you, too." She leaned back just a bit, not wanting to be too far away from his warm embrace. "The first step toward trust is sharing." Releasing a hard breath, she turned to stare at the wall. "Remember the night in your car when you asked me how he hurt me?"

He nodded. "Yes."

"Well, I think now it's time you knew."

"All right."

"Four years ago, I met a man who on the surface seemed nice, but in the end, he made my life a living hell."

Marcel frowned. "How?"

"He started out being charming, attentive, showing me all the attention a woman dreams about. I think some of my vulnerability to him was because I'd grown up in foster care and didn't have a family of my own. Two months later, things changed."

"How?"

"He became controlling and obsessive."

"I don't understand what you mean."

"He would call my job at least twenty times a day. He wanted an account of my whereabouts every minute. It became real clear that it wasn't going to work. I knew he wasn't going to change, so I called it quits." With the back of her hand, she wiped at another tear that had fallen. "But he refused to accept that it was over."

"What happened after that?"

She released a long sigh. "The phone calls increased, and he started showing up at my job. When I would come home, he'd be parked outside. It seemed everywhere I went, he was there. He stalked me. Besides my foster mother, Ms. Ruby, I didn't have a lot of close ties in New Jersey, so I decided to relocate."

"To where?"

"I asked for a job transfer and moved to Atlanta, but he tracked me down."

Wrinkles appeared on Marcel's forehead. "Tracked you down? How?"

Caitlyn nodded. "He hired a private detective. The mistake I made was using my credit cards, opening a bank account—anything in my name." She squared her shoulders and continued. "Anyway, I came home one night, and there he was waiting for me inside my condo." The painful memories caused her to jerk, and her breathing became heavy.

"Caitlyn, baby, don't shut down on me now."

She sat rigid. Her brain still processed information, but her mouth refused to cooperate with the output. She stared blankly at the wall in front of her.

"Caitlyn, come on. Baby, you've got to trust me."

She turned her tear-stained face to him and saw the distress in his eyes. "H-he…"

"Talk to me, cat eyes." Marcel pulled her against his chest and spoke over the top of her head. "We'll deal with whatever it is, together." He leaned back to see her face. "But I can't help you if you won't trust me. Understand?"

"Yes." Her voice was a whisper and she brushed away another tear.

"Wait right here." Marcel made a mad dash and brought back a box of tissue. He knelt in front of her.

Pulling out several tissues, he placed them in her hands, then took one and began wiping the tears that fell at a steady pace.

Still shaking, Caitlyn blew out a long, hard breath, and her voice trembled. "That night…" She lowered her head.

Lifting her face up, he softly asked, "What happened that night, baby?"

"He…raped me."

CHAPTER 6

Marcel's body went rigid. Emotions swirled through him so swiftly he stopped breathing for a split second. He swayed from side to side as he rose to his feet. Shock, sadness, and rage ripped through him simultaneously.

"Baby, I'm so sorry...I didn't know." He sat next to her. "We don't have to talk about this." He glanced over and saw her shake her head. Reaching over, he clasped her trembling hands within his steady ones, silently communicating that continuing the conversation was her call.

Lines formed around Caitlyn's full-lipped mouth, and she squeezed harder. "You know, it's funny, but it's still hard for people to believe that someone you're involved with can rape you." She then turned to him. "But it happens. And it happened to me over and over until the next morning." With her free hand, she swiped at her tears. Her voice was hoarse and barely audible. "No means no. And if a man doesn't accept that, then it's rape as far as I'm concerned. Anyway, he forced me back to New Jersey. I let him think that I believed him when he said it would never happen again. The only thing I wanted was out. I was no match against him physically, so I had to think of a way I could beat him."

"What did you do?"

"I outsmarted him."

Pain settled around Marcel's heart. He felt pure contempt for the man who'd violated her. He couldn't imagine any man forcing himself on a woman. As far as he was concerned, any man who would was the worst scum on earth. It took everything he had to keep his voice calm. "How did you do it?"

"It took me weeks, but little by little, I cashed out everything I had—my retirement plan, savings, stock, bonds, you name it. I packed only the things I needed and figured out an escape plan. I let things settle down for a while. One day, my opportunity came when he went out of town on a family emergency—his sister was in a car accident. I left that day, and I've never looked back."

"Didn't you have friends, anyone who could help you?"

"At first, I didn't want to bring any of them into that kind of drama because I would never have forgiven myself if he'd done anything to them. And trust me, I believe in my heart he was capable of it. I finally confided in Vic, and she was my saving grace." A half chuckle escaped. "I don't even own a cell phone. I didn't want to take the chance of him tracking me down again."

"Where'd you go?"

"Everywhere, anywhere. I never stayed in any place too long."

"But you said Vic helped you, right?"

She nodded. "She did."

He shook his head in confusion. "How? Why didn't you just come here in the first place?"

"That's what he would have expected. Vic is one of the main reasons he hasn't found me to this day."

Marcel shook his head again. "I don't understand."

"For the first year he would call her to see if she knew where I was. Of course, she'd always say she didn't know and would tell him she heard I was staying with a friend here or there. Vic quarterbacked everything with our friends, especially Tara and Chandler. So, when he'd go to check it out, they would send him in another direction."

"In other words, you guys had him going in circles."

"Yes, and thank God, it worked. It gave me just a little more time to put more distance between us."

Marcel continued to hold her hand and tried to ease the tightness in his fingers and the anger that raged inside him. "I'm so sorry, baby."

Caitlyn's breathing changed, and her voice thickened. "Through it all, I made it. But it left me just a tad short on trusting men."

Marcel had always believed negotiation was the best way to settle a dispute. But he knew if he could get his hands on the man who'd raped Caitlyn, screw negotiation. The bastard would be dead. "Who did this to you, baby?"

She lowered her head and shook it.

"What's his name?"

"Marcel, please, I don't want you anywhere near—"

"I can find out, you know."

"Please, just leave it be."

"Why?" He half shouted and rose to his feet. "Some low-life asshole who calls himself a man brutalizes the hell out of you, turns your life upside down, makes you leave everything you've worked for, and you want me to leave it be. Hell no." He stalked off to the other side of the room.

Caitlyn followed and placed her hands on his arm. "Baby, don't you see? If you find him, go after him for any reason, he finds me." She cupped his face. "Leave it be. Please."

Her endearment warmed his heart because she'd never referred to him as "baby" before. He nodded begrudgingly. "All right, I see your point. I give you my word I won't go after the son-of-a-bitch." Then he paused. "What'd you say his name was again?"

She took in a deep breath and slowly released it. "I didn't."

He knew she was upset, but she was smart, too. She wasn't so distressed that she didn't pick up on his back door way of finding out the information he wanted. He gathered her in his embrace and held her, placing a kiss on the top of her head. "Thank you."

With the fear of the past no longer a threat, she placed her head against his chest and listened to the steady beat of his heart. "For what?"

"For trusting me."

It was a long time before either said a word. Finally, he broke the silence and placed his hand on her stomach. "Had dinner yet?"

Caitlyn didn't expect the kitchen's décor to be as elegant as that of the living room she'd walked out of. A crystal chandelier illuminated the parquet-top table that could easily seat six. The mahogany cabinets had clear glass inserts and showcased an array of glassware, china and sterling silver.

After washing her hands, Caitlyn stood at the oversized island next to Marcel. "So, what do you need me to do?"

Marcel nodded toward the refrigerator. "How about tackling the salad? You should find everything you need on the second shelf."

"Got it."

"Are you allergic to seafood?"

"No." With everything for the salad piled in her arms, Caitlyn shut the refrigerator door with her foot. She glanced at the pot on the stove from which a mouth-watering aroma was coming. "Does it have shrimp in it?"

He gave her a sexy wink. "Of course. You can't have roots from N'awlins, baby, and not love shrimp jambalaya."

"Smells good."

"Trust me, it is." Marcel bunched his brows together. "You've had shrimp before, right?"

"Yes, but I only like them deep fried."

He dipped a spoon in the pot and lifted out a jumbo-sized shrimp. "Come on. Try mine. I guarantee you'll love it."

Caitlyn scrunched her nose. "Do I have to?"

"Yes." Marcel chuckled. "Come on. Open." He eased the shrimp inside her mouth.

"Um…um…um, now that's good."

During dinner, Caitlyn learned just how different she and Marcel were. She loved simplicity; Marcel relished grandeur. For the most part she was even-tempered; it took a lot to set her off and make her mad. She took things slowly. Marcel, on the other hand, could spiral off the deep end if things didn't go his way or according to his schedule. But Marcel always maintained control of his emotions, and she knew that it would take something near and dear to his heart for him to totally lose it. Amazingly, as different as they were, there were many things they had in common. Both claimed to be Wimbledon champions because of their passion for playing tennis, and listening to smooth jazz ended their days.

She'd finally gotten Marcel to admit he was a secret member of the Black Hole, the notorious but loyal group of Oakland Raiders football fans. Since he had private box seats, she accepted his invitation to the home games on one condition: that he tutor her in French, a language he spoke fluently.

While he cleared the dishes, she went to the family room and looked intently at the array of pictures. A while later, he came up behind her and settled his arms around her waist. With her back against his chest, she placed her arms on top of his.

Marcel leaned around, staring at the intense look on her face. "What's wrong, kitten?"

"Nothing's wrong."

"You sure?

"Positive." She pointed to the wall in front of her. "I was just admiring the pictures of your family. Guess it made me think about what it would have been like to have a family of my own."

"You've never told me much about your family."

She turned to face him, but didn't answer right away. "There's not a lot to tell. It was just my mom and me up until I was five. One day, she didn't pick me up from school and no one could find her. Since we didn't have any other family, I was placed in child protective services." Pain settled in her voice. "It was kind of scary, being only five and shifting from the only place you've ever called home to the home of a complete stranger."

"I can't even imagine what it was like."

"Not pretty. Trust me. I bounced from one foster home to the other. Some families were kind. Some were in it just for the money. I guess that's part of the reason I'm reluctant to ask people for help. Growing up, I had to pretty much depend on myself."

"How long would you stay at each home?"

"In the beginning, usually not long. For seven years, I kind of bounced through the system. When I turned twelve, I was placed with Ms. Ruby and stayed until I left for college. She's the only family I ever had until I met Vic and her family." She smiled. "Oh, Marcel, you'd love Ms. Ruby. She's a retired teacher and never had kids of her own. God, I don't know where I'd be if it hadn't been for her."

"You really love her, don't you?"

"Oh, yes. She's my mother in every sense of the word. You know, she could've retired the year I left for college but continued to work so I didn't have to take on a part-time job."

"I hope to meet her someday."

"That would be nice."

"Did you ever find out what happened to your mom?"

"She had a heart attack the day she didn't pick me up from school. She died that night."

He tenderly asked, "What about your dad? Do you know anything about him?"

"No. That's one of the things I've always regretted, not knowing him. I don't know who he is, or if he's dead or alive. But that's next on my to-do list, to try and find out. I want to have closure to that part of my life, if nothing more."

"Do you know his name?"

She shook her head. "His name isn't on my birth certificate."

"Perhaps I could help out."

She looked puzzled. "How?"

"I've got a friend who's a P.I. I could ask him to do some investigating."

Her eyes shone with excitement. "Really?" She thought about her budget, and just as quickly, the glimmer faded.

"What's the matter?"

"I don't have the money in my budget to spend right now. I'll wait until—"

"Don't worry about that. We'll work something out."

"But, Marcel, I don't want to be obligated to you for anything."

"Okay. Listen, if you feel uncomfortable about accepting the money, would you consider it a loan?"

"Well, I guess so. As long as we're clear that it's a loan."

He chuckled. "We're clear. And I'm sure you'll come up with a payment plan that's acceptable."

She nodded graciously at his offer. "Thank you. I'll pay back every dime."

"I trust you, kitten." He placed a kiss at each corner of her mouth.

"You need to know that I've always paid my bills on time."

"Umm-hmm." He rained kisses along her temple.

"We better go clean up."

"All taken care of," he whispered, never ceasing his actions. Burrowing his face in the space between her neck and shoulder, he bit down gently, and moments later, the warmth of his breath blew the sting away. "Tell me what you miss most about Newark."

"My two dogs." She snuggled closer to him. "I knew I couldn't take them with me, and it broke my heart to have to leave them behind. The last thing I did before I left Newark was drop them off at a shelter to be placed for adoption."

"What kind of dogs?" His tongue left a wet trail along her slender neck.

"Bichon Frise," she whispered with her head thrown back.

Marcel lifted his head and smiled. "Were you guys close?"

"We slept together every night." She saw his eyes widen in mock surprise and playfully punched his shoulder. "You know what I mean."

He grinned. "Yeah, I do."

Standing on her tiptoes, she placed a kiss against his cheek. "It's been a wonderful evening."

He wrapped his arms around her waist and walked them until her back rested against the wall. "In more ways than one."

Caitlyn reached up and drew his head down to hers. She'd dreamed of his kiss, but fantasy was nothing compared to reality. She'd longed to feel his lips on hers again. Marcel's mouth stirred sensations within her she'd never felt before and revealed a need to know what it was like to be thoroughly devoured by him and feast on everything the man who gently held her in his arms had to give.

Without shame, she molded her slender body against him and felt the unhurried gyration of his hips rolling against hers. She tightened her arms around his waist, urging him to continue to fuel the fire he'd created. Greedily, she took his tongue, not wanting the kiss to end, and savored the intoxicating intimacy they shared.

The need to breathe eventually brought the kiss to an end. Marcel released a ragged moan and placed his forehead against hers. Barely able to replace his oxygen supply, he stepped back. "Come on. I'll follow you home. I want to be sure you get in safe."

"Uh, well…okay." She looked down, then back up at him. "Marcel, what I told you about the rape…I just don't want you to think that it…" She pursed her lips and dropped her head.

"That it what?"

She shrugged. "That it left me with hang-ups about sex. I-I'm not loco behind it, okay?" She shrugged again. "You might be one of those brothers who thinks a woman's damaged goods."

"Don't even go there." He hauled her against the solid wall of his chest. "No woman should have to go through what you did. And no, I don't think you're loco." He smiled. "Your head's as hard as a boulder sometimes, but you're not loco, no way." He ran his hands up and down her arms. "And just to set the record straight here, at this moment, I want you as bad as a crackhead wants his next rock. But I made a promise to you that I'd earn your trust, and I won't go back on my word by rushing anything between us."

"So, in other words, you don't want me to stay a little longer?"

"Oh, I want that, more than you'll ever know. But if you stay, I think we both know what will happen. God knows I want you here with me tonight, but I also want something more."

"What's that?"

"Your trust. If you can honestly look me the eye and tell me I have your complete trust, this discussion is over."

She looked away. God, she wanted to say the words, but in her heart she knew it would be a lie. "I-I can't. Not right now."

"Then we wait. Besides, I'm looking forward to pampering you first."

She wrapped her arms tighter around his waist and looked up. "You pamper all your women?"

He shook his head. "No. You're the first."

"Yeah, I bet. I'm sure you have women falling down at your feet."

"Wrong presumption." His face was void of any expression.

She stared, stunned. "Really?"

"I'm not going to lie and tell you I haven't dated, but I've never wanted to pamper anyone until now."

She stared up at him, her heart warmed by his words. Placing her head back against his chest, and with nothing but a mustard seed of faith to guide her, she whispered, "Marcel?"

"Yeah, baby?"

"His name is Cole Mazzei."

CHAPTER 7

Marcel was as restless as a wild animal in a cage. He paced in the sitting area of the master bedroom. After following Caitlyn to her apartment, he'd parked, gone inside and checked the tiny space from top to bottom. His nerves were still rattled from what she'd shared earlier, and he didn't want to take any chances this Cole character would pop up on her in the middle of the night like a jack-in-the-box. In two months, she'd managed to wrap herself so firmly around his heart and had become such a part of his being he couldn't imagine life without her.

He plopped down on the bed in a spread-eagle position and thought back over his life. Of the six children, he'd always had the most compassionate and a giving heart. If he could help something or someone, he did.

Growing up, his family and friends had teased him for bringing home every stray dog he found. His desire to help others had really taken root during his senior year in high school. His track mate, Alex Robinson, had just transferred from a school out of state, and they had immediately bonded. Marcel talked his father into letting Alex and his mother move into their home when he discovered they were homeless. The day they settled in, he made a solemn vow, that rich or poor, he would share whatever he had with anyone who needed it. Although wealth and material possessions had fallen his way, they hadn't fazed him a bit. If he lost everything, so be it.

Discipline was his catalyst to achieving his aspirations, and for the last three years, he'd forced himself into a self-imposed hiatus from anything and everything that would distract him from the professional goals he'd set for BF Automotive. That included women. He hadn't missed the thrill of the hunt. His last relationship had been doomed from the start. He had always been selective in the few women he'd dated, but he'd realized early on they were more interested in how many zeros followed the first number of his bank account than him.

Not even his best friend Alex knew his heart's desire—to establish a corporate philanthropic foundation with the hope that it would make a difference in the lives of inner-city youth.

Marcel stared at the ceiling and knew he'd gone past wanting Caitlyn. She'd done what no other woman had managed to do: make him fall in love. It had taken him thirty-eight years to find love, and he knew he was in for the fight of his life. He'd never had to fight to earn a woman's trust.

He wanted to be the first man to erase the hurt from her memory. He wanted to be the only man to fill her present and future with love. He wanted to be the last man with whom she ever shared her body. But he wanted that feeling reciprocated. But before any of those things could happen, he needed to find out a little more about this Cole Mazzei. He rolled over and picked up the phone.

"Hey, partner. You awake?"

The insistent ringing had awakened Alex out of a dead sleep. "At two o'clock in the morning? Hell no!"

Besides his father and two younger brothers, Alex was the only other person Marcel trusted with his very life. He'd often reminisced of their times together while attending Tuskegee University. During their sophomore year, they'd pledged the same fraternity, Alpha Phi Alpha. After graduation, Alex spent several years as an undercover police officer with the Pennsylvania Police Department before moving to Oakland. Now he was the owner of one of the top private investigative companies in the country. Marcel knew that if anyone could find the answer to a question, it was Alex.

"Listen, Robinson, I need a favor."

Alex sleepily yawned into the phone. "Look, B, I don't do favors at this hour of the morning. But if I did, what is it?"

Marcel shared with Alex everything Caitlyn had told him about Cole except the rape. That fact was a private matter between him and Caitlyn, and he vowed he'd go to his grave with it remaining that way.

"Shit."

"My sentiments exactly. I want to know where that bastard is at all times, and make sure he isn't on her trail. Come to think of it, run a background check on him." To Marcel's way of thinking, knowing Cole's whereabouts and what he'd done since birth wasn't going back on his word to Caitlyn. He'd promised her he wouldn't go after him.

"All right."

"Listen, partner, I also need you to check out who's behind this bidding war for the new dealership."

"Easy enough. Anything else?"

"Yeah. See if you can locate Caitlyn's father while you're out there searching. Swing by the office in the morning, and I'll give you the information you need."

"No problem. What time you getting in?"

"Let's do eight."

Alex yawned again. "Make it nine, will ya?"

"All right. See you then. By the way, Robinson, all of this is a priority."

Alex chuckled. "Oh, don't worry. When you get my bill, you'll know it was priority status. Listen, B, your first two requests are a cakewalk. As for Caitlyn's dad, if he's still alive, I'll find him."

"I know. That's the reason I called you."

Marcel disconnected the call and smiled as he reclined on the bed.

His plan for Caitlyn was simple: gain her trust and make her fall in love with him.

He just hoped he didn't lose his mind in the process.

Over the next few weeks, never once did Marcel move their relationship beyond that with which Caitlyn felt comfortable. The more she thought about it, the last time Marcel had touched her was at his home the night she told him about the rape. Since then, he hadn't even kissed her. She knew what she felt for him was more than lust and whenever she hinted that she wouldn't mind moving their relationship to the next level, he would simply smile and tell her she was worth the wait. She was at her wit's end, though. If he'd deliberately set out to torture her with his hands-off policy, he'd succeed. Marcel had awakened a sexuality she didn't know existed and brought to the fore-front a passion she hadn't known. The sensuality she'd long ago buried set off a spark that she wanted to burst into flames.

Despite the non-physical contact between them, he'd made her feel sexy, desirable, and most definitely wanted by him. However, Marcel held his emotions in check with such rigidity she wondered if he was made of steel.

But did she trust him? She sighed because she knew she didn't, not yet at least.

All week, she'd looked forward to their dinner in San Francisco. With her confidence fully in control, she smiled. She planned to break through the no-touch barrier he'd erected between them. She wanted to be held, touched and kissed by him. She wanted to push him to the edge and make him lose control. She'd lost hers days ago.

She spent an extraordinary amount of time with her appearance, wanting everything to be perfect. Since it was late summer, she opted against pantyhose with her knee-length black wrap dress, which showed off her curvy body. She'd wet-set her hair, and it fell in a wavy mass to the top of her shoulders. The elegant evening sandals showcased her red toenails, and the diamond toe ring on her left foot sparkled.

When the bell rang, Caitlyn opened the door but wasn't prepared for what she saw. Her gaze roved appreciatively over the man who stood in front of her looking like a model straight off the cover of *GQ* magazine.

A black tailor-made, double-breasted suit fitted Marcel's well-toned physique to perfection. The black-and-white horizontal-stripped shirt had a contrasting white collar and French cuffs adorned with sterling crescent-shaped cufflinks and a purple silk necktie. The designer belt and black Italian leather slip-on loafers completed his ensemble.

Caitlyn's lips parted at the sight of him, and she ran her tongue seductively over them. "Almost ready. I just need to grab my purse and a jacket."

Marcel dropped his keys and stuttered whatever he was trying to say.

She playfully scolded. "Aren't you listening? I said I'm ready."

He was still stuttering his words as he followed her out the door.

Maharani, one of San Francisco's finest restaurants, was touted not only for its excellent cuisine, but also for its private dining experience in the romantic Fantasy Room.

After dinner, Marcel propped his back next to a plush pillow and rested his weight on one elbow. A smile touched his lips. "I hope you enjoyed dinner."

"I did." Caitlyn shifted to face him and a frown creased her brow. "Can I ask you a question?"

"Ask away."

"Are you deliberately holding back with our relationship?"

He met her gaze with a level stare. It was killing him not to touch her, but it was all part of his plan. She needed to know without a shred of doubt he didn't want their relationship to be based solely on a physical need for each other. Plus, he wouldn't accept anything less than her total trust in him. "Do you think I am?"

"Yes." She hated when someone answered a question with a question. For a long moment she stared at him. "You're torturing me on purpose, aren't you?"

"Torture you? Never." He smiled. "The only thing I'm doing is treating a woman the way she deserves to be treated."

"The way things have been going, it seems like we're just…"

"Just what, kitten?"

"Friends."

"I wouldn't exactly say we're friends."

"Then exactly what are we?"

"I'd say two people who are still getting to know each other." He lifted a glass of wine to his lips. "Do you trust me yet?"

She lowered her head for a moment before she looked back up at him and shook her head.

He nodded with a wicked grin. "Well, I guess my work is cut out for me then."

Sighing, Caitlyn rested against the pillow. Now she got it. All of this was a clever plan he'd come up with to make her trust him. Irritated that she hadn't penetrated his rigid control, she cut him a sideways glance. He gave her one of the sexiest smiles she'd ever seen. Sighing in exasperation, she folded her arms across her chest and blew out a hard breath.

She'd already known this man was arrogant and stubborn, but she'd just found out something else about him.

He played hardball.

"Just got word that BF Automotive has countered our bid." Louis, the car dealership CEO from New York spoke in a low, frosty tone.

Antonio shook his head in disbelief. "Let it go, will you?"

"I want that dealership."

Antonio bunched his brows together. "Why? It's just business, right?"

"Wrong. Some things are business. Some things are personal. This is personal."

Antonio threw his hands in the air. "Fine. Do what you want. I'm out of here."

Louis stared at the closed door and shook with rage. He'd waited a long time for revenge—thirty-seven and a half years to be exact. And for each year he'd waited, his hate for Alcee Baptiste had intensified. He'd wasted five years of his life sitting in a prison cell, all because of Alcee, and he wanted more than revenge. He wanted total annihilation. Getting his hands on the dealership was just the beginning. He didn't care what he had to do, but he'd see every one of the Baptistes roast in hell before he was finished.

The mood was relaxed and the red glow of the sunset streaked across the western horizon. Caitlyn stretched out on her back, her stomach too full to care what happened next. On Thursday, Marcel had invited her to a Saturday picnic, and she figured they would hang out together at a park. Never in her wildest dream did she think he'd create such a fantastic atmosphere right in his own backyard with all of her favorite foods.

"You barely ate a thing." Marcel dropped down on the blanket next to Caitlyn. "No wonder you're so tiny." He chuckled. "Do you even weigh a hundred pounds?"

The only body part on her that moved was her eyes when she glanced up at him. "I'll have you to know I weigh a hundred and one." She sighed with contentment, then rolled to her side. "This day has been wonderful, Marcel. Thank you for making it so special."

"Thank you. It's been a long time since I've taken the time to enjoy a picnic."

"Why?"

He reclined on his side and leaned on his elbow. His eyes roamed over her face to capture every facet of her beauty. "Working too hard, I suppose."

"Have you always headed BF Automotive?"

He chuckled and shook his head. "Actually, heading the business was something I never planned to do. For as long as I can remember, I've always tinkered around with cars.

You should have seen my room growing up. It was filled with every model car I could put together."

"So what did you do before you went to work for BF Automotive?"

"After I got my degree in mechanical engineering, I went to work as a design engineer for BMW."

She plucked a blade of grass. "Why did you quit?"

"Pop was able to snag up two more dealerships and business took off. We talked it over one day and knew we could take the company to the next level if we put our minds to it. So, a couple of months later, I resigned, went to Harvard and got my MBA, and the rest, as they say, is history."

She rolled onto her belly and braced her hands under her chin. Three months ago, no one in the world could have ever made her believe she would feel this way. "Marcel."

"Yes, kitten." He sat up and stared at her, watching her breasts rise and fall beneath the semi-sheer beige tank top. His gaze shifted to the thin sheen of perspiration along her top lip and he ached to lick it away. The tiny flickers of fear he'd seen in her eyes when they first met was gone. In their place was peace.

"I trust you."

He released a long breath through his nose and his smile mellowed as his voice dipped. "I hold on to what's mine."

"Am I yours?" She looked up to study him and plucked another bland of grass to keep from reaching out and touching his face. He had her on the verge of begging. She felt as if she were a stick of wax about to melt from his compelling gaze, even though the temperature was in the mid-sixties. She wanted to be possessed by him. Every day, she found herself wanting to be totally and completely dominated by his gentleness and protection.

"Yes." He allowed his gaze to burn her again before he scooted forward. His fingers traced a lazy pattern on top of her hand. "There's something you need to know."

"What's that?"

"There's no turning back."

Her fingers grazed the edge of his. She nearly gasped when his finger slid and slowly traced a lazy pattern up and down her arm. She shuddered and her nipples strained against her top. Her mouth went dry and she licked her lips in reflex. Her heart pounded wildly with anticipation. "That's good because I don't want to go back"

That's what he'd longed to hear all these weeks. Finally, she trusted him. Now he was on to phase two: getting her to fall in love with him. And he knew he was close. The way she had responded to his touch had almost sent him over the edge. He returned his gaze slowly to her face, studying the movement in her throat. Her lush mouth parted and her nostrils flared, just at the edges. Those slanted, brown eyes were nearly shut. He moved in for the kill. "Heads up. I've been courting you until now. But every chance I get from now on, I plan to seduce you. If it's too soon, tell me now."

His gray-green eyes were almost closed and his breathing labored. She indulged in a slow glance down his body and watched his stomach tense when her gaze swept below his waist. As his palm moved leisurely across hers, the thick muscles in his arm bulged and her desire for him produced sheer delirium.

She uttered her answer as a hoarse whisper. "Permission granted."

CHAPTER 8

In addition to his commitment to fund the co-op program, Marcel offered to help Caitlyn out on Saturdays as a volunteer. Since it was his first time meeting the group, he wasn't quite sure what to expect and decided to follow her lead.

"Everyone, I'd like to introduce Mr. Marcel Baptiste." Caitlyn walked into the room, her gaze scanning the group of teenagers assembled. "He's agreed to help us out."

The youth ranged from fourteen to seventeen and gave Marcel the once-over from head to toe.

"Uh, yo there, Mr. B, that there your lady?" The question was from a boy named Jamal who nodded at Caitlyn.

You're damn straight she's my lady, Marcel thought. "Ms. Thompson and I are business associates, and she said you guys could use—"

"Yeah, yeah, we done heard that before." The curt outburst was from a girl who sat on the back row.

During the rounds of high-fives and sarcastic laughter, Caitlyn walked between the chairs and looked directly at the one who'd made the comment.

"What's your name?"

The slim girl looked around mockingly as if she didn't understand the question.

Caitlyn stared at the light-skinned youth who'd challenged her. "Answer the question."

"Chanta," she replied flippantly. She was new to the center, and it was her first meeting.

"You got a job?" Caitlyn folded her arms across her chest.

Chanta stood with her hands on her hips and rolled her head. "What's it to you?"

Caitlyn released a half chuckle. "Oh, that means you don't have a job, huh?"

The others giggled, and Chanta was at a loss for words. Before she could reply, the boy who spoke first blurted the answer. "Naw, she ain't got no job."

"Jamal, be quiet." Caitlyn looked again at Chanta. "You depend on your man?"

Chanta snorted. "Don't need no man to take care of me. That's what the system's for."

Caitlyn moved to a nearby table. "I'm going show you how to stop depending on the system."

"Listen up—" Chanta waved her arm around to indicate that she spoke on everyone's behalf. "Give us a break with the sweet talk."

Caitlyn gazed intently at the entire group. "The system has pimped all of you." The group stared back with astonished expressions. "The system exploits your trifling behinds because you don't want to learn. Take a real close look at yourselves."

"Dang," Jamal whispered. The room fell quiet, and he looked over at Marcel for some backup. Marcel just gave him a confident smile and shrugged.

Chanta spoke again. "What you know about the system?"

"Excuse me?" Caitlyn planted her feet on the floor.

"You heard me. What you know about the system?" Chanta moved closer to Caitlyn.

Caitlyn looked up at Chanta. "I know what it's like to depend on the system. Had to depend on it for thirteen years myself. I know what it's like to have people think you're stupid and can't learn. They turn their noses up at you and treat you like you're trash." She started to walk off, but pivoted around with her eyes narrowed. "Cut me some slack about staying in the system, and let's figure out how you're going to make it out the hellhole you're in."

Chanta's tone was low, apologetic. "So what we got to do?"

"Tell me what you know how to do." Caitlyn patiently waited for an answer.

Jamal snorted. "They say we ain't good at doing nothing."

Caitlyn's voice held an indignant tone. "Who is 'they'? I know you can do something."

Silence.

Caitlyn focused her gaze on Chanta. "You look smart to me. Bet you're running the books for your man's money."

Chanta cocked her head sideways and slowly nodded as she grinned. "Down to the last penny."

Caitlyn fought back the twinge forming at the corners of her mouth. "You got the heads-up on his inventory, know what walks out the door, and I bet you know who owes him, right?"

"Yeah, something like that."

"Well then, sister-girl, in the business world, that's called inventory control, accounting and money management all wrapped up in one."

At the end of the session, Marcel walked up to Caitlyn and whispered next to her ear. "Cat eyes, you aren't a kitten, you're a tiger."

Caitlyn thought about Cole and shook her head at the statement. Tigers fought their predators; they didn't run from one end of the country to the other to get away from them. She noticed that Marcel had fished his car keys from his pants pocket. "Are you leaving?"

Marcel nodded. "I'm going to hang out with Jamal for a little while and talk with him." He glanced at his watch. "How about lunch at Kincaid's in an hour?"

Caitlyn smiled. "See you then."

Once she was alone, Caitlyn neatly stacked the chairs against the wall and never once regretted sharing the hardship of her childhood with the group. She'd done it primarily for Chanta's benefit and prayed something she'd said would help the girl.

She was headed to her office to catch up on some paperwork when Chanta appeared from a side room.

"Uh, Caitlyn…I mean Ms. Thompson, can I ask you something?"

Caitlyn nodded and patted the girl's shoulder. "Feel free to call me Caitlyn."

Chanta offered a soft smile. "I was thinking about what you said today, you know, about us being able to make something of ourselves."

"I meant every word. You can do it. You all can do it."

"You know, I've always dreamed of being a nurse."

Caitlyn could hardly contain her excitement. "What's stopping you?"

WHEN I'M WITH YOU

Chanta shrugged. "I don't know. Just ain't had nobody to talk to about it. I don't know nobody who's a nurse who could tell me what it's like." She lifted her round face to look at Caitlyn. "Know what I mean?"

"I know exactly what you mean." Caitlyn's eyes lit up. "Listen, if you're really serious about this, I think I can put you in touch with someone. Perhaps she could serve as a mentor." She saw the glow that brightened Chanta's face.

"You really mean it? I mean, you think she could talk with me?"

"My word on it."

Chanta hugged Caitlyn. "You know I've been making good grades lately."

"That's good." Caitlyn stared at the floor as a thought ran through her head. "Do you have a copy of your last report card?"

Chanta eagerly nodded.

"Okay. I want to see it. Can you remember to bring it to me next week when you come?"

"Yes!" Chanta's voice was filled with excitement.

"Good." Caitlyn reached out and drew Chanta into her embrace, which was equally reciprocated.

Chanta's voice was a mere whisper. "Ms. Thompson, I mean, Caitlyn, thank you."

Caitlyn pulled back and looked into doe-brown eyes sparkling with tears, but filled with hope. "You are going to make it, you hear me?"

"I hear you."

Leaning back in his chair after their lunch at Kincaid's, Marcel pushed his plate aside and watched Caitlyn with a look of total satisfaction.

"How many more sugars are you going to put in that cup of tea, kitten?"

"Huh?" Caitlyn was so engrossed in her thoughts, Marcel's question hadn't registered.

"I said…" He waved six empty sugar packets in front of him. "How many more sugars are you going to put in your tea?"

"Oops."

"That's okay." He tossed her a wink. "Just so you know, I think you're sweet enough."

She winked back. "Oh, really?"

"Yeah, really. So, lady, what's going on up in that pretty head of yours?"

With a gleam in her eye, Caitlyn propped her elbows on the table. "Marcel, I'm going to write another proposal to get some funding for mentors, you know, to regularly work with the kids at the center."

"Okay. But what brought this on?"

Caitlyn shared the exchange she'd had with Chanta. To her surprise, Marcel told her about a similar dialogue he'd had with Jamal after they left the center. Jamal confided to him that he wanted to be a doctor and had maintained excellent grades in math and science.

"All right. Just tell me what you need, and it's done."

"No."

His brow hitched. "No?"

"Baby, I didn't bring it up for you to fund it. Besides, you've already done so much for us as it is."

"I want to help. Is that such a crime?"

"It's not a crime, but I just don't want you to feel obligated to do something that ordinarily you wouldn't do, that's all."

A muscle twitched in Marcel's jaw. "Dammit, Caitlyn, why is it so difficult for you to believe that I truly want to help out?" He shook his head and raised his voice an octave. "Oh, I get it. You think I'm pimping the cause. Is that it?"

"What?"

"You heard me."

"That's not true, and you know it."

"Then tell me, Caitlyn, what is true here?"

Caitlyn let out a harsh sigh. She couldn't believe they were having this conversation in a public restaurant of all places. Through clenched teeth, she whispered, "Why do you always feel the need to be the savior of the world and pay for everything?" She regretted the reference the moment she said it. "I'm sorry. That was a cheap shot."

"You got that right." Marcel shifted in his seat and glared at her.

They both fell silent after realizing their conversation had attracted the attention of more than one table.

Caitlyn blew out a hard breath and softened her tone. "Listen, I didn't mean to imply that you weren't sincere or that you had an ulterior motive. It's just that—"

"Just what?"

"I-I just don't want to feel obligated to you for anything. That's all."

"It's not about you, Caitlyn."

"What's that supposed to mean?"

"It means that my wanting to help has nothing to do with you. This is about the youth center and the kids. Not you." He reached in his back pocket for his wallet, pulled out several bills, and threw them on the table. "Perhaps you're the one who lied to me."

She gasped in disbelief. "What?"

"You told me you trusted me, remember?" The muscles in his jaw twitched. "I'm not Cole and I would never intentionally hurt you."

Caitlyn blew out a hard breath. It was a long time before she said anything. She stared at the table when she finally did. "You're right."

"About what?"

"Everything you said. You're right." She chuckled and shook her head. "I did it again, didn't I?"

"What?"

"I allowed the past to come between us. I don't want you to think that I don't appreciate your offer because I truly do. It's just that…"

"I'm listening."

"I just don't want you to think I'd do or say anything to get inside your wallet. That's not what I'm about. My interest is in the man, not the man's money."

Marcel didn't have a comeback for that one. Other women would have jumped at the chance to latch on to his wallet. Not Caitlyn. Every day he was discovering not only was she different, she was rare, like a precious jewel, and he planned on treasuring her for many years to come.

"I don't think that." Reaching across the table, he enfolded her hand in his. I'm sorry I jumped to the wrong conclusion, and I didn't mean to yell at you."

"Well, as far as making mistakes goes, the score is two to zero in my favor, so you deserve a point. Accept my apology?"

He smiled and caressed the back of her hand. "Yes. Accept mine?"

"Yes."

He tightened his hand around hers. "I want to tell you something."

"Okay."

He kept his gaze focused on the table. "I've never shared it with anyone."

"Is everything all right?"

He nodded. "It's something I've wanted to do for a long time."

"What?"

"Start a philanthropy foundation at BF Automotive."

For a moment, Caitlyn stared, but was inwardly pleased at his willingness to share with others. Her eyes sparkled with excitement. "Really? Oh, baby, that's wonderful."

"Would you be willing to work for it?"

When she gave him a puzzled stare, he clarified his question. "Would you be willing to work in exchange for me funding your mentors?"

"How? What kind of work?"

"Didn't you tell me you used to work in corporate philanthropy?"

"Yes. I was the CEO of a large foundation."

"CEO, huh?" He grinned. "So, you could set up the foundation without thinking about it, right?"

"With my eyes closed."

He nodded. "Okay, here's the deal. You do whatever it takes to set up the foundation. In exchange for your work, I'll provide the funding for the mentors. Fair enough?"

"Oh, Marcel…"

He extended his hand for a shake to seal their agreement. "Well, do we have deal?"

She accepted the gesture. "We have a deal." Before she released his hand, she whispered softly, "Marcel?"

"Yeah, kitten?"

"You just gave me a piece of your heart, didn't you?"

"No. I gave you all of it."

"Come on, Vic. Tell me the last time I asked you for a favor."

Vic lightly tapped her index finger against the right side of her temple and looked across the table at Caitlyn. "The answer is still no."

"Vic, come on," Caitlyn pleaded. She knew Vic had recently quit her job as a top-level nursing administrator, and since she hadn't started a new position, she hoped to convince her to volunteer a few hours a week at the center.

"Hell, Caitlyn, I quit because I got tired of working with a group of dickheads who didn't know jack. Now you want me to work with a bunch of knuckleheads who think they know everything."

Caitlyn sighed because Vic had a valid point. She tried a different tactic. "But working at the center would help you get your mind off your breakup with Ron."

"Child, thinking about Ron only gives me a headache. Working with teenagers would give me a stroke."

Caitlyn laughed. "I really need your help. Pleasssse? Besides, sharing your experience as a nurse would really help Chanta."

Vic's eyes narrowed. "Who's Chanta?"

Caitlyn smiled. "A teenage version of you."

"Oh, hell no! I can't stand me sometimes, and you want me to work with someone like me with raging hormones?" Vic shook her head again. "Uh-uh. No way."

"Victoria Louise Bennett…"

Vic grinned. "You know I can't stand it when you beg. So before I say yes, what day?"

"Saturdays."

"Saturdays?"

"Yes."

"What time?"

"Nine."

Vic grimaced. "In the morning, nine?"

Caitlyn sighed. "Yes, Vic."

Vic cut her light brown eyes at Caitlyn. "All right. Just be sure to have my Tylenol handy. Extra strength at that."

"Come on, *petit frère*, I need your help on this one," Marcel pleaded for the umpteenth time.

A.J. shook his head the entire time Marcel begged, his shoulder-length ponytail swishing along the top of his broad shoulders. The easygoing pediatrician had resigned a coveted position as chief of pediatrics at Children's Hospital two years ago and was in the process of opening a family health center in East Oakland. The change allowed him more time raising his adopted twin daughters, Taylor and Tyler.

Marcel frowned. "No?"

"That's right. No. You never call me little brother, especially in French, unless you want something."

"Why won't you help out?"

"Who's going to watch the girls on Saturday mornings?"

"If I told you I'd take care of it, would you say yes?"

A.J. smiled. "Day and time?"

"Saturday mornings at nine."

"You're interfering with my Friday nights."

"No, I'm not. Now if you were Ray, then I'd have to say you were right. Besides, you haven't been out on a date in two years."

WHEN I'M WITH YOU

Raphael, their youngest brother who answered to Ray, was a world-renowned jazz musician who made Casanova seem like a monk.

A.J.'s double dimples peeked through when he smiled. "Keeping up with my love life?"

Marcel smiled back. "Hell, it's been three years since I've dated, so I've got you beat by a year."

CHAPTER 9

Sprawled across the couch with a pillow over her head and a blanket tucked to her chin, Caitlyn was tempted to remain there, but the insistent banging at her door and the question, "Kitten, you in there?" from the other side made her abandon the thought.

"Hi, baby. What's wrong?" Marcel didn't try to conceal the anxiety in his voice when she finally opened the door.

Clutching her stomach, she winced and waved him in. "Bad cramps."

Marcel closed the door with concern etched on his face. "I was worried about you. I didn't know if something happened or what. I called the center, and they said you'd phoned in sick. I've been trying to reach you here all morning and didn't get an answer."

Caitlyn slowly moved toward the couch. "I turned the ringer down. I'm sorry. I didn't mean to worry you." She clutched her stomach with one hand and rubbed at her lower back with the other.

He sat beside her. "Is it like this every month?"

"No. I'm really irregular. But when it does decide to show up," she rolled her eyes, "it comes with a vengeance." She lowered her lashes. "I'm sorry."

"Sorry about what?"

"I look like crap." She tried to straighten her Capri pants and T-shirt. "Plus, I'm embarrassed."

He shrugged. "You look fine to me. But why are you embarrassed?" Then the answer dawned on him. "Not because you're having bad cramps?"

She nodded.

"Kitten, it's the most natural thing in the world. There's nothing for you to be embarrassed about. Do you have anything to take for them?"

She bobbed her head. "But it makes me sleepy and I don't like being by myself half conscious."

Marcel took off his suit coat, tossed it on the back of the sofa and held out his hand. "Come on."

She placed her hand in his and looked up with a puzzled stare. "Come where?"

"Trust me."

He led her into the bedroom, then pointed to the bed. "Off your feet, lady, until I get things ready."

He took off his onyx cufflinks, rolled back his sleeves and put his watch inside his pocket. Once inside the bathroom, he began to fill the tub. A few seconds later, he peeked his head out the door. "Do you use any kind of bubble bath?"

She turned in bed until she could see him. "Yes. Right side of the vanity cabinet."

A couple of minutes later, Marcel was at the foot of the bed. "Where's your robe, kitten."

She looked to her right. "In the closet."

He glanced around the room. "Okay. Baby oil? Towels?"

"Baby oil, on top of the dresser, and towels are in the linen closet in the hallway. But—"

"No buts." He helped her to her feet. "The water's a little hot, but that's good for you." When she hesitated, he gave her shoulder a gentle push. "Go on before it cools off."

Walking toward the bathroom, she stopped and spoke over her shoulder. "Where did you—"

"I grew up around three sisters, remember?" Once Caitlyn began to peel off her clothes, Marcel made a half turn to the door, then stopped. "Let me know when you're finished, all right?"

"Marcel?"

"Yeah, baby?"

"Thank you."

He smiled. "You're welcome. All right, now lean your head back on that towel." He turned and quietly closed the door behind him.

Marcel searched every cabinet in the kitchen until he found several bags of herbal tea. He'd placed a cup of water in the microwave and was waiting for it to heat when he heard Caitlyn call out to him.

After her bath, Caitlyn slipped on a pair of shorts and another T-shirt and sat on the edge of the bed.

Marcel walked in with a steaming cup of tea. "I think this will help." He placed the cup on the nightstand. "Feeling better?"

"Yes."

"Good. Now stretch out for me. I'll be right back."

A few moments later he returned with two large towels. He grabbed the baby oil off the dresser, then pointed toward the bathroom. "Do you keep your medicine in there?"

"Yes. Second shelf inside the cabinet."

He grabbed the bottle, read the directions and took out two tablets. Back at the side of the bed, he held out his hand. "Come on. Take these. There's no sense in suffering with pain if you have something that will knock it out."

Lying on her stomach, she rolled to her side. "But it'll make me sleepy."

He shrugged. "I'm not going anywhere."

She popped the white tablets in her mouth and washed them down with the tea.

"What hurts most?"

She groaned. "My back."

"Okay. We'll start there first." He spread one of the towels on the bed. "On your stomach for me."

With long, tapered fingers, he gently kneaded her shoulders, and in a steady motion, worked his way down her spine.

"Umm, feels good."

"Is the pain starting to ease?"

"Yes."

"Good." He continued to gently massage the muscles that felt like knots. "Now close your eyes and relax for me."

"Thank you." She fought back a yawn. "I don't want to keep you from anything. Go on. I'll be okay."

Bending down, he placed a soft kiss at the center of her back. "Go to sleep, kitten. I'm exactly where I want to be."

After a Saturday mentoring session at the youth center, Marcel accepted a challenge from Jamal, the young boy he'd met on his first day at the center, to a game of one-on-one at the gym a couple of blocks away. Caitlyn decided to work on a couple of reports while she waited for them to return.

Two hours later, Marcel staggered into her office breathing heavily. Bent at the waist, he clutched his thighs and sweat dripped down his face. Finally, he slumped into a nearby chair.

"Whew." Marcel sounded winded.

"Poor baby." Caitlyn bit down hard on her bottom lip to keep from laughing out loud, but a snicker still managed to escape.

Opening one eye, Marcel looked at her. "What's so funny?"

"You thinking you're the twenty-year-old version of the NBA's next superstar."

He closed his eye. "I'll have you know I can hang with the best of them."

"Oh yeah?"

"Yeah."

"So, who won?"

"It was close."

"In other words, you got your butt kicked, right?"

He leaned his head against the back of the chair and stretched out his long legs as a hard sigh escaped. "Hell yeah."

"Let me see if I can make it better." Caitlyn took a seat on his lap and sniffed. She leaned back and wrinkled her nose. "Oh, baby, you stink."

Marcel chuckled. "Jamal smells just as bad."

She started to get up but a pair of strong arms held her still.

"In some countries, women like their men musty, you know."

"Sorry to bust your bubble here, but this is the U.S. of A., brother, and this woman likes a good-smelling man."

He pulled her closer and rubbed his sweaty face against the side of hers. "You mean good smelling with deodorant, aftershave, cologne—"

"Right now, I'd settle for soap and water."

They both laughed.

Marcel caressed each corner of her mouth before his tongue slipped inside. He sighed with contentment. "Listen, if we're going to keep our date, I'd better get going. It'll take me at least thirty minutes to drive home, shower, change, and drive back over to pick you up."

"Do you have a change of clothes with you?"

"Yeah," he answered with a hesitant drawl.

"Deodorant and cologne?"

He chuckled. "Yes. Why?"

"Want to shower and change at my place?"

"You sure?"

She got up, grabbed her purse and took a single key off the ring. She held it out to him. "I'm sure. I need about thirty more minutes to finish this report anyway. "

Accepting the key, he stood and pulled her close and murmured his thanks against her mouth. "*Merci.*"

She parted her lips and his tongue slipped inside. When they finally pulled away, she started to say to him "you're welcome" in English. But her French lessons had improved tremendously. "*De rien.*"

CHAPTER 10

"Marcel, you're putting the wrong fork by the knife." Brie chastened her twin brother as she watched him arrange the antique sterling-silver flatware. She looked closely at the fork again. "Yep, I was right. Boy, that's a salad fork."

"Look, Brie, right now a fork's a fork, all right?" With a little less than an hour before Caitlyn's arrival for dinner with his family, Marcel nervously scurried around the dining room table to make sure everything was perfect. His grandmother, Mama Z, had gladly taken charge of dinner and prepared several of her delicious Creole dishes. Earlier that morning, Marcel had ordered his personal house-keeping service to come in and clean his father's house from top to bottom, even though Alcee told him his cleaning service had performed the weekly task the day before.

Marcel couldn't remember how many bottles of wine he'd flown in from his favorite winery in Italy until they had arrived at his house two days earlier. He had spent a small fortune ordering a new set of Waterford crystal because he thought he saw a chip on one of the wineglasses he'd inspected the week before. When the clerk told him she couldn't guarantee his order would arrive in time, he'd explained to her in no uncertain terms he expected his order by the close of business the next day. The store manager personally delivered it before noon.

His constant appearances in and out of the kitchen forced Mama Z to issue a temporary restraining order against him for the remainder of the evening. She reassured him she had the evening's meal under control and pleaded with him to go find someone else's nerves to rattle. With less than an hour before dinner, he found his partner in crime, his ace, Brie.

His fraternal twin was older by two minutes, and Brie had absolutely no trouble reminding him he was her little brother. He'd shared her pain when she lost the love of her life, her husband of only two years, in a head-on collision. Since then, she'd channeled all of her energies into establishing a successful beauty salon and spa, Taste of Heaven.

From the opposite side of the table, Brie stiffened her six-foot frame and braced her hands on her narrow hips. She grinned. "Little brother, there're different types of forks. What if Caitlyn has more sophistication than you appear to have right now and knows the difference?"

Nervously fingering his beard, Marcel studied the placement of the forks he'd spent the last hour arranging. "Yeah…yeah…yeah. You're right." He looked up to see his sister with both hands clamped over her mouth. "Come on, Brie, and help me out here." He opened his arms wide. "I wouldn't just stand around and not help you out if you'd made a mistake."

"Yes, you would." Still laughing, Brie switched the forks.

A worried look crept into Marcel's eyes, and he slumped in a nearby chair. "God, I hope everything goes well."

"Why wouldn't it?"

"Brie, you know how crazy this family is."

She took a seat next to him and patted his shoulder. "You really like her, huh, little brother?"

Marcel didn't answer.

Brie leaned over and whispered in her brother's ear. "I know you, and that's a yes. Boy, I ain't seen you this nervous in my life."

"I'm not nervous." Marcel proceeded to fold the linen napkins in front of him at the wrong angle.

She chuckled. "Yeah, right. You haven't been this excited about a female since you told me that Kennedy what's-her-face let you kiss her back in the seventh grade."

"What?" He laughed at the reminder.

"You heard me." Brie placed a soft kiss against his cheek. "Everything's going to be fine. At least Ray isn't here."

Marcel sighed with relief. "Thank God for small favors, huh." Ray, their youngest brother, was touring with his jazz band, but had promised to be back home by the second week in October when the family celebrated what they referred to as Baptiste family week.

They both laughed.

With a gleam in her gray-green eyes, Brie casually offered Marcel her usual assistance. "Don't worry. I'ma help you run interference tonight."

"Brie." Marcel's voice had a warning tone.

"What?" Brie scooted her chair in closer. "No, now listen, *petit frère*. You know this crew as well as I do. Moni will be asking fifty million questions." She shook her head and sighed. "Heaven knows what kind of mood diva Aimee will be in when she gets here."

Marcel pinched the bridge of his nose and faced Brie. "That's what I'm worried about. I asked Caitlyn to join us for dinner, not come and witness a three-ring circus. You know, sometimes all of you people can be as uncontrolled as animals in the wild."

She cut her gray-green eyes at him. "I know you're not talking about me."

"You included." He smiled and thumped the end of her nose. "At least I can count on you controlling yourself better than the rest of them."

She slapped the table. "See, that's exactly what I'm talking about. I've always had your back. Now just leave all inquiries to me." Without hesitation, she pointed her thumb at her chest. "I'll field all questions tonight."

"Oh, no, you won't."

"Why not?"

Marcel had known since they were teenagers that Brie always tried to run interference between him and the women he dated. God love her, but more often than not he had to remind her he was perfectly capable of handling his woman.

He chuckled and stood. "No." He placed a kiss on both her cheeks.

"Why not? Look, you need me to at least—"

"No." He really wanted to tell his sister her interference in his love life was wearing on his last nerve. At the moment, the only thing he was interested in was making a good impression on Caitlyn and getting through dinner without her feeling she'd spent half the evening in a psych ward.

"Marcel?" Brie followed him toward the kitchen.

Marcel turned in mid-stride. "Brie, stay out of grown folk's business."

Everyone was seated at the huge dining room table enjoying Mama Z's red beans and rice, chicken-and-okra gumbo, jambalaya and Creole cornbread. For dessert, she'd made beignets.

Alcee and Mama Z sat at each end of the table. A.J., his daughters Taylor and Tyler, and Aimee, the youngest sibling, sat on one side of the huge dining room table while Brie, Moni, Moni's husband Zach, Marcel and Caitlyn sat on the opposite side.

"Unca Marcel," Tyler giggled.

Marcel looked across the table at his niece. "Yes, cupcake. What is it?"

The four-year-old looked at Caitlyn. "She pretty."

Marcel smiled. "Thanks, sweet pea." He glanced over at Caitlyn and gave her a loving look. "I think so, too."

Caitlyn offered a soft smile. "Thank you, Tyler."

Tyler bobbed her tiny head up and down. "Welcome, Caitlyn."

Mama Z softly cleared her throat and whispered to Tyler who sat next to her. "That's not right."

"Oops, I soorie." Tyler formed a huge O with her mouth. She stood and cupped her hand next to her great-grandmother's ear. "What I say again, *arrière grand-mère*?"

Mama Z smiled and whispered back. "Ms. Caitlyn, sweetheart."

Tyler's doe-brown eyes lit and she nodded, then shifted her gaze back to Caitlyn. "Welcome, Ms. Caitlyn."

Caitlyn nodded and smiled.

A pregnant Moni was seated to Caitlyn's left and turned with her elbow propped on the table. "So, Caitlyn, how long have you lived in Oakland? Where are you from? How long have you and Marcel been seeing each other?"

"Moni." Zach, Moni's husband, spoke somewhat forcefully as he reached for a second helping of red beans and rice.

Moni turned to him. "What?" When he didn't respond immediately, she innocently shrugged. "Did I do something wrong?"

Brie peered around Zach. "Yeah. You asked the woman a zillion questions without coming up for air. I'm sure if there's something Caitlyn wants us to know, she'll tell us."

Moni looked at her sister with her hand up defensively. "Listen, Brie, I was just trying to make friendly conversation. That's all."

All the adult family members countered back as if on cue, "No, you weren't." Afterward, a few of them mumbled under their breath their displeasure at Moni's questioning.

"Son, ya needs to get a handle on ya woman there." Mama Z nodded to Zach while she looked sternly at her granddaughter. The family matriarch's skin tone was as smooth and rich as butter, but the deadpan expression on her face was as hard as cement.

A smiling Caitlyn intervened. "Moni, to answer your questions, I've lived here about nine months. I'm from Newark, New Jersey, and I've known Marcel a little over three months."

Moni clapped gleefully. "Okay, now, let me ask you this—"

"Monique Desiree Baptiste Tate." Zach's tone was crisp.

Moni straightened up and didn't utter another word.

Marcel lowered his head and chuckled. He'd always gotten along with Zach, even before he and Moni married six years ago, but at the moment, he loved him for whatever techniques he'd employed to curtail Moni's propensity to gossip. He figured those skills came from Zach's job as a lieutenant with the Oakland Police Department.

Aimee gasped in amazement. "So, Zach, is that all we need to do to keep her quiet?"

Zach continued eating and tossed Aimee a quick wink. "Requires a little more than that, sister-in-law."

Brie chuckled. "Well, let us in on the other half of your secret, brother."

After dinner, Mama Z served the beignets, and Alcee helped her serve coffee. While they were eating, Aimee looked over at Marcel. "You're still keeping your promise to help me move Saturday, right?"

Marcel lifted his brow in surprise. "Aimee, I never made you that promise. Besides, Caitlyn and I have plans for Saturday."

Aimee poked out her ruby lips. "Well, how am I supposed to move my stuff?"

Brie rolled her eyes. "Girl, stop whining, please."

Aimee snatched her napkin from her lap and tossed it on the table. Brie, I'm not whining. Marcel said he was—"

"No, you said that," Marcel shot back. "Not me."

Caitlyn smiled as she glanced back and forth between the squabbling siblings. She finally knew what family was all about. She patted Marcel's hand. "Don't worry about Saturday. I think we should help Aimee." She looked over at Marcel's sister. "Perhaps some of my kids from the center could help you as well. We try to encourage volunteerism, and I'm sure they wouldn't mind."

Aimee snorted. "I don't know any of *those* people."

Caitlyn's smile quickly faded. "They don't know you either."

Brie leaned over and looked down the table at Caitlyn. "G'on, girl." Looking over at Aimee, she taunted, "Hmph. What you got to say now?"

A.J., Marcel's second youngest brother, fingered the diamond stud in his right ear. "Listen, Aimee, I work with those kids on Saturdays, and they're a good bunch. Besides, I think it was generous of Caitlyn to offer you the help in the first place."

Aimee glanced around the table at angry eyes. "Listen, I wasn't trying to be rude. It's just that I'm not used to having a bunch of people around my stuff. I don't know…"

Caitlyn's eyes narrowed. "Aimee, I can assure you my kids won't take any of your things, if that's what you're worried about. They're not looking to steal, just searching for a chance."

Marcel's tone was icy. "Aimee, stop being a brat. I'm with A.J. on this one. It was more than generous of Caitlyn to even make the suggestion in the first place. We'll be there bright and early Saturday morning with our kids. You just be ready."

Aimee lowered her head and a few seconds later said, "Caitlyn, I apologize if I was rude. I didn't mean to imply anything negative about the kids."

Caitlyn nodded. "No need to apologize."

Brie snorted and looked down her side of the table again. "Marcel, see there. I told you, you should've—"

"People, we have a guest here tonight, all right?" Pinching his nose, Marcel glanced around the table and tried to keep his temper in check. His family's wacky behavior was exactly what he'd been afraid of.

Alcee spoke in a stern voice. "Marcel's right. There's a guest in my home and at my table." He glanced around the table. "Unfortunately, none of the people I claim as children—" he paused and narrowed his eyes at each of them, "have shown good manners this evening."

Brie glared at Aimee across the table. "Well, it's all Aimee's fault, Daddy."

Aimee shouted back. "Me?" She pointed at Marcel. "He's the one that started all of this."

The napkin in Marcel's lap landed on the floor when he tried to stand but was stopped by Caitlyn's hand on his arm. "What? Look, you started this mess with your pouting and whining."

A.J. defended Marcel, too. "Look, Marcel didn't start anything. If Moni hadn't been asking a zillion questions, none of this would have gotten started."

Zach stopped eating his third helping of red beans and rice and turn to face A.J. "Now wait just a minute there, brother-in-law. My baby just asked a couple of questions, that's all." He glanced at Moni. "Ain't that right, baby?"

Moni tilted her head high. "That's right. All of this is Caitlyn and Marcel's fault."

Caitlyn turned to stare at Marcel with her mouth wide open, then turned back to Moni. "What?"

Marcel shook his head in disbelief. "For the love of God, how?"

Mama Z's eyes narrowed and she issued a stern warning. "Marcel Xavier, watch ya mouth. Ya knows better than to use God's name in vain."

Marcel nodded. "Sorry, Mama Z." He looked at Moni again. "How, Moni?"

Moni waved her hands in a circle. "This whole fiasco started when the two of you agreed to help Aimee move Saturday."

Caitlyn turned back to Moni with her hands planted at her hips. "Now listen here, Moni. He said he didn't tell her that. I'm not going to sit around and let somebody say he said something when he said he didn't."

Mama Z chuckled. "I likes that."

Everyone stopped talking and turned toward Mama Z.

"Like what, Mama Z?" Marcel finally asked.

Mama Z smiled and nodded at Caitlyn. "A woman who takes up for her man." She winked at Caitlyn. "That's a good thang, child." After a moment of complete silence, everyone burst into laughter.

Taylor held her hand high in the air and waited.

A.J. turned to acknowledge her. "What is it, pumpkin?"

"Daddy, what's a brat?"

A.J. stammered. "Well…uh—"

"You know, it's what Unca Marcel calls us sometimes." Tyler lifted her gaze to the ceiling and placed a chubby finger against her head. "So it's good. Right, Unca Marcel?"

The only thing Marcel could do was smile. His nieces never ceased to amaze him. From the moment A.J. adopted them two years ago, he'd fallen in love with the dynamic duo, and it didn't take long for the family to figure out the mischievous mirror images would make them voluntarily commit themselves to the nearest mental institution.

Caitlyn placed her hand over her mouth to keep from laughing.

Marcel chuckled at Tyler. "Listen, sweetheart, I'll explain it to you later.

Alcee looked over at Caitlyn. "Marcel tells me you have an investment program at your center."

Caitlyn nodded. "That's correct."

Alcee cupped his chin in his right hand. "Listen, I dabble a little with stocks and I've got a little free time on my hands these days. If you'd like, perhaps I could come over and work with that program."

"Oh, Alcee, that would be wonderful," Caitlyn exclaimed. "Thank you so much."

Moni reached out and touched Caitlyn's arm. "You know, I taught high school before Zach and I got married. I could help out with tutoring, if that's all right."

Caitlyn beamed. "Moni, it would help. Thank you so much. I'll give you a number where you can reach me before I leave. We can talk tomorrow about the details."

Aimee cleared her throat. "Caitlyn, I could help tutor them in math, if you'd like." Then she glared at Moni. "On the opposite days she's there, of course."

Caitlyn chuckled. "I'll make sure the schedule doesn't present a conflict for you and Moni."

"Listen, since my beauty shop is closed on Mondays," Brie offered, "maybe we could arrange to get the girls over to get their hair and nails done. I'll even bring some barbers for the boys. What do you say?"

Caitlyn's eyes glossed with tears at the generous offers. "Thank you. Thank you all so much."

After dinner, Marcel drove Caitlyn back to her apartment. Standing in the middle of her tiny living room, he ran his hand across his face. "Kitten, I hope you weren't embarrassed by that crazy clan I claim as family."

Walking over, she stood in front of him and looped her arms around his neck. "Thank you for inviting me. And no, I wasn't embarrassed at all. In fact, they made me feel very welcome." She laughed out loud. "And Mama Z is something else."

"Yeah, she's a feisty one." Marcel chuckled. "I hope I'm that spry when I hit seventy-five."

"Seventy-five?" She gasped amazed. "Well, she certainly looks good for her age."

WHEN I'M WITH YOU

He chuckled when he saw the look in her eyes, as if a calculator were going off in her head. He knew what her next question would be, so he beat her to the punch. "She was fifteen when she had my mother."

She stroked the right side of his face. "You're blessed to have a wonderful family. You know that, don't you?"

"I know."

The lamp on the nearby table highlighted her features, which appeared more exotic than he remembered. Feasting on her beauty, the same jolt of awareness Marcel felt the moment he first saw her hit him with such intensity he found it difficult to breathe. He loved this woman more than he ever thought possible.

His confession of love hung on the tip of his tongue. He knew Caitlyn cared for him, but caring wasn't good enough. He wanted her unconditional love, and until she was ready to make that same confession, discipline intervened and eradicated the words. The woman had him at a breaking point, and more than anything in the world, he wanted to be buried so deep within her she couldn't imagine him not being a part of her. But he had to be absolutely certain she was with him every step of the way. Once words of love were exchanged between them, there would be no turning back.

He wrapped his arms around her, reminding himself of his promise to earn her trust, and until she was ready to accept his love and place her confidence in him, he would take things slow and easy. If he had to wait until eternity, he would. She was worth the wait.

He meant for the kiss to be gentle and tender, but when her tongue sought his and she opened completely, his control snapped. His hands fused to the back of her head as he deepened the kiss and pressed her petite body closer. Without reservation, he allowed her to feel what she did to him.

A ragged moan surfaced, and he was barely able to catch his breath. "Sweet dreams, kitten."

Outside, he rested his taut body against the door, and the coolness of the night's air washed over him. Fumbling with his keys, he raced to his car. He needed a cold shower in the worst way.

CHAPTER 11

Marcel stopped by the youth center a little after six the next evening and knocked lightly on Caitlyn's office door.

"Hi, baby."

"Hi yourself, handsome." Caitlyn came around the desk and planted a kiss on his cheek. "What are you doing here?" She glanced at her watch. "I thought we agreed I'd come over to your place around eight."

"I know, but I have a surprise for you." He motioned for her to sit down. "Close your eyes—and no peeking, all right?"

"Yes, sir." She giggled and obeyed his order with a salute.

Marcel returned moments later with a huge box and took out the contents. "Okay, kitten, you can look now."

Caitlyn opened her eyes to see two white Bichon Frise puppies racing toward her and covered her open mouth with both hands. "Oh my God, Marcel. They're beautiful!"

"I saw them and truth be told, I fell in love with them myself."

Reaching down, she lifted them onto her lap. "But where am I going to keep them? There's a no-pet policy where I stay."

"I've got that covered. They can stay with me."

She hitched her brow. "And who's going to take care of them?"

He beamed. "We are."

"We are?"

"Yeah. I figure since we'll be spending a lot of time working on the foundation, you can come over and check on them in the evenings. I've got the morning shift covered." He grinned.

Caitlyn offered him a chagrined smile. "I get the feeling there's an ulterior motive somewhere."

He'd chided her before about accusing him of a hidden agenda. However, in this instance, she was dead on the money. He couldn't lie to her. "You, kitten," he kissed one cheek, "are a very smart woman." He repeated the gesture on the other cheek.

By that time, both puppies were trying to steady themselves on Caitlyn's lap as they licked her face. "Okay, so what are their names?"

Marcel plucked the female, who had a pink bow around her neck, off Caitlyn's lap. "This one is Kenji, and I figured she needed some company. You've got Max." Max had a matching blue bow.

"Male and female in close quarters? Marcel, I don't know. They might—"

"No, they won't. I took care of it." Marcel looked between the two dogs. "Didn't I, gang?" They barked in unison.

Caitlyn threw her head back and laughed. "Okay, I see whose side you guys are on."

"I've got something else for you."

"What?"

Marcel walked out the room with Kenji trailing behind. They returned a few seconds later and he handed Caitlyn a smaller box.

Opening it, Caitlyn carefully lifted out each item and laid them on her desk. "Hmmm…let's see. A cell phone, company credit cards with my name on them." She took out one other thing. "Oh, my…your ATM card." With a soft smile, she looked up at him. "Anything else?"

"Baby, I just don't like you running around carrying a purse full of cash. It's not safe." Shuffling his feet, he stuffed his sweaty hands inside his pockets. "And you need a way to communicate with someone—you know, me." Taking in a deep breath, he rushed to add, "And everything there is safe. Cole will never be able to trace anything back to you."

Caitlyn blinked back tears and didn't say a word as she placed everything back inside the box.

"And…uh…well, we can settle up the bill however you want." He ran his hand across his bearded face. "Kitten, tell me something here."

She handed Max to Marcel, then she stood on tiptoe and kissed his left cheek. "Thank you so much."

He felt the tension seep out of him. "You're not upset?"

She smiled and shook her head. "Nope."

He released a long sigh of relief and placed Max on the floor next to Kenji. "I just didn't want you to feel…"

"Feel what?"

"Feel like I don't respect your need to be independent. And I'm not trying to be controlling or obsessive, nothing like that."

"I don't feel like that." She grabbed her clutch purse and walked out of her office.

Marcel took off behind her and skidded up to the door. He called out from behind. "What do you feel?"

She turned and winked at him "*Je t'aime.*" She motioned for Max and Kenji. "Come on, guys so I can get you home and settled in." She tossed Marcel a sultry look. "Once I get my little babies settled, then I'll work on settling my big baby." She walked out the building.

I love you. Marcel pumped his fist in the air. "Houston, we have landed!"

Marcel loved watching the joyful expression on Caitlyn's face as she fussed over and pampered Kenji and Max. After dinner, she'd taken them for a walk while he cleared the dishes. It wasn't until he had finished cleaning the kitchen and entered the family room he discovered she'd curled up on one end of the couch with her hand tucked under her head snoring, as Kenji and Max snuggled on the floor in front of her. Stepping around them, Marcel effortlessly lifted his precious bundle from the couch and headed to his bedroom in the east wing with both puppies in hot pursuit.

His bedroom was decorated in crisp, cool white. The two custom bedside tables, plush area rug and silky sheers at the windows made the space seem like a billowing sea of white clouds. The most spectacular feature was the bed with its semicircular headboard in the middle of the room. A white mosquito netting suspended from a circle of wire wrapped the entire custom king-size bed in a cozy cocoon of privacy.

Caitlyn stirred once when Marcel placed her in the middle of his bed, but didn't awaken. He slipped off her sandals and stepped away. For the life of him, though, he couldn't leave. He stood motionless, watching her breasts rise and fall beneath a semi-sheer white top. Then his gaze shifted to her hair, which was cascading across the pillow like a blanket of black velvet. The look of complete contentment on her face when she rolled onto her back, throwing her arms over her head, caused a shudder to race through him. Her lush, slightly parted lips breathed out a steady stream of air he swore he could feel from where he stood.

The sight of her lying there in his bed, less than an arm's length away, made goose bumps appear on his arms. He had to get out of there. Watching Caitlyn had reduced him to the unthinkable—begging.

A couple of hours later, Caitlyn awoke to find Kenji and Max lying at the foot of the bed.

"How are my babies?" Scooping them to her chest, she glanced around at her surroundings. After a quick trip to the bathroom, she climbed in the middle of the bed with her legs drawn beneath her. Snuggling her nose into the pillow that held Marcel's scent, she whispered to herself. "I love him."

Caitlyn's heart pounded at what felt like a thousand beats per minute as the reality of her confession set in.

Three months ago, no one could have made her believe not only would she learn to trust another man again, but that she'd fall in love. As stubborn, arrogant and possessive as Marcel was, she loved him. She loved him for his gentleness and for his willingness to share whatever he had. He could be down to his last fifty cents, but she knew he'd always make sure she had a quarter. Although he could have, he hadn't wooed her with material things, but with the desires of her heart. Even when she didn't think so, he'd listened to her during the long hours they'd sat and talked, something no man had ever done. She was bound and determined before the break of dawn to not only tell him she loved him, but to show him.

"Where's Marcel?" Her laughter filled the room when Kenji and Max jumped off the bed and raced toward the closed bedroom door, tails wagging as they barked in unison. Scooting to the edge of the bed, she peeled off everything except her underwear and slipped into Marcel's black silk robe lying at the foot of the bed.

Since it was the first time Caitlyn had been in the upper level of Marcel's estate, it took her a while to get her sense of direction. She finally made her way downstairs and found him in his study looking over a stack of inventory reports at his desk.

"Marcel."

He lifted his head and beckoned her to come. "Have a good nap?" He patted his lap for her to sit, and when she complied, he placed a kiss at her temple.

She looped her arms around his neck. "Very good. But I didn't mean to crash on you. Why didn't you wake me up?"

"Figured you needed the rest." He fingered the collar of his robe and smiled.

She looked down and asked in a silky tone, "You don't mind, do you?"

"Uh-uh. You look good in it." He looked around the floor. "Where're Kenji and Max?"

"In their room."

Marcel had redecorated one of the guest bedrooms down the hall from his. He'd purchased beds, gold-plated, engraved feeding dishes and everything in between, along with a double doggie stroller.

"You're spoiling them, you know. Especially Max."

She chuckled. "No, I'm not. I'm not doing any more for them than what you do for me. Besides, Kenji feels she owns you."

"Max doesn't want me within a foot of you, I'll have you know. He needs to learn how to share."

She tightened her arms around his neck. "There's no need for you to be concerned about Max." She shifted in his lap. Gently palming his face, her fingers stroked his beard. "Marcel Xavier Baptiste, you are the man in my life."

"Thank you." He gave her a warm smile. "Now that we've got that settled, tell me what it is you'd like your man to do for you now."

The huskiness and desire in his voice coupled with the hardness of his arousal prompted her next words. "Discuss us."

Now that she'd confessed her love to him, the only thing he wanted to know was how fast they could make it to his bed. But the decision needed to be hers, though. He hung on to his promise not to rush, barely. He trailed his finger down the side of her cheek until he reached the opening of his robe. "What do you want to discuss?"

"Where we go from here."

"Where do you want us to go?"

"To the physical. I want us to have sex."

Marcel caressed her cheek. "Sorry, but that won't happen, cat eyes."

"I see." She turned her face away to try and hide her disappointment at the impact of his words. For weeks, she'd hoped he'd break his ironclad control. She'd even told him she loved him and meant every word. What was this man trying to do to her?

With his index finger, he turned her face back to his. "We won't ever have sex, kitten." His lips brushed across hers. "We'll make love. There's a big difference."

"Marcel?"

"Yeah, baby?"

"I'm ready to make love."

Pulling back slightly, he looked into her eyes. "So am I, kitten. And you're ready to accept everything that goes along with that? Meaning, this isn't temporary, and you can't wake up one day and decide it's over between us. You're my woman, and from this night forward, what we share is for keeps. I told you before, I keep what's mine."

Staring back into his smoldering gaze, she nodded. "You are the man that I love, the man I trust, the man I want to make love with."

They'd shared kisses before, but this one was different. It was hot and deep. His tongue swept hers, tenderly at first, then moments later her tongue matched the strokes he made, and before either could pull away, tongues dueled, teeth clashed, and lips formed a seal so tight not even air could escape.

"I'm getting a little warm." Caitlyn stood, slowing loosening the sash on the robe.

"That can be fixed."

Walking backward to the door until she could go no farther, she purred, "Perhaps a nice long bath would help cool things off."

He shook his head. "I don't believe so." He reached to rid her of the robe.

The silk material glided down her body and pooled at her feet. "Perhaps if I took this off, that would help." She reached up to release the front of her bra. "Or this." Her matching thong quickly followed.

Standing before him completely nude, she wrapped her arms around his neck, seductively moving against him. When he captured a taut nipple, then circled it with his tongue, desire raced through her with such force, nerve endings short-circuited.

He nuzzled his lips along her neck as his hand palmed her damp center. "All mine?"

"All yours."

She followed him with her eyes when he dropped to his knees, his tongue trailing a wet path along her navel, down her hip, ending with a kiss against her curly patch. Moisture pooled at her center and threatened to spill forth, and her nails left their imprint on his shoulders.

Marcel stood, scooped her into his arms, and once in his bedroom, lowered her onto the bed. He watched her gaze follow him as he quickly undressed, never taking his eyes from hers. Nude, he proudly stood before her so she could see exactly the state he was in whenever she was near. "I want our first time to be better than good, and we'll go slow."

He placed one knee on the bed, committing her beauty to memory. Every exquisite detail of her body was exposed without inhibition. Firm breasts, chocolate-tipped nipples, a narrow waist that connected to slender hips, and even the tiny gold ring that pierced her navel were imprinted forever in his mind. Crawling on all fours, he lifted her petite feet to his mouth and kissed his way up, searing her silky skin with the warmth of his breath and branding her with such pleasure she writhed against the sheets. He crouched over her, his palms flat against the mattress. "I don't want you to ever be afraid of making love with me. I want nothing between us—no fear, no doubt, no shame. One day soon, I want to come inside of you. I want the love we make to fill you with my *bébé*. I want this house to become our home."

God, he hadn't meant to propose to her in the heat of passion. His declaration of commitment was supposed to be on bended knee after a candlelight dinner. But the moment he stared into her eyes that reflected her complete trust in him, the words burst forth like a volcanic eruption.

He reached to retrieve a condom from the nightstand, but the hand on his arm halted his efforts.

"In a minute." She nipped at the tiny buds hidden by the triangle of hair on his chest, and her hands roamed the smooth, hot length of his arousal.

His arms strained and trembled from his weight, yet he closed his eyes and surrendered to the magic of her touch. Feeling the first moisture drop squeeze through, Marcel knew things could end before they began.

"Kitten, hurry…baby, please." Whatever words he'd thought to add gave way to the sensation of her nails raking lightly over his moisture-beaded head.

"Not yet." She gently squeezed him until he moaned, his hips rocking in mid-air.

"Baby, now," he hoarsely pleaded.

"Fair exchange." She relented and rolled the condom in place.

He dropped his weight and gathered her close. He lovingly punished her mouth with his for the delay, then moved to a nipple, drew it in and sucked hard.

"Marcel, please."

"I will, baby…just stay with me." Tonight, his only mission was to brand her as his. Not one part of her was to be left unclaimed. Finally, he lifted her hips and started his entry. The brief flinch that flashed over her face stilled him. "It's okay, kitten. I'd never hurt you. Relax and open for me."

With trust in her eyes, she did.

Inch by tantalizing inch, he filled her, stretched her until he'd settled in. "Aaah, kitten, *Je t'aime.*" A hard, deep moan rumbled from his chest when she clamped herself tightly around him. Marcel savored the feeling of finally being united. Pulling Caitlyn's arms overhead, he laced their fingers together to start an expression of love designed exclusively for them.

"I love you, too." She wrapped her legs around his waist and tightened her hold on his fingers. "Marcel…"

He eased back, then slowly pushed forward, establishing a leisurely rhythm. His strokes deepened, and he knew if he died right then and there, he'd enter the pearly gates with a smile.

When he set out to seduce her, he'd never imagined he'd end up seduced. Nor did he ever imagine he'd come to her a virgin. But that was exactly what he was. Before, he'd had sex. But for the first time in his life, he made love. And it was the most soul-stirring, intoxicating lovemaking imaginable. It simply didn't get any better than that.

He never took his eyes off her and before long, heard her soft whimper. Listening to the small catch in her voice, he knew her release was moments away. He increased their rhythm, their bodies pumping frantically, wildly, and he didn't stop until he felt her shudder beneath him, softly whispering again and again, "*Je t'aime.*" Hearing that, his control snapped and he surrendered to the rapture of their love.

They stayed connected, neither wanting the inevitable separation to take place. He was a large man, and as tiny as she was, he needed to be certain he hadn't hurt her. He planted a gentle kiss at her temple. "You okay?"

She palmed his face and nodded. "*Oui*."

He kissed the tip of her nose. "This is usually the point where a brother becomes concerned."

"Why?"

"He wants to make sure his woman was satisfied."

She smiled. "All right, I'll scream a little louder next time."

"And before your mind goes there, I'm not on a macho trip here." Resting on his left elbow, he trailed his finger along her cheek. "I just need to be sure I didn't mess things up, and that it was good for you."

She ran her hand up and down his back. "Was it good for you?"

He smiled. "Maybe I need to roar a lot louder next time."

She palmed his face and the love she felt for this man brought tears to her eyes. "Marcel?"

"Yeah, baby."

She glanced at the tiny, car-shaped gold charm dangling from the chain around his neck. A tear slipped down her cheek at the thought of how an old, raggedy car had brought her so much happiness. She whispered softly, "*Merci*."

Exhaustion finally laid claim just before dawn, after Marcel misinterpreted Caitlyn's early morning request to go riding. They'd often driven around late at night, with him serving as her personal tour guide. He quickly discovered his error. Straddling him, Caitlyn took him on the ride of his life. She rode him hard. She rode him long. She rode him with so much passion his white-knuckled grip loosened the fitted sheet from the mattress. His release hit him with such intensity he roared her name in English, made up another name for her in French, and invented an entirely different language, which he went to sleep trying to figure out.

When morning came, he stared down at the woman lying next to him, and a smile touched the corners of his lips. He was just about to pick up where they'd left off a few hours earlier when he heard the ringing of his private line.

Frustrated by the disturbance, he answered on the first ring. "What?"

"Marcel, it's Moni. Have you seen Caitlyn? I've been trying to reach her all morning."

Marcel felt Caitlyn snuggle closer. Talking to his sister was the last thing he wanted to do. "Yes, Moni, I've seen her."

"Well, I was trying to see if she wanted to go shopping with me. Besides, we missed each other yesterday to discuss the tutoring schedule."

Marcel opened his mouth to speak, but Moni interrupted him. "That's okay. I'll try her at home again. Bye."

A few seconds later, the phone rang again. Caitlyn had remote forwarded her phone to Marcel's. "What is it, Moni?"

"Marcel, where's Caitlyn? What's going on over there?"

He pinched the bridge of his nose and rolled his eyes. "Look, Moni, that's more information than you need to know."

"But why are you answering her phone at this hour of the morning?"

Marcel spoke with forced patience. "I didn't answer her phone. I answered mine."

"Well, how…"

"Listen, Moni, I'll let you figure that out for yourself. I'll give Caitlyn your message."

CHAPTER 12

"Brie, I need your help," Marcel said.

"All right. Shoot."

Marcel explained that Caitlyn's birthday was two days away. Even though he'd spent weeks planning for it, he felt he'd missed something. He wanted her day to have a personal touch—his touch. Everything had to be perfect because he intended for this birthday to be one she'd never forget.

"Oh, *petit frère*, I've got the perfect plan."

Marcel listened intently, and even he became excited. "You really think so?"

"I know so. Just leave everything to me."

"Brie, have I told you lately that I love you?"

"Nope. Been too damn busy seducing your woman." She released a hearty chuckle. "But I forgive you. She's worth it."

"Thanks, Sis."

"Love you, too."

Morning sunlight crept through the bedroom window and awakened Caitlyn from a short, but peaceful slumber. She stretched as a slow, sexy smile crept over her face.

She'd tried in vain all week to find out what Marcel's plans were to celebrate her birthday. He'd steadfastly refused to divulge any information, saying she needed to trust him.

And she did.

The ringing of the phone brought Caitlyn back to reality. Before she met Marcel, only Vic would phone at six in the morning.

"Good morning, beautiful."

Caitlyn rolled to her back and spoke in a low, sultry voice. "Good morning."

"Did I wake you, baby?"

"No."

"I miss you."

She chuckled. "How can you miss me when you saw me less than six hours ago?"

"It could only be six seconds ago, and I'd still miss you."

"I'm looking forward to tonight." She propped her pillows against the headboard and rested her back against them. "Can't you give me a teeny-weeny little hint?"

"Uh-uh."

"Well, how do I know what to bring or what to wear?"

"Do you trust me, kitten?"

"You know I do."

"Good. Just remember to be ready by ten, okay?"

"All right."

"By the way, what do you have on?"

"What?" Her giggle was soft and sultry.

"I mean right now, what are you wearing?"

"Your earrings and my bracelet." She'd finally gathered enough courage to allow Brie to pierce her ears as a birthday present to herself. Marcel had rewarded her courage with a pair of two-carat pink diamond studs.

"Anything else?"

"Nope."

"I better let you go," he hurriedly responded.

"Marcel, is everything okay?"

"Yeah, baby. Everything's okay."

After a long pause, she whispered, "I love you."

"Love you, too. Make love with me later?"

"Count on it."

At ten o'clock sharp, Caitlyn answered the intercom. "Ms. Thompson, your car awaits you." The voice belonged to the chauffer Marcel had hired to pick Caitlyn up.

Fifteen minutes later, the immaculately dressed chauffeur arrived in front of Taste of Heaven, Brie's beauty salon. He assisted her out, and Brie greeted her at the door.

"Brie, what's going on here?" When she didn't get a response, Caitlyn said again, "Brie—"

Brie tossed a quick wink. "Just relax and enjoy."

After a continental breakfast of croissants, juice and herbal tea, Caitlyn undressed, slipped on a white satin robe and received a facial and neck massage.

None of the staff uttered a word. They smiled, catering to her every whim, and extended the most exquisite care of her life.

In a candlelit room, Brie provided a ninety-minute massage that lulled Caitlyn into a peaceful slumber. It was well after two in the afternoon before she woke to a late lunch of smoked salmon, fruit, cheese and crackers. Afterward, she received a manicure and pedicure that left her fingernails and toenails a shiny candy-apple red.

Her final stop was the stylist's chair. Jennifer, one of the salon's stylists, shampooed, blow-dried and arranged her hair in an upsweep coiffure and Candace, the esthetician, applied her makeup to perfection.

Brie answered a knock at the salon door and moments later returned with a long garment bag slung over one arm and a smaller one in her hand.

"Come on, lady. Time to get you dressed." She handed the smaller bag to Caitlyn. "Here. Use the changing room in the back to put these on." She gave Caitlyn's shoulder a gentle push. "Go on, now. We're running on a tight schedule."

Caitlyn came back a few minutes later clutching the robe tightly in front. "Brie, you didn't give me a bra."

The only two items in the bag were a pair of black, lace boy panties that barely covered her cheeks and an ultrasheer pair of black, thigh-high stockings with a back seam.

"Honey, you won't need one with this." Brie unzipped the larger bag and pulled out a black silk corset-style strapless evening gown with a sheer mesh bodice to showcase the tiny gold ring in her navel.

"Oh, my God, Brie…" Caitlyn's eyes began to fill with tears.

"Oh, no, you don't." Brie quickly grabbed a tissue and dabbed softly at her eyes. "You can't be messing up our hard work."

"Brie…"

Brie smiled. "Go on now and get dressed."

Caitlyn returned a few moments later and stood in front of Brie. "You look absolutely beautiful." Brie was about to walk away but stopped. "Oh, Lord, I almost forgot." With a quick snap of her fingers, Candace and Jennifer took their place on each side of Caitlyn while Brie stooped to slip a pair of jeweled T-strap heels on Caitlyn's feet. "Now you can look."

Caitlyn couldn't believe she was the woman reflected in the mirror. She felt beautiful. She felt happy. She felt loved. "Oh, my God, I don't know what to say."

"You don't have to say anything."

A second later, there was a knock. "Ms. Thompson, are you ready?" asked the same chauffeur who'd driven her over earlier.

The limousine pulled into the circular driveway of Marcel's estate, and the chauffeur assisted her out and to the open front door.

"Happy birthday, kitten." Marcel stood in the doorway, handsomely dressed in a white dinner jacket, mandarin collar shirt and black trousers. "Did you enjoy your day?"

Overcome with happiness, tears spilled down her cheeks. Not trusting herself to speak, Caitlyn simply wrapped her arms tightly around Marcel's waist and nodded. Once she had recovered, she obeyed his instructions to close her eyes as he led her by the hand to the garage. When she opened her eyes, she found the red BMW convertible she had given back to him wrapped with a huge red bow, and her tears flowed once again.

Her total submission to his plan got her thoroughly kissed.

Later that night, it got her thoroughly loved.

CHAPTER 13

Caitlyn and Vic's conflicting schedules interrupted the time they spent together on Sundays. So, after attending service at Vic's church, they returned to Caitlyn's apartment for lunch.

With mischief twinkling in her eyes, Vic walked into the kitchen and sat at the table. "Glad you could come up for air and share some time with a friend."

"I know. Except for the days you're at the center, we really haven't had a chance to hang out together. I'm sorry."

"Sorry for what? Sweetie, I don't have to see you for the next decade as long as you keep that glow on your face."

Flashing the smile of a woman in love, Caitlyn turned to her best friend. "I'm happy, Vic."

"That's all that matters."

Caitlyn stood at the kitchen counter. "Listen, thanks again for helping out at the youth center. You know I appreciate it." Caitlyn stopped preparing the tossed salad and looked over her shoulder. "What in the world were you and A.J. fighting about yesterday?" Picking up the salad bowl, she placed it on the dining room table. "I thought you two were getting along."

From the kitchen, Vic bellowed, "Getting along? Caitlyn, the man is crazy."

"Vic, come on."

Vic came from the kitchen and stood next to Caitlyn. "Don't come-on-Vic me. Do you know what he had the nerve to tell me?"

"What?"

"That if a woman is married, she doesn't need a career, that her place is in the home."

"Oooh, I bet that ruffled your feathers."

"Ruffled, hell. How about plucked right out?"

Caitlyn giggled. "What did you say?"

Vic's placed her hands on her hips. "I told him, Negro, please." She shook her head and rolled her eyes. "Girl, the man's definitely not in the twenty-first century. And you know what else gets on my nerves? He calls me 'honey.' "

"Come on. Vic. Be nice."

"Oh, I'll be *real* sweet. I'm just going to ignore his chauvinist behind." Vic sat and plucked a carrot from the salad bowl. "You better hang on to that man you've got. I'm telling you, he's a rare commodity."

Caitlyn stared. "A rare commodity?"

"Yeah."

"How so?"

Vic bent back her fingers with each point she made. "Thirty-eight, no babies, college educated, and ain't spent time in jail…"

Caitlyn heard the knock at the door first. "Who is it?"

"It's me, kitten."

"Hi." Caitlyn stood aside and let Marcel enter.

"How's my girl?" Marcel pulled her into his embrace and buried his head against her neck, breathing in her fragrance.

Caitlyn moved seductively in his embrace. "I'm wonderful. But baby…uh…Vic is here."

"I see her. But a smart man prioritizes." He proceeded to kiss her with such thoroughness her legs gave way. He grabbed her hand, and they walked to the table.

"Hi, Vic." Marcel leaned down and placed a kiss on her cheek.

"Hi, yourself." Vic put a forkful of salad in her mouth and chewed. "I heard what you just said back there, brother. You ain't getting no complaints from me about handling your business. Besides, from the looks of things, my girl might want to consider giving you a promotion."

"Promotion?" Marcel gave Vic a puzzled look.

"Yeah. Move-in rights." Still smiling, Vic winked at Marcel. "Listen, you take my spot. I'm out of here."

Marcel placed his hand on her shoulder. "Oh, no you don't. I'm not going to stay. Actually, I'm glad you're here. I want to know if I can talk you both into joining me for Baptiste family week."

Vic shook her head. "Marcel, that's sweet of you, but I'm not family."

Marcel shook his head in disagreement. "Yes, you are. You're a part of my kitten's family, and her family is my family. So, will you join me?"

All Caitlyn could do was smile. She was touched by Marcel's generosity, that he would invite Vic to his family gathering because of her. If she didn't love him before, she sure loved him at that moment.

Vic smiled. "Is there another one like you anywhere around?"

Marcel's puzzled gaze volleyed between Vic and Caitlyn.

Caitlyn offered an explanation to clarify things. "Vic thinks A.J. is a chauvinist."

"Ain't no thinking to it…he is," Vic hissed.

Marcel smiled. "You and everybody else think along the same lines, so join the club. But to answer your question, no. My other brother, Ray, is even worse. He's at the other extreme. Skirt chaser. Guess I fall somewhere in the middle."

Caitlyn and Vic looked at each other, then back at Marcel, saying at the same time, "And that is?"

"Uh…well, I admit I can be arrogant at times…"

"At times?" Caitlyn mocked.

"A little stubborn…"

"A little?" Caitlyn rolled her eyes.

"Be quiet, kitten." He blew a kiss her way. "Let's see. I don't take no for an answer…"

Caitlyn nodded. "Oh, you got that one right."

"But I'm a firm believer in chivalry."

Vic chuckled. "Good save. Your hole was getting a little deep there, brother."

After a moment of laughter, Marcel sat in the chair across from Vic. "Listen, don't pay any attention to A.J. I've been telling him for years that what he needs is a good sister to put him in check. Well, what do you say? Will you come to family week?"

Vic smiled. "Sure. Thanks for the invite."

Marcel turned and looked across his shoulder at Caitlyn who stood behind him. "What about you, kitten?"

"Maybe." She turned and walked toward the kitchen, purposely swaying her hips.

In fast pursuit, Marcel walked up and pinned her against the counter. "Just maybe?" He trailed his tongue along the space between her neck and shoulder. "Can you take a week off?"

"If I do, what's in it for me?" She moaned as Marcel cupped her breasts.

"Can't let you in on all my surprises, but I guarantee you won't be disappointed."

"God, that feels so good." Feeling Marcel massage her nipples through her silk blouse made her knees buckle.

"I aim to please."

The movements of his lips and tongue accompanied by the rubbing of his hard erection against her caused Caitlyn's eyes to flutter shut and her head to fall against his chest. "I'm not family, you know, just a friend."

He inched back slightly and placed her hand on his crotch. "Baby, friends don't make me feel like this."

"Bad boy."

"Oh, you ain't seen nothing yet."

"You need to show me."

"First, you show me those moves you were doing at the center the other day." Caitlyn really wanted to encourage the girls at the center to exercise, so she'd started a belly-dancing class.

"You mean like this?" She slowly gyrated her hips.

"Yeah, that's it."

She moved in closer and pressed hard against him. The feel of his hips rolling with hers caused her breathing to quicken. "Marcel..."

His head dropped back and slid his eyes shut, all the while rotating his hips in perfect sync with hers. "Whatever you do, don't stop."

From the dining room, Vic shouted, "Caitlyn, you coming or what?"

Caitlyn gripped Marcel's thighs as she reached the peak first. "Hmm-hmm."

A few moments passed before Vic shouted out again. "Marcel, come on now."

Marcel clamped his hands down on her hips right as he slipped over the edge. "I did."

It was a beautiful Sunday afternoon when everyone gathered at Alcee's home for the official start of Baptiste family week. The family was committed to coming together every year during the second week of October in commemoration of Angelique, the Baptiste children's late mother. It was a symbol of their strength as a family, bound not only by their love for her but for one another.

Early Monday morning, Caitlyn smiled as she stood alongside Mama Z doing her best to stifle her yawn. Only she and Marcel knew the reason for her exhaustion—they'd made love until dawn once she finally found the room he was in. She'd always had a poor sense of direction, especially when she had to rely on someone else's verbal instructions. On Sunday night, she had eased down the dark hallway trying to follow the directions Marcel had given her to his room until she realized she was lost. She ended up in Mama Z's room.

Caitlyn was so sleepy that she struggled to understand the recipe for jambalaya, which she was reading for the third time. Before meeting Marcel, the extent of her culinary skills had consisted of popping a frozen potpie into the oven. Even though her first two attempts at jambalaya had been a disaster, she was thankful for Mama Z's patience and encouragement. She was determined to get one of Marcel's favorite meals right.

Mama Z smiled. "Caitlyn?"

Caitlyn jerked her head up. "Ma'am?"

"Where're Kenji and Max?"

"Oh, Kenji is taking her nap." Caitlyn shrugged. "And Max…well, uh…Max is in time-out."

Vic, Brie, Moni and Aimee sat at the table with puzzled looks, staring at Caitlyn.

Vic frowned. "Time-out. Who put him in time-out?"

"I did." Caitlyn sheepishly lowered her lashes.

Vic opened her arms. "For the love of God, why are you putting the dog in time-out?"

Wiping her hands on the nearby dishtowel, Caitlyn released an exasperated sigh. "He's having a hard time at school. He's not sharing well with the other dogs." Caitlyn had enrolled Kenji and Max into a doggie camp so they wouldn't be bored during the day. Marcel dropped them off each morning, and she and Marcel alternated evenings picking them up. She chewed on her bottom lip. "Marcel is going to have a talk with him after family week is over."

Moni's eyes bulged. "Oh, my God. He is?"

Caitlyn bobbed her head.

"Lord, have mercy." Brie rolled her eyes at the ceiling. "Marcel is going to talk to Max, you mean like father to son?"

Caitlyn nodded. "Umm-hmm."

Aimee chuckled. "Jesus H. Christ. I've heard just about everything now."

Mama Z leaned over the counter with her hand near her heart.

Shouting her name, everyone rushed to her side. "Mama Z."

Mama Z shook her head and made the sign of the cross. "Mary, mother of Jesus."

Everyone froze at Mama Z's words.

Mama Z laughed out loud. "In all my years, ain't never heard of no dog having a father-and-son talk. Jesus help 'em."

They all burst into laughter.

Caitlyn was ecstatic when Brie invited her, along with Mama Z, Moni, Aimee and Vic, to spend the rest of the day at Taste of Heaven getting pampered from head to toe.

Brie finished Caitlyn's manicure and placed her hands inside a nail dryer. "I'm really glad you're here with us this year."

Caitlyn beamed. "Thank you for having me."

Brie's eyes twinkled. "You know, this is the first time in twenty-four years Marcel's ever invited anyone to family week."

Caitlyn sat up with such a jolt her wet nails bumped the inside of the dryer. "Darn it."

Brie eased Caitlyn's hands out to assess the damage to her right pinkie. "No problem. You just nicked the side of it." She reached for the bottle of red nail polish. "Here, let me touch it up for you."

"No one else?" Caitlyn whispered, leaning in closer. "I mean, you know, another woman?" She cupped her hand against the side of her mouth. "No one?"

Brie smiled. "You hold that distinct honor."

"Distinct honor for what?" Moni asked from across the room.

Aimee snorted and looked at Moni. "Moni, I swear to God, you have radar ears."

"Aimee." Mama Z's voice was stern from her chair at the other manicure station. "Ya don't use the Lord's name in vain."

Caitlyn inwardly chuckled when she thought back to earlier in the morning when they were all in the kitchen and how Mama Z had done the same thing. But she wasn't about to remind the woman of her choice of words. No way.

Aimee nodded. "Sorry, Mama Z." She turned back to Moni. "Like I said, Moni, you have radar ears."

Moni wrinkled her nose and didn't comment. Instead, she looked at Caitlyn. "So, you and my brother have become quite the couple."

Before Caitlyn could string two words together, Brie was on her feet. "Moni, put a lid on it. Why is it that you seem to get into everybody's business? Doesn't having a baby keep you busy enough?"

Moni sat next to Vic and wiggled her French-manicured toes. "Brie, I'm not being nosy." She turned to Vic. "Right, Vic? You don't think I'm being nosy, do you?"

"Nosy, no. Real nosy, yes." Vic answered back.

Moni released a huff. "Well."

Vic turned in her chair to face Moni. "Listen, I'm just a friend of a friend, okay, and I'm not really in a position to say much. But I know my girl, and I think she's got the situation under control."

With a wicked grin, Moni tilted her head and slowly nodded. "Oh, I see. So I guess the conversation you and A.J. were having yesterday at dinner was under control?"

"No...she...didn't." Vic gritted her teeth as her chest heaved and she gripped both arms of her chair.

Caitlyn giggled. "Yes, she did."

Brie nodded at Vic's hands. "Careful now. They're still wet." Pausing, she placed her finger against her temple. "Well, now that Moni's brought this up, y'all were kind of tight yesterday, Vic."

Vic stood, placed her hands, wet nails and all, against her hips. "For the record, ladies, A.J. and I were simply discussing our mutual interest—you know, our mentoring at the youth center." She sat back down. "That's all."

"Umm-hmm," everyone said at the same time.

Caitlyn giggled. "We believe you, Vic."

"Uh, yeah, Vic, it looked that way to me, too." Brie hid a snicker behind her hand.

Mama Z barely contained her chuckles. "Ya keep on believing that, child."

Aimee laughed out loud. "And pigs fly."

Moni opened her mouth, but Vic looked over and gave her a warning look. "Don't you say one word. Not one."

After fifteen seconds of complete silence, they all burst into laughter. Moni looked over at Caitlyn. "Now tell the truth. You don't think I'm being nosy, do you?"

"Yes, I do," Caitlyn replied calmly. "Moni, I heard you when you asked your question the first time."

Moni frowned. "Well, you didn't answer me."

Caitlyn smiled. "Yes, I did."

Moni shook her head in confusion. "How?"

"It's called silence." Caitlyn winked at Vic. "In other words, no comment." Smiling at Mama Z, she added, "For you that means none of your business."

Brie took her right index finger and made an imaginary stroke in the air. "Point in favor of Caitlyn."

Moni pouted. "But, Caitlyn—"

Aimee sighed loudly. "Jesus, Moni, give it a rest."

"Aimee." Mama Z's warning held a sharp edge. "I told ya once about using the Lord's name that way. Ain't gonna say it no mo."

Aimee placed her hand over her mouth. "Sorry."

Moni looked at everyone. "I was just—"

Mama Z's voice was crisp. "Monique Desiree Baptiste Tate, silence. Caitlyn may not think ya being nosy, but I certainly do, young lady. Ya needs to concentrate on handling yo' business with Zach." She tossed a loving wink at Caitlyn. "I'm sure Caitlyn and Marcel can handle theirs."

"Amen to that." Brie sighed.

"Thank you, Jesus," Vic added.

On Tuesday evening after dinner, the family gathered in the backyard. Marcel, A.J., Ray and Alex huddled together near the patio table nursing their Coronas as they watched Caitlyn and Vic introduce A.J.'s twin daughters, Taylor and Tyler, to some belly-dancing moves.

"Oh, *mon frère*, now she's a beauty." Ray nudged Marcel in the side, tilting his head in Caitlyn's direction.

Marcel looked over at Ray and chuckled. He was an all-out ladies' man, and if it wore a skirt and had a split, it was on. He was the only one who'd inherited their mother's love for music. At thirty-six, he'd already earned two Grammys.

Marcel watched the undulating movements of Caitlyn's hips with sheer delight. "Yeah, she's a beauty that's all mine."

Ray whistled. "Tiny, but damn, got all the curves a man likes."

"Ray," Marcel admonished.

"No disrespect." Ray patted Marcel on the back and chuckled. "Ain't never known you to be possessive, not over a woman anyway." He palmed the beer between his hands. "You know I love me an ebony-skinned sista." He took another swallow. "Besides, you know what they say, the blacker the berry, the sweeter—"

"Watch it, Ray," Marcel barked.

With a wide-eyed stare, Ray's mouth dropped open. "Oh, don't tell me you done jumped up and fell in love with Little Bit."

Marcel sighed loudly. "Her name's Caitlyn, Ray, not Little Bit." He stared at Ray. "How long are you home?"

"Till the end of the year." Ray shrugged. "Why?"

"Damn. I don't know if I want you around Caitlyn that long."

Ray put his bottle on the table, bent over with his hands wrapped around his stomach, and burst into laughter. When he straightened, he shook his head. "*Mon frère*, you really are in love with Little Bit, huh?" All humor left his voice, and he nudged A.J., who was standing next to him. "Homeboy's in love. Well, I'll be damned."

Marcel knew despite his protest, Ray would always refer to Caitlyn as Little Bit. Marcel couldn't remember the last time Ray had called him by his given name. They were both alike. Once they settled their minds onto something, nothing between heaven and hell could change it. "Is that such a crime?"

Ray polished off the remainder of his beer. "Nope. Just glad it's you and not me."

Marcel pinched the bridge of his nose. "Ray, I pray to God I live to see the day when the right woman comes along and finally snags your rusty ass."

Ray tossed his empty bottle in a nearby trash bin. "Guess you planning on living into eternity because it ain't going to happen." Ray turned around to A.J. "And what you over there snickering about? Don't let me start on the way you been looking at Vic all day."

A.J. shrugged. "I don't have the faintest idea what you're talking about."

Alex chuckled as he lifted his bottle of Corona to his lips. "What a convenient time to come down with temporary amnesia."

"Oh, so I guess them stars floating around in your eyes and that drool running out your mouth every time you look at her is nothing, huh?" Ray's black dreads hung over his shoulders and he cocked his head. "Look at that, full hips handling a shimmy like a pro. *Daaayuuum.*"

Marcel looked over at A.J. and laughed. "He's got you on that one, *petit frère.* You have been staring awfully hard at Vic."

"She's not my type," A.J. defended quickly.

"Naw, naw, brother." Ray took two steps back. "Naw. Naw. She's just your type. After talking to her at dinner today, she's about the only sista I've ever met who can get you over that caveman mentality of yours."

Ray exchanged a high-five with Marcel. "Come on, *mon frère.*" Ray beckoned Marcel toward the lawn. "Need to find out a little more about my future sister-in-law."

"Ray, behave yourself. I'm warning you," Marcel growled.

Ray continued walking with a grin. "You pop the question yet?"

"That's none of your business, all right?"

"That's a no, I take it, huh?

"Ray, handle your business, and leave mine alone, okay?"

Ray came to a dead halt. "Got it. I know ya, and that means soon." He resumed his long strides toward his destination. "All right then. My lips—" he broke off mimicking zipping his mouth shut, "are sealed."

On Saturday, the last day of family week, Marcel was filled with pride when Caitlyn told him after breakfast she had spent the entire week learning how to make jambalaya and wanted everyone to try out her dish at dinner that evening. But his delight was short-lived and turned to sheer panic when he learned about forty-five minutes before they were to eat she had prepared the meal unsupervised. He had firsthand knowledge of her cooking skills, and after the one and only meal she had prepared for him by herself, he had gone to bed with an empty bottle of Rolaids on the nightstand. Since then, he'd taken over the cooking duties for them. While he loved her dearly, he knew despite her best efforts, she couldn't cook.

Once everyone had seated themselves at the huge dining room table, and after Alcee blessed the meal, the only thing Marcel could do was stare at the platters and bowls Caitlyn had arranged in the center.

Caitlyn happily announced, "Well, everybody, dig in before the jambalaya gets cold."

Marcel swallowed hard. "Uh, kitten, it looks…umm…sort of…different."

Caitlyn nodded in agreement. "I know. It's not exactly like the picture in the recipe book, but it's good."

"Oh, Caitlyn," Moni exclaimed, "It looks great, the same way mine does when I make it."

Brie lifted her brow and stared at the food. "Yeah, Moni, you're right. It does."

Marcel swallowed real hard this time. He knew Moni's cooking was worst than Caitlyn's. "Uh, kitten, you followed the recipe, right?"

Caitlyn smiled. "Umm-hmm."

Aimee glanced across the table at her brother and winced. "You try it first, Marcel."

Marcel stared first at the platter with the rice—well, what was supposed to be rice—and shuddered. Instead of being fluffy, it was gooey. He turned and looked up at Caitlyn. "Baby, you know, I think the meal would taste better if we had some uh…hot sauce."

Everyone scrambled from their chairs, including Taylor and Tyler loudly volunteering, "I'll get it."

Caitlyn waved her hand down for them to return to their seats. "No, no. Everyone go ahead and eat. I'll get it."

Once Caitlyn was out of earshot, Alcee stared at the platter with the jambalaya. He leaned over and whispered in Marcel's ear. "Uh, now what did she say this was supposed to be again?"

Marcel shrugged and lifted a shrimp with his fork. "Jambalaya." He twirled the fork completely around to inspect what was supposed to be a shrimp—"I think." He sighed. "What are we going to do?"

"We give it to Kenji," Taylor suggested.

Tyler nodded. "Yeah, Max, too."

Max growled and Kenji whimpered, and they both scurried out the dining room.

Zach chuckled. "Listen up, brother-in-law. Let me give ya some words of wisdom here. All ya can do at this point is when she asks how it tastes say umm…umm…good."

Moni looked at her husband and pouted. "You never say that when I cook jambalaya."

Zach leaned over and whispered something in Moni's ear as he rubbed her expanding belly. "But I make it good in other ways. Ain't that right, baby?"

Moni released a long sigh of contentment and smiled.

Ray voiced his opinion loudly. "Whatcha mean what *we* gonna do? Look, she's yo woman. I don't know what you gonna do, but as for me…Burger King is two blocks up."

"Hush up, all of ya," Mama Z said. "That there child worked hard fixin' this food, and we goin' eat it—every bit of it." She tightly clutched the rosary beads around her neck with one hand and made the sign of the cross with the other.

Marcel peeped around to be sure Caitlyn wasn't on her way back to the dining room. "At least we have two trained medical personnel in the house."

"Trained is the operative word," A.J. advised. "And there's a limitation to that."

Seated next to A.J., Vic whispered from the opposite side of the table. "Marcel, I can't believe you let her roam in the kitchen by herself. Boy, don't you know by now that's dangerous?"

WHEN I'M WITH YOU

Marcel rubbed his stomach and winced. "Vic, trust me, I know." He looked around at everyone, and issued a stern order. "Send your doctor bill to me tomorrow. Let's eat."

CHAPTER 14

"Marcel…"

Caitlyn's strained, trembling voice on the cell phone made the hairs on the back of Marcel's neck stand at attention.

"Baby, what's wrong?" He was driving across the Bay Bridge and had just passed Treasure Island. He had another fourth of a mile to go before he'd exit toward Oakland.

"My…my apartment. Someone's been in here."

"Is anything missing?"

"Nothing is missing, but Marcel, someone's been in here. I know it. My jewelry box is not the way I left it."

Marcel stared out the windshield straight ahead. If he didn't know anything else about Caitlyn, he knew how neat and organized she was, especially with her jewelry. He'd watched her enough to know that she placed each piece in a particular arrangement. "Where are you now?"

"Inside."

Cole. "Get out now," he shouted. "Go outside and stand on the corner where people can see you. Give me fifteen minutes." When he didn't get a response, he shouted into his mouthpiece again. "Caitlyn, did you hear me?"

"Yes."

"Go on, baby. Right now."

He disconnected the call and punched in another number.

"Zach, it's Marcel. Listen, can you get a car over to Caitlyn's place? Somebody's broken in." He quickly recited the address. "Dammit, Zach, I don't know who, what, when, where, but I'm headed there now." He nodded at Zach's words. "Thanks."

As soon as Marcel disconnected the call with his brother-in-law, traffic slowed. All he could see was a sea of red taillights and eventually every car came to a dead halt. Nothing but an accident or stalled vehicle could cause such a massive traffic backup. He didn't know how long he'd be stuck on the bridge. In addition to the police, he needed to find someone who could get to Caitlyn fast. As his heart thudded inside his chest, he reached down and punched in the number to his service technician at the Oakland dealership.

"Sean, can someone cover you right now?" He was relieved when Sean said yes and gave him Caitlyn's address. "Stay with her until I get there. Don't let *anyone* near her. Understand?"

Marcel rounded the street corner forty-five minutes later doing forty miles per hour. When he spotted Caitlyn and Sean, he slammed the gear into park, rocking the car violently. He was out and running toward them before the motion stopped. He hauled her against him. "You okay?"

"I am now." She looked at her apartment building. "The police came."

"I called Zach and told him what happened."

"What if?" Caitlyn cried against his chest. She looked at him with unshed tears in her eyes. "What if it's Cole? What if he's found me?"

180

He didn't tell her it that was the first thing that had popped into his mind. He stroked her cheek with his thumb, his gaze of reassurance speaking volumes, his voice soothing. "You let me worry about Cole. Your days of running from him are over. You hear me?"

She nodded.

He extended his hand to Sean. "Thanks, man. I owe you for this."

Sean nodded. "No problem, boss man."

Wrapping his arm around Caitlyn's waist, they walked back to her apartment. "Come on. Let's see what the police have found out. We'll get some of your things, and you're coming home with me. I'll come back for the rest of your stuff later."

After Caitlyn phoned Vic that evening and told her someone had been inside her apartment, Vic demanded to speak with Marcel. It took him more than thirty minutes before he finally convinced her Caitlyn was safe. Their conversation ended with Vic agreeing to meet Marcel at Caitlyn's apartment around eight the next morning to pack the rest of Caitlyn's clothes. He'd used every skill he had to convince Caitlyn to stay with him until he could find out the person who was responsible for all of this.

Marcel didn't allow Caitlyn to do anything. After dinner, he gave her an hour-long massage topped off with a pedicure, after which, he personally blew her toes dry. Once she was ready for her bath, he undressed her and with a smile, watched as she sank into the bubble-filled, black marble tub. Mesmerized, he leaned against the doorframe and watched bubbles float over her like billows of clouds.

She called out to him and with a provocative look, watching him slowly make his way toward her with two huge velour towels. Her eyes held his when she rose from the tub with water and white fluffy foam cascading along the smooth, dark surface of her skin.

His hot, potent gaze roamed her from head to toe and finally landed at the spot she wanted him to touch more than anything in the world. Her body came alive. Stepping from the tub, she obeyed his gentle command: "Come to me."

Her eyes fluttered while he dried her upper body with extraordinary tenderness. Kneeling before her, he started at her feet and slowly trailed the towel upward deliberately lingering in some places. As he worked his way up her body, the towel became a trusted ally in his sensual assault, moving in and out, up and down until her breathing became shallow. A shimmer of heat passed through her when he whispered, "Do you trust me?"

"Yes."

Her dark brown eyes bore into his gray-green ones as he glided his hands up to cup her breasts. A moan whose origin began in her abdomen tore from the back of her throat when his fingers circled her nipples, making them harden like tiny pebbles of granite. Feeling her body burst to life at his unhurried strokes along her stomach and thighs, she bucked at the finger skating ever so slowly over the tiny bud tucked beneath her dewy patch. She closed her eyes, parted her lips and surrendered.

A deep whimper she recognized as her own replaced the silence in the room the moment Marcel's mouth touched her there. Somewhere from deep in her subconscious, she heard him groan right before his tongue shocked her like an electric current. It swept along her wet folds with such gentleness she didn't realize she'd reached down and held his head securely at her spot. Before long, her purrs escalated to a roar.

It wasn't until loving fingers replaced the magic of his tongue that she opened her eyes, and through a hazy, passion-glazed fog, locked her gaze with his while his fingers plunged in and out of her. The familiar tightening at her center blurred her vision even more, but hearing Marcel's passionate whispers caused her to soar. Sensations built to such intensity, she begged for the pleasure to never end. She tried hard to stave off the magic his mouth created and hang on to what his fingers prolonged. It wasn't meant to be. His voice loomed in the stillness of the room.

"Come for me."

And she did.

Trailing his damp finger between the valley of her breasts, he stopped at her parted lips. "Know how you taste, kitten?"

"No."

He gently stroked his finger over her quivering lips. "Open."

She tasted herself and accepted his kiss, causing tears to sting her eyelids.

"Marcel?"

"Hmm?"

183

"Well…how do I taste?"

"Mighty sweet, baby. Mighty sweet."

Early the next morning, Marcel eased out the bed while Caitlyn was still sleeping and anxiously headed downstairs. He'd been restless all night trying to figure out why someone would enter into Caitlyn's apartment and not take anything. Plus, he needed to check in with Alex and find out Cole's whereabouts. If the bastard had somehow found out where she was, he couldn't promise he wouldn't commit bodily harm against him, or worse. He shut the door to his office and picked up the phone.

"Robinson, wake up."

Alex yawned. "B, do you know what time it is?"

Marcel glanced at the clock on his desk. "Yeah, it's four." He didn't apologize for the intrusion. "Robinson, this is urgent. You've been tracking Mazzei, right?"

"Yeah. Why?"

"Somebody got inside of Caitlyn's apartment yesterday."

"Is she okay?"

"She's scared shitless."

"Hell, I don't blame her. Dealing with a stalker is nothing to play around with, partner. But trust me, it wasn't Mazzei."

"I don't care. Put somebody on Caitlyn twenty-four/seven." Marcel trusted Alex to a fault and accepted what he said as gospel, but he wasn't willing to take any chances with Caitlyn's safety. He planned to stop at nothing until he found out who got into her apartment.

"Do you know where Mazzei is?"

"Yeah…New York? Why?"

Marcel breathed a sigh of relief. He went on to tell Alex everything that had happened.

"Listen, B, Zach and his boys are good, but I'm better. I'll swing by your office later this morning and get the key to Caitlyn's crib. I want to check things out myself."

"Thanks, Robinson." Marcel placed the phone back on the receiver and frowned. If it wasn't Cole who had gotten inside of Caitlyn's apartment, then who?

A little before eight, Marcel met Vic at Caitlyn's apartment. Vic neatly placed several outfits in an open suitcase atop the bed. Marcel strolled in a few moments later and peeked over to find a pair of black G-string panties with a rhinestone design on the front. He held them up with his index finger. "She calls these panties?"

Victoria turned around and laughed. "Yeah, and if you keep looking, you'll probably find a pair that'll put those to shame. I'ma let you in on a little secret. If you let her, that girl would spend every penny she's got shopping at Victoria's Secret."

Marcel nodded and tucked what Vic just said into his memory blank. "Vic, I'm glad you were there for her."

Vic smiled. "She's the sister I never had."

WHEN I'M WITH YOU

Vic inclined her head and looked straight in his eyes. "Marcel, she's gone through a lot the last three years. Most women would've given up or caved in, but she held on."

"I know that, Vic. Her stubbornness is what I love most about her."

"You really love her, don't you?"

"Yes. And I will do *anything* to protect her and keep her safe."

"I'm happy for you guys." Vic hesitated a second. "Marcel, I ain't trying to get into ya'll's business, but…" She waved her hand. "Forget it. Let's finish up here."

Marcel led Vic over to the edge of the bed and squatted in front of her. "Come on. Finish what you were about to say."

"Uh, she told you about Cole—"

"Yeah. That bastard. She told me." Marcel's face twisted into a frown. He folded Vic's hands inside of his and looked off into the distance. "I'm not sure what I'd do if I ever stumble on him."

"You know, Marcel, it wasn't until she went through all that crap that I truly realized how strong she is."

"Why do you say that?"

Vic chuckled softly. "That little-bitty person is the most resourceful woman I've ever met."

Marcel rolled his eyes and chuckled back. "Tell me something I don't already know."

"Seriously, my girl can stretch a dollar until it snaps. You know, I remember when we were in college, and she had the discipline to manage her money down to the penny. Hmph, the rest of us graduated faced with student loans. She came out debt free."

Marcel chuckled. "Oh, I can believe that."

"Ain't never seen a person who could take one chicken and feed twenty folks, but that woman of yours sure can. You know, until she could get out here, she lived on practically nothing so she wouldn't have to ask folks to help her out." Vic looked up at Marcel. "Just promise me that you'll love and protect her."

"You have my word."

"Marcel?"

"Yes?"

"If you ever need me for anything, just call, okay?"

He placed a kiss against her cheek. "Thanks, Vic. I'll remember that."

Without fail, Marcel and Caitlyn dedicated every Wednesday night to a scrumptious feast of sushi at Yoshi's, which had the best in Oakland.

Marcel glanced around, hoping their waitress would return with their order soon. "You know, I've been meaning to ask you this for a while. How did you know to send your proposal to me?"

Caitlyn shook her head and smiled. "I didn't send it to you. I gave it to Fran. She said she knew someone in her family who might know someone who'd be interested in funding it."

"But I got your proposal from Marilyn." Marcel frowned and palmed the side of his face. "Besides Russ, the only other family Marilyn has is a sister-in-law she can't stand."

Caitlyn's brow lifted. "Do you know her name?"

"Yeah. It's Francesca."

They both looked at each other and said at the same time, "Fran."

Marcel leaned back in his chair. "So how are things with the foundation?"

"Great. I—"

"Marcel, darling."

They both turned to stare at the long-legged woman with light-brown skin who'd stood at their table. Marcel's square jaw grew rigid, but he stood out of courtesy. "Tiffany."

Tiffany gave Caitlyn a slow perusal, then shifted her gaze to Marcel. "I didn't know you like them so young and…" She took a step closer, tapping her long fingernails on the table's edge. "Let's see, how should I say it?" She shot an evil look at Caitlyn. "Dark."

The napkin in Marcel's hand landed in the center of the table. "Tiffany, I believe you owe Ms. Thompson an apology."

Tiffany raised her brow. "Oh, Ms. Thompson, is it?"

Steam rose from the back of Caitlyn's neck. Marcel had told her about Tiffany and the brief time they had dated, but she'd had no idea the woman was so vain or so rude. She was as pretentious as her full, stay-in-the-beauty-shop-all-day weave. So what if she was dark-skinned? As long as Marcel liked it, that was all she cared about. She didn't want to embarrass Marcel or herself, for that matter, but she was ready to dust Tiffany from one end of the restaurant to the other. This was her man, and no woman was going to disrespect her in front of him.

With a wry smile, Tiffany glanced first at Marcel, then Caitlyn. "Surely Marcel could have found someone with a little more class. Honey, you're so…tiny. You aren't a midget by chance, are you?"

"Tiffany." Marcel spoke in a warning tone. "That's enough."

"Oops." Tiffany mockingly covered her mouth with her hand. "My apologies."

With a gentle pat on Marcel's arm, Caitlyn, who never took her eyes off Tiffany, declared with warrior confidence, "I got this one, baby." She stood. "No need for an apology. No doubt it would be as fake as you are."

A red blotch appeared on Tiffany's cheeks, and her eyes widened. "Now listen here—"

"No. You listen." Caitlyn's finger took dead aim front and center in Tiffany's perfectly made-up face. "You have until the count of three to move away from this table."

Tiffany rolled her neck. "And if I don't?"

"Then your narrow behind and that fake piece of hair are going down. Understand?" Caitlyn started her count. "One…"

Tiffany was outraged. "Marcel…"

Marcel lifted his chin proudly. "You heard the lady."

Caitlyn continued counting. "Two…"

Tiffany turned and made a beeline for the door.

"That witch. She ruined my appetite." Caitlyn took her seat and scooted her chair up toward the table.

Marcel's grin stretched from ear to ear.

"And you..." Caitlyn chided with a half grin of her own. "...can put a check on that over-active ego of yours."

"That's my boo." Still grinning, Marcel placed a kiss on her cheek.

"That's right, and don't you forget it." Palming his face with both hands, Caitlyn swiped his mouth with a thorough kiss that left no doubt in either of their minds as to her status—his woman.

Marcel looked down and smiled at the woman snuggled securely at his side. He shook his head and wondered how someone so little could snore so loudly. He relished the sound and looked forward to hearing it every morning for the rest of his life. The ringing of his private line snapped him back to reality. Not wanting to disturb Caitlyn, he reached over and picked up on the first ring.

"Yeah."

"B, what are you still doing in bed at this hour? What's going on over there?"

Marcel chuckled at the question his best friend posed and looked down at Caitlyn who was sound asleep. "Robinson, when you find the right woman, you'll understand."

"Oh, man, I'm sorry. I didn't mean to disturb you guys. Listen, B, I've finally been able to track down the information you wanted and I know who was in Caitlyn's apartment."

"Talk to me, Robinson."

"Naw, man, this isn't a conversation we need to have over the phone, especially with Caitlyn there. How about lunch this afternoon?"

"All right. Why don't you swing by the office, and I'll have something brought in for us?"

"Sounds good. Oh, B, by the way, I don't do sushi. I'll leave that dish to you and Caitlyn."

Marcel chuckled. "I get your message loud and clear. I'll have Marilyn order sandwiches."

After Marcel disconnected the call, it dawned on him this was the second time someone had called him on his private line and interrupted him while Caitlyn slept contentedly by his side. Once was okay, but twice? He didn't think so. The phone didn't disturb her because, as he'd come to realize, she could sleep through a tornado whirling through the house. But it did disturb him. So, without a second thought, he reached over, grabbed the cord, and with one powerful jerk, ripped it away from the wall jack.

CHAPTER 15

Alex arrived at precisely noon and walked straight into Marcel's office. Marcel was on the phone and motioned for Alex to take a seat. After he hung up, he smiled. "Hungry?"

Alex nodded stiffly. "Starved." He lifted a thick binder from his briefcase and placed it in the middle of Marcel's desk.

"Damn, Robinson, I swear you could find a snowflake in a pile of salt." Marcel leafed through the papers without really reading anything and placed the binder back on the desk. "That's the Hollywood premiere, but you're going to give me the two-minute trailer, right?"

With his face drawn, Alex offered a bogus smile. "Yeah. Let's eat first, all right?"

They polished off a couple of submarine sandwiches and washed them down with lemon-flavored Snapple. Alex finished first and wiped his mouth with a napkin. "Okay B, what order do you what to hear things?" He touched one index finger to the other as he named them. "Mazzei, rival for the dealership, or who was in Caitlyn's apartment?"

Marcel stiffened. His best friend's question was an easy one to answer. Somebody had dared to frighten his woman. He wanted to know who and why. "What do you think?"

Alex stood, fished a tie clip out his pants pocket and handed it to Marcel. "Look familiar?"

"It's Ken's." Marcel's eyes flared as he stared at the sterling silver tie clip with an onyx stone that he and Alex had designed, along with a pair of matching cufflinks, for Ken's sixtieth birthday. He snatched his head up at Alex. "Where did you find it?

"Underneath that little vanity table in the corner of Caitlyn's bedroom where she keeps her jewelry box. I almost missed it myself, so I can see how Oakland police overlooked it."

Marcel's eyes narrowed and he shouted out, "What the hell was Ken doing over there in the first place?"

Alex shrugged. "Partner, only Ken can give us the answer to that question."

Marcel slipped Ken's tie clip inside his shirt pocket and patted his hand to it. "Oh, you can be damn sure I'll get the answer from him."

Despite his fury at Ken, which he somehow managed to control, Marcel settled more comfortably in his chair with his left index finger braced to his temple. "All right. Let's open doors one and two."

Alex scooted to the edge of his chair. "One and two are connected, B."

"How?"

"Does the name Louis Hennings ring a bell?"

Marcel appeared deep in concentrate for a moment. "No. Why?"

"Hennings is the one behind the bidding war for the dealership."

"Okay, so how does Hennings connect to Mazzei?"

"Mazzei is trying to nab some high-powered position with Hennings's firm." Alex paused, then cleared his throat. "B, I got word this morning that another woman filed a complaint against him, too."

Marcel's back became rigid and he sat upright. "Did he stalk this woman, too?"

Alex nodded. "Not only that, she alleges that he raped her." He shook his head sadly. "She got cold feet and dropped the charges. Looks like our boy walks away scot-free again. He's one lucky dog."

Marcel narrowed his eyes. "Why do you say that?"

"The woman who filed the charges against Mazzei is the daughter of a prominent judge. Word on the streets is that daddy dearest wants friend under the jailhouse, but his hands are tied because he can't talk his daughter into re-filing the complaint."

No good bastard. Marcel felt his stomach plummet and swallowed back the lump in his throat because he knew in his heart the woman's allegations were true. This woman no doubt wanted Cole out her life at any cost, the same way Caitlyn had. He agreed a thousand percent with the way they felt, but if Cole wasn't stopped now, some other woman would suffer the same fate later down the road. "Do you think this woman's father believes the allegations?"

Alex nodded. "Based on everything I heard, I'm positive he does." He lifted his brow. "B, are you sure you've never heard the name Louis Hennings before?"

"No, Robinson, I haven't. Right now, the only thing I want to know is why this Hennings character has been so relentless in going after our bid."

"Apparently, Hennings hasn't always lived in New York. He's from New Orleans."

"A homeboy, huh?"

"Right. But before he moved to New York, he got convicted of a crime down there he swears he didn't commit."

Marcel shook his head. "I'm still not making the connection."

Alex swallowed hard. "B, Hennings and Alcee know each other. They went to college together at Dillard University. From what I can gather, there was never any love lost between them. Anyway, after they graduated, Hennings went to work for one dealership, and Alcee went to work for another. The owner of the dealership Hennings worked for got busted for financial fraud right about the time Alcee and Angelique moved to Oakland." Alex leaned forward. "The owner where Hennings worked lied and implicated him. They both went up in smoke. Seems like the one person who could've cleared Hennings was Alcee."

"I'm certain that if Pop knew Hennings needed him to clear his name, he would've done it."

Alex ran his hand across his face. "I'm almost certain word never got to Alcee. Anyway, Hennings did some time at a federal prison. After his release, he moved to New York."

Marcel laced his hands behind his head. "Does he still have connections in New Orleans? Friends? Family?"

Alex released a weary sigh. "Not exactly."

"Not exactly?" Marcel spread his arms out above his head. "Come on, Robinson. What's that supposed to mean?"

"He has a half brother."

"Well, who is he? Where is he?"

Alex gave Marcel a long, penetrating stare before he answered. "The brother lives here in Oakland. B, his brother is Alcee."

"Oh, shit." Marcel bolted from his chair and paced behind his desk. Suddenly, he whirled and faced Alex. "Pop has never mentioned a thing to any of us about having a brother."

"Listen, man, I about came out of my chair when word came down to me. Hennings and Alcee had the same mother, but different fathers. My sources are good, and from what they passed along to me, they never got along."

"Why not?"

"That one, I can't answer." Alex cleared his throat. "Listen, partner, there's more."

"Talk to me, Robinson!"

Alex nodded at the chair. "B, you need to sit down.

"What now?"

"Another PI has been making inquiries about Caitlyn."

Marcel's eyes flared. "Who?"

"Friend of mine. Name's Charles Perkins."

"Well, who the hell hired him?"

Alex swallowed hard. "Alcee."

Marcel stood straight up, his body shaking. "What the hell for?"

"Alcee hired Perkins to determine who Caitlyn's father was."

"Why would Pop want to know who Caitlyn's father is? He already knows who Caitlyn's mother is. She told me herself he asked her. So why in God's name would he need to know who her father is?"

Alcee shook his head. "I'm not sure."

Marcel gripped the back of his chair and stared at Alex as his eyes filled with an emotion that bordered on sheer agony. "Dear God." His voice dropped to a whisper, his mind racing a hundred miles an hour at the harsh possibility. Was his father Caitlyn's father, too? If that were so, then the woman he loved more than life itself could be his…He willed himself not to let the bile he felt rising spew out.

Marcel stared blankly at Alex. "Do you think Pop is…Caitlyn's father?"

"B, I honestly don't know."

"Robinson…" Marcel's voice became feeble. His knees buckled and he sagged to his chair.

"I know, man. I know. I would have given my right arm not to have to tell you this."

"Caitlyn could be my…"

Alex walked around the desk, squatted next to Marcel's chair, and lifted a comforting hand to his friend's shoulder. "Listen, partner, don't jump to any conclusions yet. The first thing you need to do is talk to Alcee and find out the facts."

Marcel sat alone on the front pew of the chapel and did something he didn't do often enough.

He prayed.

He had stormed out of his office and headed straight to his father's house. But once he arrived, he learned from Mama Z that Alcee wasn't home. He was a man with everything money could buy, yet, money couldn't buy the one thing he needed most at the moment: the truth.

He felt hollowness so deep inside nothing mattered to him anymore. His head fell back in frustration, and a deep rumble in his chest made its escape in the form of a wail. The only thing he could do was pray. Pray he and the woman he loved more than his own life didn't have the same bloodline. His hands shook as he ran them down his face. God, how could this be? What had he done in life to deserve that fate?

Marcel went to the altar and knelt before it, making the sign of the cross. He prayed as if his life depended on it—because it did. He wept so hard his shoulders quivered. He knew there was a God somewhere, and at that moment he needed Him to answer only one question: Was Caitlyn his sister?

Marcel prayed for strength. He prayed for guidance. But above all, he prayed for the truth.

"Why did you hire a PI to investigate Caitlyn?" Marcel slammed the door so hard the walls vibrated. As he stalked to Alcee's desk, he loosened the knot in his tie and slipped the top button of his shirt. "Pop, start talking," he demanded. When Alcee hesitated, Marcel's voice escalated. "Now, dammit. Now."

"Son…please," Alcee pleaded.

" 'Son, please' is not what I want to hear, Pop." Marcel braced his hands on the desk. "You better talk—and fast." He straightened with his eyes narrowed. "Do you have any idea how I felt when I found out you'd hired a PI to snoop into Caitlyn's background?" He threw his hands in the air. "Why?"

Alcee stood. "I did it for Ken."

"For Ken? I don't understand."

"Marcel…" Alcee's voice was a mere whisper. "Both of us had to know the truth."

"Know what?" Marcel bellowed. "Are you Caitlyn's father?"

Alcee stood and shook his head vigorously from side to side. "No, Son. I'm not her father."

Marcel had held his breath as he waited for the answer, and when he heard his father's denial, the air inside him escaped so fast, he sounded as though he were having an asthma attack.

"What makes you sure you're not?"

"I *never* had a relationship with Caitlyn's mother."

Marcel's eyes bulged at the thought that hit him right between the eyes. He'd been so consumed with the horror that Caitlyn might be his sister that he'd blocked everything and everyone from his mind. "You mean Ken…"

Alcee nodded. "Yes, Son. We both believe Caitlyn is Ken's child."

"Did you know Ken broke into Caitlyn's apartment?"

"No, I didn't know that, but I'm not the least bit surprised."

"Why?" Marcel stopped pacing and faced his father, then told him what Alex had discovered about the break-in. "That little stunt scared the shit out of her, Pop."

"I'm sure that was never Ken's intention." Alcee walked around the desk and stood in front of Marcel. He patted him on the shoulder and motioned to the sofa. Once Marcel sat, he sat next to him. "Remember the night we were in your office and Caitlyn came to meet you for dinner?"

Marcel nodded.

"The moment I set eyes on Caitlyn, I thought I was seeing a ghost from the past. Then I noticed the bracelet she had on and knew who she had to be. There was little doubt in my mind that the Della who was Caitlyn's mother was the same Della Ken had fallen in love with almost forty years ago."

"Ken popped in that night, too." Marcel gasped. "I introduced him to Caitlyn."

Alcee nodded. "Tell me about it. After you and Caitlyn headed out, Ken came down to my office white as a sheet. We talked about how much Caitlyn resembled Della. He hadn't noticed the bracelet Caitlyn had on, but I told him about it. That's when he began to suspect that Caitlyn was his child."

"B-But the bracelet?" Marcel looked confused. "What's so significant about Caitlyn's bracelet?"

Alcee smiled. "Ken gave that bracelet to the Della he fell in love with. She was a friend of your mother."

In the past few hours, so much had been thrown at him, Marcel felt as if he were on information overload. Nothing made sense at that moment. He braced his arm along the back of the couch. "Okay, start at the beginning and tell me everything."

"I've never told any of you kids…but I have a half-brother, Louis. We are only eighteen months apart. My biological father died when I was just three months old. Mama didn't have any skills and took whatever jobs she could just to keep food on the table." Alcee paused to gather his thoughts. "I'll go to my grave believing that she didn't love Louis's father, that marrying him was a means to an end." Shaking his head at the irony of it all, he added, "It was a way to make sure I didn't go without. Anyway, she died in my arms. I was fifteen, and my world turned upside down. That's when the real trouble started. Seems like overnight, nothing I did was good enough. Ben, Louis's father, never let me forget that Louis was his flesh and blood and me…I was just some other man's child he had to care for. That's when the beating started." Alcee stared at Marcel, and his eyes were filled with pain. "I took it for as long as I could."

Marcel winced at his father's words.

"The day I turned eighteen, I left and never looked back. I had a scholarship to Dillard." He stared at his hands. "I had to work like a dog at any job I could find to get through school, but I was determined to graduate."

"But when…how…did you meet Caitlyn's mother?"

"I met Della and your mother a year later. They were in the freshmen class. By that time, I was a sophomore. Della and Angelique were best friends. Louis was in their class and dated Della."

"Did *Mère* know that Louis was your brother?"

Alcee nodded. "Yes, your mother knew."

"So what happened between Della and Louis?"

"For about a year or so, things seemed to be going okay. Then one night, Della came to your mother's dorm beaten to within an inch of her life. Your mother called me, hysterical, and I went to check things out. Louis always lived on the edge, loved to flirt with danger. I confronted him, but he told me the situation was between him and Della."

"Then what happened?"

"Della knew she had to get away from him, so she dropped out that year."

"What happened after that?"

"Louis stalked her." Alcee shook his head. "Don't know if you know someone who's had to go through that, but it's not pretty."

Marcel knew all too well what that was like. His Caitlyn was living proof of the horror. "Then what?"

"Della transferred to a small college in Memphis. That's were she met Ken." Alcee shook his head in amazement. "God, she loved him. A few months later, your mother and I went to Memphis to visit them. Ken wanted to ask Della to marry him, but he didn't have the money to get her an engagement ring. Instead, he gave her a bracelet that had been his grandmother's. Della loved that bracelet more than anything. It's the bracelet Caitlyn wears."

Confused, Marcel asked, "So why didn't Ken and Della stay together?"

"A few days after we left, Louis found out where Della was. He told her if she didn't come back to him he would hurt Ken. She loved Ken with all her heart and was determined not to go back to Louis. To keep Ken safe, she packed up and left Memphis in the middle of the night."

"Do you think Ken knew Della was pregnant?"

"I'd stake my life on the fact he didn't know. Maybe Della didn't even know right then. After she left, it was like she went underground. She didn't even keep in contact with your *mère*." Alcee sighed. "The first thing Ken and I did was get a copy of Caitlyn's birth certificate, but the name of the father wasn't listed. That's probably why Ken snuck into Caitlyn's apartment. I suspect he needed to see that bracelet for himself. When he couldn't find it, he called me, and in turn, I hired the PI. Son, you have to believe me when I say that's the only reason I did what I did. Ken and I were hoping the PI could retrace history to determine if Ken really is Caitlyn's father."

Marcel leaned forward. Verifying that fact through DNA was easy enough and he planned to do just that. He shifted his thoughts away from Caitlyn's parentage for a moment. "You and Louis…why haven't you told any of us this before now?"

"Louis thought your mother and I talked Della into running away, and he hated us for it. I could live with the hate because I knew we'd done nothing wrong. But one day, he decided to take his frustrations out on Angelique."

"What did he do?"

Tears spilled over the rim of Alcee's eyes. "He tried to rape her." He brushed the tears back with his hand. "That's where I drew the line. God, I hated him for what he almost did to her. My own flesh and blood, but I hated him. I knew if I ever laid eyes on him again, I'd kill him, brother or not. From that moment on, I cut him completely out of my life."

Marcel sat motionless. Finally, he stood and opened his arms to Alcee. They shared an embrace for a long time.

"Pop, I'm sorry. I—"

"Don't apologize, Son. If I were in your shoes, I probably would have thought the same thing and would have reacted no differently." He chuckled. "I know what it's like to lose all sense of reasoning in order to protect the woman you love. Now do you understand why I didn't tell you kids about Louis?"

Marcel looked his father straight in the eyes. "Totally." He blew out a hard breath and pinched the bridge of his nose. There's something you need to know, though."

Alcee frowned. "What is it?"

"Louis is our rival for the new dealership."

"Damn."

"Did you know he did time in prison?"

Alcee stared, stunned. "No."

"Well, he did. Five years, as a matter of fact."

"Do you think Louis is seeking revenge and that's why he's been after us?"

"I don't know. But I plan to find out."

"Caitlyn has to be my child, Marcel." Standing, Ken braced his hands on the edge of his desk to steady himself. "She just has to be. She's all I have left from Della."

"From everything Pop has shared with me the last hour or so, the probability is in your favor." Marcel sat in the chair in front of Ken's desk. As soon as he left his father's home, he headed straight to BF Automotive. "Trust me, we'll find out soon enough."

Ken sat in his chair and stared with his jaw slack. "How?"

"A DNA test. I don't want to say anything to Caitlyn until we're absolutely sure you are her father. First thing in the morning, I'll make arrangements for the test to be performed."

"Does Caitlyn know any of this?"

Marcel shook his head. "Before I tell her anything, there has to be a certainty that you are her father. I'm going to send a hair sample from Caitlyn to the lab. I need the same from you."

Ken nodded.

Marcel fished out the item in his pocket and handed it to Ken. "I believe this is yours."

"B-But how?" Ken stammered, trying to collect his thoughts as he looked at his sliver and onyx tie clip. "W-Where did you find it?"

Marcel offered a sympathetic smile. "Alex found it underneath Caitlyn's vanity table."

"Marcel, I didn't take a thing, I swear. I was just trying to find the bracelet Alcee told me about. I thought if I could see it I'd know if Caitlyn's mother was my Della. The bracelet belonged to my grandmother and the night I asked Della to marry me, I gave it to her. I couldn't afford a ring."

Marcel flashed a smile. "You probably don't know this, but shortly after we met, Caitlyn asked me to help her find her father."

Ken's eyes lit up. "Really?"

Marcel nodded. "I started the ball rolling at the same time I asked Alex to investigate who was behind the bidding war for the dealership." He cleared his throat. "Ken, Louis is responsible for that ruckus."

Ken shot to his feet and angrily shouted, "That son-of-a-bitch."

Marcel knew he had to keep the focus on Caitlyn instead of re-opening a wound inflicted years ago, one that obviously still hadn't healed. "Listen, Ken, I understand your anger, but right now it won't help me to keep Caitlyn safe."

"Safe?" Ken's gaze darted wildly around his office before landing back on Marcel. "What do you mean, safe? What's going on? Did Hennings do something to Caitlyn?"

"No. It wasn't Hennings, but a man named Cole Mazzei."

"What did he do to her?"

There was no way on earth Marcel was going to reveal to Caitlyn's father of all people what Cole had done to Caitlyn. "He's a stalker. She's been on the run from him for three years."

Ken paced behind his desk and rubbed at the tension in his neck. "Whether she's my child or not, I swear, if I ever lay eyes on Mazzei, I'll kill him."

"Right now our concern should be focused solely on Caitlyn," Marcel reminded Ken.

Ken nodded. "I-I understand." Suddenly, tears formed in his eyes. "What happened to Caitlyn all those years?"

"She lived in foster care from the time she was five."

"Dear God." Ken sat down and held his head in his hands. "If I had known, I never would have let her go into foster care."

"I believe you. But everything worked out, and you're going to love her once you really get to know her." Marcel scooted to the edge of his chair and braced his elbows on his knees. "Ken, let me tell you here and now, I love Caitlyn more than life itself, and I will do anything—and I mean anything—to protect her and keep her safe. You understand me?"

Ken offered a genuine smile. "Marcel, I know that. You're an honorable man, and you and your family have always done right by me."

Marcel flashed a wide grin to the man who'd been a part of his life for as long as he could remember.

Ken stared at the wall, and after a pregnant pause, spoke. "Caitlyn's mother—Della—I fell in love with her the moment I laid eyes on her. After I got out of the service, I settled in Memphis—that's where we met. Della told me about Louis, but she never went into any great detail about what happened between them. I kinda sensed that it was too painful for her to talk about, so I didn't press the issue. The only thing that mattered was that she was with me." He stood and swallowed back a lump. "Then she left. It was like she'd disappeared from the face of the earth."

"Did you try to find her?"

Ken nodded and stuffed sweaty palms in his pockets. "When I couldn't, I figured she went back to Louis." He shook his head. "Since there was nothing left for me in Memphis, I headed back down to New Orleans. Alcee and I worked at a car dealership for about a year until Angelique graduated." He shrugged. "And well…you know the rest."

Marcel stood, walked behind Ken's desk and patted his shoulder. "Listen, you go home and get some rest. As soon as I get the results of the DNA test, I'll let you know."

CHAPTER 16

Once Marcel left BF Automotive, he went back over to Alcee's house. With everything that had gone on today, he wanted to clear his head before he headed home and faced Caitlyn. He stood alone inside his father's study at a huge picture window with both hands behind his back.

"Son, what's wrong?" Mama Z stood at the door's threshold and posed her question.

He didn't bother to turn around. "Nothing, Mama Z."

Quietly, she closed the door and walked to the front of the desk. "Don't ya lie to me, boy. Don't never see ya do what ya doing unless somethin' troubling your mind."

Marcel turned to her. "Do what?"

She chuckled. "Stand at that there window with yo hands behind your back. Ya know, ya looks just like yo daddy standing there. When his mind's troubled, he do the same thang."

He cast a half-smile. "You know me pretty well, huh?"

"I better. I raised ya from fourteen, remember?"

He walked over and placed a kiss against her left cheek. "I remember." He released a frustrated sigh. "Just got a lot on my mind, that's all."

Mama Z's eyes narrowed. "You and Caitlyn all right?"

"We're fine. It's…it's just that…"

"Just what, Son?"

"There're some things I need to tell her, and I don't know how." He plopped down on the black leather couch with both hands covering his face. "I don't know whether to tell her the truth. You see—"

"Uh-uh. Don't tell me." Mama Z held up a silencing hand. "Ya needs to tell Caitlyn. Y'all both is grown, and I don't get into grown folks' business. That child needs to hear it first."

With his arms on his knees, Marcel leaned over with his head down. "I can't lose her, Mama Z."

She grabbed both his hands and tugged until he looked at her. "Do ya love her?"

"With all my heart."

"She love ya?"

"Yes."

With a gentle smile, she declared, "Then that's all that matter. Whatever ya gots to tell her, no matter how hard ya think it is, no matter how much ya think it will hurt, y'all be protected by the love ya has for one each other."

"But—"

"No buts, child. I knows what I'm talking about here. Remember, I gots more years behind me than in front of me." Reaching up, she stroked the side of his face. "Trust is the best proof of love. If ya love her, then you gotta trust that whatever ya tell her she can accept, and ya needs to be there for her. Understand me?"

Marcel kissed the tip of her nose. "I understand." He scooted over to wrap his arms around her neck. "I can't see my way through this one, Mama Z," he whispered.

"Yes, you can, Son. Ya might not know it now, but ya got everything ya needs to get through this right in front of ya. God don't place ya in no situation and not gives ya a way out. Just needs to ask Him to show it to ya, that's all."

"I hope you're right."

"Trust me, child. I knows I'm right."

After Mama Z left, Marcel sat back on the couch and lifted up a silent prayer for guidance of how to tell Caitlyn everything that was going on.

Suddenly, a vision came into view, and without warning, he bolted upright. His plan of action flashed before him step by step. Only one problem existed: time. Telling Caitlyn he'd found her father wasn't an issue, but bringing Cole back into her life, if only for a little while, would be a challenge. But it was a gamble he'd risk if it meant Caitlyn would be rid of Cole once and for all.

Marcel walked into his bedroom and stopped dead in his tracks. Since the break-in, he'd convinced Caitlyn to stay with him until he could find out who was responsible. She walked toward him and the sight of her in a sheer white robe caused his knees to buckle. The soft light from a small lamp cast a glow around her, and the translucency of the robe enabled him to delineate every sensuous curve. Her smile darn near caused him to go into cardiac arrest. Before she could issue a greeting, he kicked the door shut. He grabbed her wrist, spun her against the door and kissed her with a possessiveness he'd never felt for any woman. She was his, and he wouldn't lose her without a fight.

He slid his mouth along the scented column of her neck. "You know I love you and I'd never hurt you, right?"

"I know that."

He tugged at the sash until the robe parted and pushed it over her shoulders where it pooled on the floor. He trailed his hands up her arms and cupped her face as his tongue played along the seam of her lips before plunging deep to taste the sweetness inside.

"Tell me." His voice was low and husky. "Tell me you trust me."

"I trust you," she said softly, wrapping her arms around his waist.

"And you love me?"

"Absolutely."

"Show me."

He watched her loosen his belt, unfasten his pants and slide them and his silk briefs down his hips. In one swift motion, he ripped her white thong away.

He wrapped both arms beneath her bottom, and lifting her off the floor, entered her hard. He held himself in check for a moment, focusing at a pinpoint on the door, trying to regain what little control was left. Love, passion and protection for the woman in his arms soared beyond boundaries, eradicating all levels of comprehension. At that moment, he was her prisoner and would gladly live a lifetime locked away as long as she was with him. This woman, his woman, had him shackled, mind, body and soul.

"Marcel…"

His gaze locked with hers. "Tell me you love me."

"I love you."

He thrust again, deeper this time, reveling in the sensations only she could bring forth. "Again."

"I love you."

"Say it again." His voice was gravelly, and he hardly recognized it as his own. He stroked her, impaled her, and savored her sighs and groans. He pumped harder with an urgency that bordered on desperation, to protect her against what lay before them. He felt the sting from her clawing at his back, but he didn't care. He held her, and she clung to him with all the strength she could muster.

"Marcel, *Je t'aime*."

That was all he needed to hear. Those words provided the catalyst to put his plan in motion.

"Baptiste, you didn't tell me you were bringing your posse along with you." Louis directed the sarcastic comment to Marcel as he strolled into his office and glanced at him, then Alcee and Alex.

Louis glared at Alcee. "It's been a long time."

Alcee offered a chilly response. "You're right. A long time."

Then Louis looked in Alex's direction. "And our other guest is…"

"Alex Robinson."

Seated behind his desk, Louis drummed his stocky fingers against the top. "Robinson, Robinson. Now why does that name ring a bell?" He snapped his fingers. "Could it be the Robinson of Robinson's Investigative Services?"

Alex's expression was stoic, his voice flat. "One and the same."

With a smirk, Louis looked at Marcel. "So, Baptiste, is this how you found out that I was your competition for the dealership?"

Marcel's expression was bland, his tone laced with wrath. "That's a moot point, Louis." The anger in his voice was controlled. "Let's get down to the business at hand."

Louis reared back in his chair, releasing a deep, cynical rumble. "So, gentlemen, exactly what is the business at hand? Concession perhaps?"

"Save the sarcasm, Hennings," Marcel warned. "We're here for two reasons. Just so you know, BF Automotive withdrew its bid for the dealership this morning."

Louis smirked. "So, Baptiste, what brought about this change of heart?"

The only evidence of the storm raging inside Marcel was a piercing gaze. "What's at stake now is far more precious."

"Come on now," Louis taunted. "I figured you to be a more astute businessman than that. You didn't get to where you are by simply walking away from a golden opportunity, right?" When he didn't receive an immediate response, he added, "Or perhaps you've taken after your old man here."

"Louis." Alcee's tone held a violent warning. "Whatever bad feelings you have for me, I can live with, but leave my son out of it."

Louis ignored Alcee's comment and looked dead at Marcel. "Maybe I don't want just one dealership. What if I want all of BF Automotive? You're willing to give that up, too?"

Leaning slightly, Marcel braced his hands on the edge of the desk, his voice so low he barely heard himself. "I'm willing to give up every penny I've got."

Louis's eyes narrowed and he exploded. "That's a crock of bullshit, Baptiste, and you know it. No man with the power and wealth you've got wakes up one day and decides to walk away from it."

Marcel flashed a flinty smile. Where Caitlyn was concerned, he'd go broke and become homeless before he'd let any harm come to her. "Try me."

With his gaze narrowed, Louis steepled his hands in front of him. "You said there were two reasons you were here. What's the second?"

Marcel took a seat. "I want you to hire Cole Mazzei."

Louis was stymied. "How do you know him?"

A wry smile turned the corner of Marcel's lips up. "I make it my business to know my enemies."

Louis cast a skeptical look. "Why?"

Marcel answered bluntly. "Three years ago, he hurt my woman. It's payback time."

"Three years is a long time for a woman not to recover from a broken heart." Louis propped his feet on his desk and laughed. "Surely your lady's not still upset with him after all this time."

"No, she's upset because the bastard has made her life a living hell," Marcel shot back.

"Baptiste," Louis uttered through a contemptuous laugh, "I've got better things to do than sit here and listen to the drama going on in your love life. Besides, it's not my concern."

Marcel's jaw tightened. "Well, guess what. You better make it your concern.

Louis's eyes flared as he planted his feet on the floor and stood. "What did you just say?"

Marcel remained seated and released a soft, dangerous smile. "You heard me. Hire him."

Louis shot an angry glance at Marcel. "And if I don't?"

Marcel slowly rose to his feet, tightened the knot in his silk tie, and answered in a condescending tone, "If you don't, before the ink dries on my check, your company will be mine."

Alcee cleared his throat. "Louis, you owe us this much."

"I owe you nothing, Alcee," Louis spat back. "If anyone owes, it's you."

Alcee moved swiftly in front of Louis. "Owe you for what?"

"For coming between me and Della, that's what." Louis's hands balled into fists.

Alcee stood mere inches from Louis's face and hissed between his teeth. "You never had Della. Perhaps if you had treated her right, things would have worked out differently."

Marcel stepped between his father and Louis. "Shut up. Both of you." He held them apart with hands against their chests and glanced between them. "At the moment, I don't give a rat's ass about something that happened so long ago neither of you probably remembers exactly right. I've got three concerns." He put his hands down and bent his fingers as he named them. "Keeping my woman safe, taking Mazzei out, and planning my future with Caitlyn." He narrowed his gaze at them both. "Do I make myself clear?"

Louis and Alcee begrudgingly nodded and retreated to opposite sides of the room.

After a short silence, Louis spoke again. "So, I guess you and Angelique are still convincing Della that I'm no good."

Louis's reference to Angelique shook Alcee to the core and a veil of sorrow covered his face. "We haven't talked to Della, Louis."

"Why not?" A questioning look drifted over Louis's face.

"Angelique and Della are dead," Alcee quietly advised.

Louis's knees buckled, and his breathing became wheezy as he sat in his chair. "W-what?"

Marcel saw the painful expression on his father's face and offered an explanation. "Louis, my mother has been dead for twenty-four years." He took the seat in front of Louis's desk again. With his arms on his knees, he leaned forward. "The woman I plan to marry is named Caitlyn Thompson. Della was her mother."

Louis was dumbfounded. He asked no one in particular, "Is Caitlyn my…"

Marcel knew what Louis was about to say before he uttered the words, but until he had absolute proof that Ken was Caitlyn's father he opted to answer the question in a different way. "Caitlyn was born two years after you and Della split."

"H-How do you know all of this?" Louis stuttered.

Marcel looked to Alcee and saw the brief nod he gave. "I hired Alex to find out who was behind this bidding war with the dealership. After Caitlyn and I met, she told me she wanted to know if her father was dead or alive. I agreed to help her."

Alex cleared his throat. "During my investigation, I discovered that I wasn't the only one checking into Caitlyn's background."

A confused frown etched across Louis's face. "I'm not following you."

Alcee's admission broke the silence in the room. "I hired a PI, Louis."

Louis narrowed his eyes. "Why?"

"I wanted to help find Caitlyn's father," Alcee admitted.

Louis's anger flared, and he leaned forward in his chair. "Oh, you could help Caitlyn, but when I needed help, you couldn't help me. Is that it?" Louis stood and paced. "I rotted away in a jail cell for five long years, all because of you, Alcee."

Marcel came to his father's defense. "Listen, Pop wasn't responsible for what happened to you, Louis."

"He may not have been responsible for what happened—" Louis broke off and tossed a blazing glare at Alcee, "but he was certainly responsible for not clearing my name."

Alcee shook his head. "Louis, I didn't know until a couple of days ago that you tried to get word to me. I swear to you on our mother's grave, I never knew. God knows, after what you tried to do to Angelique, I hated you, but I would have helped you, if I had known. Despite everything, we are family."

Looking skeptical, Louis glanced around the room at Marcel, Alcee and Alex. "How do I know this isn't some kind of setup, some kind of revenge against me?"

Marcel stood and pulled two items out of his wallet. "You look at these and tell me if this is a setup."

Louis took the photographs of Caitlyn and her mother from Marcel's outstretched hand. "My God. She looks just like Della." He walked to the window and said over his shoulder, "What is it you want me to do?"

Marcel cleared his throat. "I want you to hire Mazzei. Once he's in, I need you to make it known to him that you know Caitlyn and where she is."

Louis turned around and a frown knitted his brow. "How?"

"Place a picture of Caitlyn on your desk," Marcel suggested. "Say she's your goddaughter, niece, cousin, I

219

don't care. The only thing I want is for him to know there's a connection."

Louis shook his head. "I don't want to get involved in this."

Marcel relaxed his long frame in his chair. He needed to convince Louis to see things his way. Without violating the confidence of what his father had told him about Louis's abusiveness to Della, he opted for a different tactic. He braced his left index finger at his temple. "Hennings, let me ask you something. Have you ever known a woman who's been traumatized at the hands of a man?" His brow rose when he saw the emotions that played across Louis's face and he pressed on. "Ever known a woman who had to leave behind her dreams, her family and her friends to escape the person who should have provided her protection?"

Louis swallowed a lump in his throat. "W-What did Mazzei do to her?"

There was no way Marcel would betray Caitlyn's trust in him by revealing Cole had raped her. It was a private matter between the two of them, and the decision to reveal it to anyone was strictly Caitlyn's. "He's a stalker, and she's been on the run from him for three years."

Louis nodded. "I'll follow your instructions to the letter." He cleared his throat. "Maybe in some way this will make up for the wrong I did in the past." He extended his hand to Marcel. "Go after that dealership. You have my word that I won't interfere again. And I don't want a penny of your money."

The tension that had threaded through Marcel for the last few hours ebbed away. He shook Louis's hand to confirm the truce. "Alex will have his men close by at all times. The moment Mazzei makes a move out of New York, I want to know about it."

"You know, Marcel," Louis paused, "a man can sometimes learn from his mistakes. I'm living proof. If I could take back the things I did to Della," he looked at Alcee, "and Angelique, I would. I learned from my errors. So, when Mazzei finds her, what do you plan to do to him?"

Although Marcel's eyes were cold, deadly and angry, he smiled. In the calmest tone imaginable, and with the gentleness of a caress, he communicated the solemn vow he planned to make good on. "Ensure he doesn't make The same mistake thrice."

He quickly glanced at his watch. His next stop was to see the father of Cole's latest victim, the Honorable John Ramsey.

As Caitlyn sat in the middle of Marcel's bed, her mind drifted to the previous night. She tried to close her heart to the feeling within her that something was wrong. She knew Marcel would never hurt her, and that he loved her. Still, she couldn't help but wonder why he'd made love to her the way he did. It was as if some wild, unexplainable force had driven him to the brink. Even though he hadn't said it aloud, she knew something wasn't right, and that whatever it was involved her.

WHEN I'M WITH YOU

Right before she drifted off to sleep, Marcel had told her he had to make an unexpected business trip to New York, but promised to be home later that evening. After receiving his text message earlier in the afternoon that simply read, 'I love you,' she felt a little better and tried not to concentrate on the nagging suspicion something wasn't right. She was determined to stay up and greet him, at whatever time he made it in. She wondered if he'd tell her what was bothering him. Would he eventually be able to trust their love enough to share the secret she knew rested within his heart?

Around eleven that evening, Caitlyn stood at the bottom of the dual staircase and turned when she heard the front door open. She threw herself into Marcel's outstretched arms and held him tight and whispered against the solid wall of his chest, "I missed you." When he pressed his lips to her cheek, she felt scorched, but when he kissed her with such gentleness, she softly purred.

She lifted her head to peer into his eyes. His gaze locked with hers and told her what they shared was real. In his eyes, she saw hope for tomorrow and a determination to banish all the hurts of yesterday. The expression in his eyes was so remarkably tender, so profoundly passionate, it caused her insides to shiver. But she saw something else, too. She saw fear, something she'd never seen before. Terror rose up inside her because the happiness she felt at that moment was in jeopardy. Wrapping her arms around him even tighter, she gently rested her head against his chest, praying that whatever had caused the distress would be over soon, and that their love would see them through. She listened to the steady rhythm of his heartbeat as he caressed her shoulders.

"Missed you, too, kitten," Marcel whispered softly.

She glanced up and became concerned when she noticed the dark circles underneath his eyes. "Come on. Let's go to bed. You look like you're about to pass out."

He chuckled. "That's the best welcome home your man can get?"

The look of anxiety she'd had before transformed into a sultry gaze of desire and a sexy smile touched her lips. Caitlyn enfolded Marcel's large hand inside hers and led him up the left side of the dual staircase and into the bedroom. Then she spoke with the boldness of a woman deeply in love. "Take everything off."

He stood nude before her, and she inhaled the woodsy fragrance of his cologne, which mingled with the scent of man. She marveled at everything she'd come to expect from him: warmth, tenderness and protection. Right now she wanted more. She wanted to take a slow, all-night tour of him. She wanted to feel the texture and taste of him.

The sash on her robe gave way, and she continued until, like him, she was nude. Then she knelt before him.

"Oh, man." His voice quivered as her tongue laved its way around his navel.

Raising her head, she saw him gasp for air when her palms landed flat against his thighs.

"Marcel." She purred softly against his erection before the warmth of her mouth closed over him and loved him in the same tortured way he'd loved her in the past. Slow, rhythmic motions enabled her to take him in deeply and his hips rocked against her lips.

"Have mercy." His fingers wrapped around the soft, wavy curls at the top of her head.

Warm, loving hands replaced her mouth and stroked him with such gentleness, he moaned. Somehow, his hand found hers, and together they moved in perfect sync.

"Touch me harder," he whispered.

For Caitlyn, realization finally set in that she'd lost him moments earlier because his hands had clenched at his side, his eyes had rolled back, and his head had slumped to touch his shoulders. Pleasure washed over her, and she lowered her mouth again.

"Baby...I'm not going...to make...it..." His words were strained and he braced his palms against the wall.

Lifting her mouth, she stroked him harder and faster. "Come just for me."

Her sensual attack didn't stop until he'd convulsed in an earth-shattering climax and spilled down the valley of her breasts. She didn't bother to wipe away his essence. Instead, she reached for his hand and placed it against the creamy-pearl substance on her.

His head hung so low it almost touched his chest, and he struggled to breathe.

Her smile was followed by two simple words. "Welcome home."

LACONNIE TAYLOR-JONES

All rationale left Marcel. He looked wild, primitive, his eyes narrowed and glittering. Perhaps reasoning fled when the flashback rolled through his head of the agonizing hours when he'd feared his love for the woman standing before him was forbidden. Or maybe it took flight because she'd just loved him in the most intimate way a woman could love her man. Whatever the reason, it didn't matter and he didn't care.

Without hesitation, he scooped her off her feet, swung her across his shoulders, and carried her in a fireman's hold to the bed. He didn't bother to search the nightstand for a condom. He just spread her thighs and settled himself in between, caressing her silken folds until she hummed.

"Lift." He buried himself in her warmth and rolled his hips. His pace started out slow and gentle, but his restraint unraveled when she whispered in his ear, "No mercy."

Withdrawing, he rose to his knees, hooking his arms under her legs. He braced his hands on the mattress with her thighs wide, draped over his arms. He drove deep and his shoulders hunched from the effort, hammering and slamming into her until she shouted his name at the top of her lungs over and over and over.

Together, they were on a one-way journey to paradise. He roared and she purred. He gave and she took. She convulsed around him, and a second climax made her shudder. When a third threatened to erupt, Marcel withdrew all the way and joined them once again with a forceful thrust that touched her womb, yet accentuated his love.

"Now, baby," he growled. That final surge caused him to explode. "Let's come together...now."

CHAPTER 17

Three days after he gave the laboratory the hair samples from Caitlyn and Ken, Marcel contacted lab and told them he needed the results of the DNA test immediately. The lab technician reminded him the testing usually took seven business days. Marcel didn't even bother to argue. He simply hung up. His next calls were to several business associates who owed him favors. Within two hours, he was back on the phone to the lab. This time, he spoke to the president. He demanded the results of Caitlyn and Ken's test within twenty-four hours, and informed the lab's top man that if he didn't get them, he, along with several business investors, would head a hostile takeover. He received the results before the close of business the next day.

"Ken, I'm really glad you could join Marcel and me for dinner tonight." Caitlyn smiled as she filled his cup with coffee. "Marcel's told me a lot about you."

Marcel had asked her whether she minded if a guest joined them for dinner. Initially, she was disappointed they wouldn't spend the evening alone, but once he assured her that in a few days they'd spend as much time together as she wanted, she quickly recovered. She figured it was a good opportunity for her to demonstrate the progress she'd made with her culinary skills, especially shrimp jambalaya, one of

Marcel's favorite meals. Since family week, she'd practiced every day preparing it, and that night's meal was superb. She was the perfect hostess and enjoyed Ken's presence immensely.

"Thanks for having me." Accepting the cup, Ken offered a genuine smile and nodded to his hosts. "You and Marcel seem very happy together."

Seated next to Marcel, Caitlyn pulled her legs beneath her yoga style and beamed. "We are. It took me a while but I finally found the love of my life." She laced her fingers with Marcel's. "And he has a wonderful family I've come to love as well. So, tell me more about yourself. Do you have a family?"

Louis shook his head. "No…I'm an only child." He swallowed, then cleared his throat. "Recently, I found out I have a daughter, though."

Caitlyn nodded when he said he was an only child, but shook her head and frowned at his last statement. "I'm sorry. I don't mean to be rude, but how could you not have known you had a daughter?"

"It's a rather complicated story," Ken softly replied.

With a look of assurance, Marcel glanced over at Ken. "But it's great you've located her, and the two of you will be reuniting soon, right?"

Ken leaned and placed his cup on the table. "A little over thirty-nine years ago, I met a woman with whom I fell in love the moment I first laid eyes on her. I thought we could make a go of it, but unfortunately that didn't happen."

"I'm sorry." Caitlyn paused a moment and tried not to sound too nosy. "Did the two of you remain friends?"

Ken shifted in his chair. "No, we didn't. She left and relocated north."

Caitlyn was still baffled. "I see. And you never heard from her again?"

"No," Ken whispered.

In a gentle tone, Caitlyn asked, "So, did she know she was pregnant with your child when she left?"

Ken shook his head. "I doubt she knew when she left, but once she found out, she never told me."

A shocked expression spread across Caitlyn's face. "And she never tried to contact you once she had the baby?"

Ken released a long sigh filled with regret. "No. Now I know I should have tried harder to find her. It's a mistake that will haunt me the rest of my life. Anyway, she relocated to New Jersey."

Caitlyn nodded.

Ken stood and paced in front of the fireplace. "I would give anything to turn back the hands of time."

Caitlyn scooted to the edge of the couch. "So, you eventually did find out what happened to your daughter?"

Ken looked first at Marcel, then at Caitlyn. "I found out she had to live in foster care after her mother died."

Caitlyn suddenly felt tears settling in her eyes, and she placed her hand over her heart at Ken's statement, reflecting on her childhood. "I know what that's like. I lived most of my life in foster care as well."

Ken's gaze locked on Caitlyn's face for what seemed like an eternity. "You have to believe me, sweetheart, when I say if I had known Della was pregnant with you, I would have moved heaven and hell to find you both."

Caitlyn's hands flew to her face. "Oh my God, you're my…"

"Yes, baby, I'm your father." Ken reached in his wallet, and with trembling hands handed a black-and-white photo of Della to Caitlyn, along with a copy of the DNA results.

With her hands over her mouth, Caitlyn gasped. Tears ran down her face and she sat staring at the picture. She vaguely remembered her mother, but seeing the dated photo and realizing the striking resemblance between them sent waves of disbelief, joy and anger through her all at the same time.

Ken squatted in front of Caitlyn. "Caitlyn, you have to believe me when I tell you that I loved your mother…"

With her head hung, Caitlyn's emotions were so fragile she was scared to say anything.

"Baby, there's something else we need to tell you," Marcel uttered in a hoarse voice.

Swiping at the tears that ran down her face, she faced Marcel. "What is it?"

"Cole Mazzei is back in the picture." Marcel's heart ripped in two when he stared into Caitlyn's terror-filled eyes glassed over with tears.

"Oh, my God." Caitlyn clamped her hand tightly over her mouth. She stood and walked to the other side of the room, then whirled to face him. "That's what was wrong the other night, wasn't it?"

Marcel remained on the couch and lowered his head. "Yes."

"W-Why...why didn't you tell me before now?"

"Kitten, you have to believe me when I tell you I wanted to." Marcel stood and walked across the room. He placed his hands on her shoulders. "From the moment everything started to unravel, I wanted to tell you." He glanced back at Ken. "But I had to be sure that Ken was really your father. We wanted to tell you together and I didn't get the DNA results until yesterday."

Ken came over and stood next to Caitlyn, rallying to Marcel's defense. "Sweetheart, don't blame him. He's not at fault here." His words had come out so fast, he had to stop and catch his breath. "Marcel has gone through just as much agony as you're going through right now."

Marcel folded her in his embrace, resting her head on his chest. "Kitten, remember the night I offered to help you find your father?"

"Yes." Her voice was strangled.

"Well, I asked Alex to try and locate your father. Baby, when Alex reported his findings to me, we discovered Pop had also hired an investigator to check into your background."

Stunned, Caitlyn could only stare with wide eyes.

For the first time in his life, Marcel stumbled over his words. "Do you recall the night you came over to San Francisco to meet me for dinner?"

"Y-Yes," Caitlyn finally managed to say. "You introduced me to Alcee and Ken for the first time."

"Meeting you led to Pop hiring an investigator." Marcel explained everything in detail about the past and how their two families were involved, leaving nothing out.

231

"There's something else," he added. "I also asked Alex to investigate the bidding war for the dealership. He found out that Cole Mazzei is trying to get a position with Louis's dealership."

"Oh God…" Caitlyn wrapped her arms around her waist and stared at the wall in front of her.

"Baby," Marcel took a deep breath, "I told Louis to hire him."

"You did what?" Caitlyn jumped away from Marcel so fast her feet tangled together. "H-How could you? You promised me that you wouldn't try and find him."

Marcel rubbed at the tension in the base of his neck, "Kitten, I kept that promise. I didn't go looking for him."

"Don't play semantics with me, Marcel. I don't know what will happen if Cole ever finds me."

"Kitten, trust me, he may find you, but nothing is going to happen to you. I promise you that."

She didn't acknowledge Marcel's promise and stared at him for a long time. "How can you be so sure?"

Marcel grabbed her hand and walked them back to the couch. He sat and effortlessly lifted Caitlyn onto his lap. He told her every detail of the plan he'd come up with that would get Cole out of her life once and for all. "Kitten, this is a sure way for Cole to confess what he did to you."

Her eyes darted over at Ken who paced in front of the fireplace. "You told my father what he did?" Her voice was a cracked whisper.

"Never that." He squeezed her tight and whispered low enough so only she could hear. "That's between me and you."

Caitlyn's body trembled and she rose to her feet. "I-I need to be by myself right now."

"Trust me." Marcel watched Caitlyn grab her purse and keys. "Kitten!" He heard the front door open. He shot across the room to go after her.

"Caitlyn," he shouted again as the door slammed shut. He opened the door to go after her, but the hand on his shoulder stilled his movements.

Ken patted his shoulder. "Let her go, Marcel. We've put a lot on her today. Give her some time. I'm sure she'll come around."

Caitlyn sat on the edge of Vic's bed, her arms wrapped tightly around her waist and rocked. Two days ago, she'd landed on Vic's doorstep. Since then, she'd cried so hard and so long her eyes were beet red and almost swollen shut. She told herself not to shed another tear. The next thing she knew, she was pulling another tissue from the box as she wiped another wave streaming down the slopes of her cheeks.

After leaving Marcel's estate, she had driven through parts of Oakland she didn't know existed, until her vision blurred. Her thoughts jumbled, and she couldn't put a rational concept together if her life depended on it. The only thing of which she was confident was that she had to leave Oakland. But just the thought tore her heart in two. When she'd had to run before, she hadn't had a choice. It was either run to stay alive or end up physically abused or worse. Before she hadn't been leaving a man who meant the world to her, but she'd leave Marcel and his family in a heartbeat if it meant they would be safe from Cole.

Vic walked in with a cup of herbal tea and held it out to Caitlyn "Here. Come on now, drink this for me."

Caitlyn shook her head. "No thanks, Vic. I'm not thirsty."

Vic sighed, set the cup on the dresser and took her seat next to Caitlyn. "Sweetie, you've barely had anything to eat or drink for two days. You're going to waste away to nothing."

Caitlyn managed a weak smile through her tears. "Well, you sure know how to cheer a friend up."

Vic smiled back. "Scoot over." She wrapped her arms around Caitlyn's shoulders. "When are you going to call him?"

Caitlyn looked down at her lap. "I-I can't call him."

"Why not?"

Caitlyn dabbed at her eyes with a tissue and then softly blew her nose.

"And just what do you plan to do?"

Caitlyn shook her head and sighed. "The only thing I can do: leave and try to let Marcel get on with his life."

"What!" Vic was on her feet in an instant. "Caitlyn Renee, do you really think that man is going to let you go?"

Caitlyn sniffed in response.

"Caitlyn, Marcel loves your dirty drawers."

"I know."

"And his family loves you, too. You do know that, don't you?"

"I know." She sniffed again. "Vic, I *will not* drag Marcel and his family into this mess with Cole. It's better that I leave. If I were them, I certainly wouldn't want to be bothered with me."

Vic chuckled.

Caitlyn looked straight ahead at their reflection in the mirror atop the dresser. "What's so funny?"

"That crazy family of his loves and wants you as much as Marcel does. Hell, they've been running your center for the last two days."

Caitlyn turned and faced Vic. "Oh my God, the center. I've been so miserable the last couple of days, I totally forget about the center."

"Well, them Baptistes didn't forget. All of 'em—and I mean every single last one of them—have been over there making sure things don't go to hell in a hand basket."

Caitlyn's mouth dropped open. "Really?"

Vic nodded and sat back on the bed. "Yep. Even got me over there with them."

Caitlyn leaned over and placed her head on Vic's shoulder. "Thank you."

Vic pushed aside a strand of hair. "I need more than some thanks after having to put up with A.J.'s chauvinist behind."

Caitlyn lifted her head and smiled. "Vic…"

"Well, it's the truth."

"He likes you, you know."

Vic grabbed Caitlyn's right hand. "I don't want to talk about that Baptiste right now. I want to talk about the one you need to call."

Caitlyn shook her head. "I can't. You of all people know that I never wanted to burden anyone with my drama involving Cole." She shook her head again. "I'm not going to call."

"Well, if you love Marcel, you'll call him."

"No!"

"Caitlyn, don't let me have to hog-tie, gag and drag you to his house."

Caitlyn gave a half smile. "Vic, you wouldn't do that."

"Humph, try me."

"Vic…"

"Listen, I harbored you away once, and for damn good reasons, but if you think I'm going to let you leave Oakland and make the mistake of your life, you're crazy."

Vic scooted up the bed and leaned over toward the nightstand. Picking up the phone, she held it out to Caitlyn. "Call him."

Caitlyn shook her head, refusing to take it.

Vic rolled her eyes. "I swear to God, you are the most stubborn person I've ever loved."

Caitlyn watched as Vic walked out the bedroom mumbling something under her breath about calling in backup.

The next evening, Caitlyn and Vic sat on opposite ends of the couch watching a movie. Caitlyn looked up at the sound of the doorbell.

Vic hurriedly hopped off the couch and headed to her bedroom. "Sweetie, get that for me. About time they got here with that pizza. I'm just going to grab some cash."

Caitlyn opened the door and looked straight into a pair of piercing eyes.

"Mama Z, what—"

"I come here to find out two thangs, understand?"

"Yes, ma'am."

"Ya tired of running?"

Tears welled in Caitlyn's eyes. After family week, she'd really gotten to know Mama Z and finally confided in her how she'd been stalked and how she'd ended up in Oakland. She glanced up at the loving expression on Mama Z's face and tears slipped down her cheeks. She was so very tired of always looking over her shoulder and wondering if Cole had somehow managed to find her. "Yes, ma'am."

Mama Z nodded. "That's good. Ain't gotta run no more 'cause ya gots a man who loves ya. That boy will protect ya or die trying."

"I know, but Mama Z—"

"Hush." Caitlyn lowered her head. "Yes, ma'am."

"Ya love him?"

"Yes, ma'am."

Mama Z nodded. "That's good. I'ma leave now. Charles gonna bring me back in one hour."

Caitlyn's head jerked up and her eyes widened. "Who's Charles, Mama Z?"

Mama Z smiled. "My man. Expecting ya to be with yo man when I get back here. Understand?"

Caitlyn nodded.

"I didn't hear ya. Speak louder."

"Yes, ma'am."

"Woman needs to be with her man. Man needs to with his woman. Besides, them there babies in ya gonna needs their father."

Caitlyn's eyes flared. "Babies? What babies?"

"The one's you gots in ya right now."

"But Mama Z…I'm not pregnant."

Mama Z smiled. Without another word, she turned and hurried down the walkway toward the passenger side of her white BMW 525i held opened by a man Caitlyn assumed was Charles.

Forty-five minutes later, Caitlyn used her key and unlocked the front door at Marcel's estate. She watched as he made his way down the stairs and walked to stand in front of her.

Her chest heaved and her voice cracked. "I'm tired of running."

He reached out and folded her in his embrace, planting a kiss on the top of her head. "I know you are and I promise you won't ever have to run again. I knew you needed some time and I didn't want to rush you." He pulled back and glanced down at Max and Kenji. "They've missed you, probably as much as I have, and they told me to tell you they want you to come home."

She smiled even though she cried. "Marcel, they can't talk."

LACONNIE TAYLOR-JONES

"Yes, they can. Tell her guys." Both puppies barked on cue.

"I'm so sorry for everything, you know—this whole mess with Cole."

He gazed at her with a loving expression. "There's nothing for you to be sorry about."

"I've got a lot of baggage."

He shrugged. "And I've got a nutty family, so we're even."

"Your plan...you really think we can pull it off?"

Marcel's eyes locked with Caitlyn's. *"Vous faire me fie?"*

"Oui!" Caitlyn responded without hesitation. She trusted him with her life.

He nodded. "Good. But we need one more person to make the plan work."

With her arms still wrapped around his waist, she glanced up. "Who?"

Marcel snatched his cell phone from his waist, punched in a number and listened to two rings. "Vic, I need to call in that marker."

CHAPTER 18

"Louis." Cole Mazzei sat in front of Louis's desk and pointed to the picture of Caitlyn positioned on the edge. "Uh…the lady in this picture. Do you know her?"

Louis had hired Cole as his vice president of sales development the day after his meeting with Marcel. It was now a couple of weeks later, and Louis was flipping through the pages of a strategy proposal Cole had submitted. Louis placed it to the side and lifted his head from the pages he hadn't even bothered to read. "Yes. She's the daughter of a close family friend."

Cole nodded. "I see."

"Good job, Mazzei. I'm impressed with your proposal." Walking toward the window in his office, Louis turned his back to Cole and formed a wry smile. "If you're interested, perhaps I could introduce you to Caitlyn."

"Yeah, I'd like to meet her. Does she live in the area?"

Louis's back was still to Cole. "No. She lives in California now…Oakland. She decided to move out there to be close to one of her friends."

"Her friend. Do you know the name?"

"Let's see now." Louis paused as if he were trying to recall the name. "Oh yes, Victoria. But I believe Caitlyn calls her Vic."

With a crafty smile, Cole nodded.

Louis walked back to his desk and stood behind it. "Tell you what. Since you did such an outstanding job on this proposal, perhaps I could arrange for you to take my corporate jet out to California this weekend to meet her. I could give her a call and let her know—"

"Uh…no. This…uh…weekend is not good. Besides, you know women don't like men to just pop up on them. If you have her contact information, I'll give her a call and try to set something up." He shrugged. "Never know where things might lead."

You stupid bastard. "You're right," Louis agreed. "You never know." He picked up his Palm Pilot and touched the stylus to the screen. "Hmm. I'm not sure if this is Caitlyn's number or Vic's. He shrugged. "Shouldn't matter, though. I'm sure you'll be able to reach Caitlyn regardless." He went on to recite the telephone number to Cole.

Cole jotted the number on a piece of paper and tucked it in his shirt pocket. "Thanks." He turned and walked out the office.

Louis trembled as he picked up the phone, punched in a number and waited.

"Marcel, make things happen on your end. Mazzei took the bait."

With Caitlyn seated on his lap, Marcel sat next to Vic with the cordless phone in his hand and gave her a look of confidence. "Okay, you know what to do, right?"

Vic picked up the other phone from its base and took a deep breath. "I got it."

They were at Vic's house with Alex and A.J. Marcel had just provided last-minute instructions to Vic on what he wanted her to say.

"Cole...Vic."

Cole chuckled. "Long time, no hear. You know, I was going to call you. Ran into an acquaintance of mine recently and he said Caitlyn might be living in Oakland."

"She was the *last* time I saw her."

"Exactly what do you mean by last time?"

"I'm looking for her. Has she contacted you?"

"No, why?" He paused. "Sounds like you're mad at her."

"Ya damn skippy. I'ma kick her ass when I find her."

"What did you just say?"

"You heard me. Think Tara or Chandler might know where she is?"

"Beats me. What did she do?"

"She pulled an M&M on me."

"A what?"

"My man and my money. She screwed around with both."

"Where was she living at the last time you saw her?"

Vic looked at Marcel who had the cordless phone glued to his ear, and he nodded. She recited Caitlyn's address. "If you hear from her, call me, all right?"

"Yeah...if I hear from Caitlyn, I'll let you know."

With tears rolling down her face, Vic ended the call. Her hands shook as she placed the phone back on the base, and slumped back on the couch. "Oh, Lord, I've never been so scared in all my life."

"Good job, Vic," Alex commended.

A.J., Marcel's brother sat next to Vic and wrapped his arms around her. "Honey, I'm really proud of you."

Still seated on Marcel's lap, Caitlyn leaned over and wrapped her arms around Vic's neck and planted a kiss on her cheek. "Thank you so much, Vic."

Marcel took Vic's trembling hands in his. "Vic, I don't know if I can ever repay you for what you just did."

Vic gave him a weak smile. "You just nail Cole's ass for me, and we'll call the score even."

With his arm still around Vic, A.J. looked over at his older brother. "What now?"

Marcel's jaw twitched as he tightened his hold around Caitlyn's waist. "Wait him out."

After Vic's call, Marcel moved quickly to put his strategy in motion. Two days later, after he and Caitlyn returned from Atlanta, he called Alex, Ken, his brothers A.J. and Ray, his brother-in-law Zach, as well as his father, and told them a meeting was scheduled at six o'clock that evening at the corporate office of BF Automotive.

Marcel allowed everyone to settle inside his executive suite and then said, "We need to be ready to move into action as soon as Mazzei lands in Oakland."

"How soon do you think it'll be?" Ken nervously asked.

Marcel shook his head. "Could be as soon as this weekend."

Ray blew out a hard breath. "Listen, *mon frère*, you sure Little Bit will be able to pull this off?"

Marcel offered his youngest brother a smile of confidence. "She can and she will." He glanced across at Alex and Zach. "Is everything set up with your people?"

Zach answered first. "The Oakland Police have already coordinated everything with New York and Atlanta police. My men are ready to move as soon as Alex gives us the word."

Alex nodded. "My people are over at Caitlyn's apartment as we speak setting everything up." He looked around at the others. "There's been an undercover team guarding her for several days now."

"I don't know…" Ken frowned. "Your plan sounded great at first, but now——" He broke off and glanced at Marcel with hesitation. "It's like we're leaving my child wide open for this maniac."

Alex shook his head in disagreement. "Trust me, Ken, she's safe. As soon as Mazzei steps off that plane in Oakland, his ass is grass."

A wrinkle burrowed itself into the middle of Alcee's forehead. "How?"

"It's called jail time, Pop." Marcel leaned back in his leather chair and offered a crafty smile.

A.J. shook his head, confused. "I'm not following you here, Marcel. I thought you told us that Caitlyn never went to the police and filed charges against Mazzei?"

Marcel glanced over at A.J. "She didn't at first, but she has now. When I asked Alex to find out who was behind the bidding war for the dealership, I also asked him to run a check on Mazzei. I wanted to know everything he'd ever done. Pop always told us that everybody has something tucked deep down in a closet somewhere. Mazzei recently pulled his stalking stunt with another woman. She filed a complaint, but later withdrew it. When I went to New York, I spoke with her father. After Caitlyn agreed to our plan and spoke to the woman personally, she agreed to re-file the charges. Plus, Mazzei's got two other prior convictions for different crimes on his record. Three strikes law. He's going down."

Alcee frowned. "But it's been three years since he stalked Caitlyn. Isn't there a statue of limitations?

Marcel's eyes twinkled with victory because he'd had the best team of legal experts to thoroughly examine Georgia laws. There wasn't a statue of limitations for crimes involving sexual assault in that state. He knew Cole's previous crimes, coupled with the new charges against him, would land him in jail for a very long time. Smiling, he laced his hands behind his head and propped his feet on his desk. "Nope."

Alcee smiled. "Son, I know that look. You've crossed your t's and dotted the i's, haven't you?" You're going to prove it, aren't you?"

"Kitten's going to prove it." Marcel's voice was filled with confidence.

A.J. bunched his brows together. "But how?"

Marcel smiled. "I don't want to take any chances on Mazzei denying the charges down the road. We're going to make him confess. Trust me on this."

Ken glanced over at Marcel. "And you're absolutely positive your plan will keep this crazy bastard away from my child for good?"

Marcel nodded.

Alex walked over and patted Ken's shoulder. "Trust me, Ken. No harm will come to Caitlyn. My men are close enough to her that if Mazzei even thinks wrong they'll be on him like a fly on shit."

Raphael walked up to Alex. "Okay, so we get him in our backyard, then what? You really think he'll go after Little Bit?"

Alex chuckled. "Oh, I know he will. He's probably scared to go after the other woman because he feels her family is too well-connected. Remember, he still assumes that Caitlyn doesn't have any family to back her up. Since he knows where she is, as soon as he's off that plane, I'm betting dollars to a doughnut he'll be at her door. Ray, I know you're concerned." He turned and waved his hand around the room. "We all are. Mazzei wants revenge. This is friend's MO—preying on women he feels wouldn't put up a fight against him. The problem for him is that he struck out with Caitlyn. There's no doubt in my mind he's pissed off enough with her for outsmarting him that he'll come after her. If nothing more, he'll want to prove to her he's in control."

"We have the warrant ready for his arrest on our end," Zach supplied.

Marcel scanned the room. "Jail time is a drop in the bucket for what I really want and that's for Caitlyn to live in peace and not have to worry that Cole's slime-ball behind will come after her again."

Alcee snorted. "You're a better man than me, Son. If it had been my woman, trust me, Mazzei would have his behind beat, bayou style."

Marcel remained silent.

"Listen, Pop," Ray chimed in. "Don't even think my man's going to walk away scot-free here. Naw, naw, his ass is going to get beat down before Zach hauls him off."

Zach tossed Ray a chastening look. "Listen here, brother-in-law. It's bad enough I gotta get one criminal off the streets. Don't need to be hauling kinfolk off to jail, too."

Ray snorted. "Well, you best make sure five-o stays on him then." He pounded his fists together. "*Nobody* messes with a Baptiste woman."

Marcel chuckled. "She's not officially a Baptiste—yet."

Ray grinned. "Mere technicality, *mon frère*. Mere technicality."

A few moments later, Marcel glanced over at Alcee, A.J., and Ray who were huddled together. "I want you three to know how much I appreciate your support. It means a lot." Out of the corner of his eye, he saw the wry look Alcee exchanged with Ray and A.J. Waving his finger back and forth at them, he issued a stern warning. "Listen, you three, if anything goes down, I'll handle it.

Understand? Besides, the three of you have been known to get into a fight or two in your day."

Alcee jerked his head up at Marcel. "Don't worry about us. You just make sure you keep Caitlyn safe. She's ours, you know."

Marcel smiled. "Thanks, Pop."

Alex flipped his cell phone closed and walked over to Marcel's desk. "Everything's set on our end."

Marcel nodded and stood. With a look of total trust, he stared Alex dead in the eyes. "I'm placing my life in your hands, Robinson, because Caitlyn is my life. I'm counting on you. Whenever things go down, protect her."

After a walk to get some fresh air, Caitlyn arrived back at her apartment just before dusk. She inserted her key and turned the lock. She froze at the voice behind her.

"Well, well, well. It's been a long time, Caitlyn."

She whirled and stared straight into the eyes of the man she had feared so long. "What do you want, Cole?" Her voice was strong and steady.

Cole's dark eyes shone with anger. "You." His cynical grin made his lips curl upward. He moved in front of her and opened the door. Then grabbing her left arm, he shoved her. "Get inside."

Marcel sat on the passenger side of an unmarked van across the street from Caitlyn's apartment, along with Zach, Ken, A.J., Ray and Alcee. With headsets strapped across their ears, they listened intently, their eyes glued to the surveillance screens and their emotions reacting to the activities unfolding across the street.

On the edge of his seat with his elbows on his knees, Marcel unconsciously jiggled his legs. "If he touches her again…" What he saw flash across the screen made him cringe, and he looked over at Zach. "Did you see that?"

Zach lifted the right side of his headset. "Brother-in-law, I'm warning ya, one more word, and ya outta here."

Cole fumbled to find the light switch. "Go pack your things and hurry up. We've got to get out of here."

"*We?*"

"Yes, we." He jerked her by the right arm and yanked her next to him. "You're going with me. Understand?"

For the first time in three years, anger replaced fear. Caitlyn snatched her arm free and took two steps back. "It's not all right. You've made my life hell, and it stops right now, Cole. Right now!"

Cole narrowed his eyes. "What did you just say?"

"You heard me, you crazy son-of-a-bitch. The buck stops here."

He wrapped a fistful of her hair around his hand and yanked so hard her head bent backward. "Don't ever talk to me like that again." He released her hair and shoved her. "Now go pack."

WHEN I'M WITH YOU

"Why should I go anywhere with you, Cole?"

"Because you have nothing and nobody, that's why." Cole balled his fists, but kept them at his sides. His tone was icy as he advanced on her. "You ran, and I don't like my women running away. Now let's go."

"No." Caitlyn stared at Cole. "You raped me. It landed me in the hospital for two days, and now you want me to go with you? You must be a fool, Cole."

"I told you I never meant to do it." Cole shrugged. "Besides, you can never prove it. Your word against mine, baby."

"So, you admit you raped me?"

Cole sighed. "All right, it wasn't consensual, but sweetheart, you aren't the only one it happened to, so don't get all bent out of shape. Now go pack your things so we can go."

"What do you mean, I'm not the only one?"

Cole sighed. "You know, all of you women are just alike. Another chick back in New York claims I did the same thing. Now move it."

She remembered the instructions the police had given her. *He has to say her name.* Caitlyn shrewdly lifted her brow. "I'm sure me and…what did you say her name was again?"

"Allyson. Now hurry up and go pack!"

"Go to hell, Cole."

"That bastard," Ken roared. He was seated directly behind Zach and failed miserably in his attempt to bolt from the van because A.J. and Ray reached out and restrained him. "I'll kill him."

Zach lifted his headset from his ear again. He turned all the way in his seat and peered around at Ken. "*Sssh*. The same thing I told Marcel goes for ya, too." He turned back, readjusted the headset and scribbled on a note pad: *one count of aggravated rape.*

Cole released an eerie chuckle and glanced around at the apartment's simple furnishings before he examined Caitlyn from head to toe. "Getting awful bold here, aren't you, Caitlyn? Tell me what you gonna do, huh?" He cocked his head to the side, his arm lifted high in the air. "Run away again?" He drew back his fist to strike. "Tell me, what do you have in Oakland that makes you want to stay?"

"Alex, move in. Move in now." Zach yelled into his mouthpiece. "She's in trouble. We got what we need."

Marcel snatched his headset off and bolted from the van. The others followed swiftly. Armed police officers raced from all directions and flooded the walkway to Caitlyn's apartment. Zach led the pack with his gun drawn with Marcel a heartbeat behind.

"If you touch her, you're a dead man." Alex's 6'6" frame stood rigid in the entrance connecting Caitlyn's living room and hallway, his legs braced apart, his gun pointed at Cole's head.

Caitlyn pivoted at the sound of Alex's voice. The next thing she knew, her back was pinned against Cole and he had his right arm anchored around her throat.

Marcel burst open the front door. "I'll tell you what she's got here. She's got more money than God, a family who loves her, and a man who will kill you if you don't turn her loose." Marcel's words were smooth, yet deadly. "I'm only going to say this once, Mazzei. Turn her loose. Now!"

Oakland police officers entered with guns pointed and inched to opposite sides of the apartment. Marcel walked inside.

"Marcel…" Caitlyn cried out.

"Shut up." Cole held Caitlyn in front of him as a human shield. "Get out of here, all of you." Trickles of sweat clung to Cole's olive-toned skin.

Zach inched forward. "Turn her loose, Mazzei. You're in enough trouble as it is."

"W-What do you mean, I'm in trouble?" Cole stuttered.

Zach reached inside his coat pocket and withdrew a piece of paper. "We have a warrant for your arrest."

"For what?" Cole shouted.

Caitlyn answered as she struggled against his hold. "For rape. Now turn me loose."

"You ain't got nothing on me." Cole blinked, once, twice in disbelief as he looked up to the surveillance camera Marcel pointed to overhead. He leaned around and spoke to Caitlyn's profile. "Y-You bitch. You set me up, didn't you?"

"You heard what Marcel said, Cole." Zach took a step forward. "This is the last time any of us are going to say this again. Turn her loose."

Cole tried to reach inside the waistband of his pants.

"Don't even think about it. My trigger finger's a little twitchy over here." Alex issued the order from a crouched position. He had a double-handed grip on his Glock, which was pointed at Cole's head.

Cole spoke low against the side of Caitlyn's neck. "You better tell all of them to get the hell out of here."

Without taking his eyes off Caitlyn, Marcel issued a final order. "Robinson, if he blinks hard take him out." He motioned for Caitlyn with a nod.

Caitlyn bolted, and the sudden movement caused her to stumble. Regaining her footing, she made a mad dash straight to Marcel's arms. He crushed her against him, his embrace so tight she thought her ribs would snap.

"Marcel," she cried against his chest.

"*Sssh*. It's okay. It's over, and trust me, he'll never come near you again." The rage inside Marcel made him shake. "I just need to hold you," he whispered, burying his face against the side of her neck.

Cole stood in the middle of the room, his face red from rage and pointed at Caitlyn. "I should've beat your ass when I found you in Atlanta."

"Oh, *naw*, partner." Ray stood with his back against the wall, feet crossed at the ankles. He made a tsking sound and shook his head. You should have *never* said that."

Lunacy overruled lucidity and Marcel lunged for Cole.

"Marcel, stop it," Caitlyn shouted as she darted after Marcel and yanked the back of his shirt, pulling him away from Cole. "He's not worth it."

Marcel's balled left fist halted in midair. "Come near her again, and you wake up dead."

"Get this scum out of here and read him his rights." Zach issued the order to his officers and they led a hand-cuffed Cole toward the door.

"Yo, partner, let me holler at ya here for a minute." Ray winked when Cole halted. "Be seeing ya around."

Two days later, Caitlyn rushed through the doors at the BMW dealership in Oakland.

"Marcel Xavier Baptiste." Caitlyn stood in the middle of the empty service bay and shouted at the top of her lungs.

She knew he had to be here since the doors were unlocked. She glanced down at the text message she'd received from him about thirty minutes earlier. It read, *Hired someone to head the foundation.* Caitlyn narrowed her eyes, fuming. He had some nerve hiring someone without discussing it with her first. After all, she'd worked hard setting the darn thing up. Rushing behind the service desk, she stumbled as she tried to avoid step-ping on Max and Kenji. But just like the first time she'd almost fallen in this same spot, a strong pair of hands grabbed her at the waist. Only this time, she knew who it was.

Caitlyn straightened and indignantly asked, "Who did you hire?"

Marcel smiled. "A woman."

Her hands landed against her hips. "A woman?"

Grinning, he hitched his brow. "You jealous?"

She shrugged. "Of course not." Then she asked in a less-than-enthusiastic tone, "What's her name?"

Marcel chuckled. "I think you know her, and I believe you'll really like her. She's smart, witty…has tons of expe-rience running a foundation."

Caitlyn was seething.

"Just so you know, we'll probably be spending a great deal of time together—private time that is."

"What?" Caitlyn's voice escalated to a shout.

"Settle down, tiger. You see, after she's had some time to get to know her father better, I believe she'll be ready to head up our foundation."

"Oh, Marcel…"

"Well, are you up for the challenge?"

Caitlyn pulled her bottom lip between her teeth. "What about my center?"

"I'm positive you'll find a qualified replacement. Well?"

"Yes."

"Yes what?"

She sighed with a smile. "Yes, I'll run the foundation. Happy now?"

"No."

"No?" She stared, stunned.

"There's one more thing."

"What is it?"

Marcel reached inside his pocket and pulled out a ring and held it in front of him.

Caitlyn widened her eyes and formed a perfect "O" with her mouth as she stared at the round four-carat pink diamond in a platinum setting. It had several smaller princess-cut diamonds on each side. She reached out to retrieve it, but Marcel pulled it back.

"Uh-uh. Not so fast here. The last time I tried to give you a loaner, you rushed out the door like the building was on fire. I love you and I'm loaning you my heart for eternity. I need to be sure you're not going to rush out on me again. Let's get married tomorrow."

"I want to wait until after I testify at Cole's trial. I want us to start our lives together with that nightmare behind us."

Marcel grimace. "That might not be for a while, though. I can't wait that long."

Caitlyn frowned. "What do you mean, 'a while'?"

"Cole's recovering."

"Recovering? From what?"

He held up a defensive hand. "Now kitten, all of this is secondhand, of course, but after his bail was posted, he had a little accident."

"Bail?" Caitlyn lifted her brow. "Cole's bail was over a million dollars, Marcel." She folded her arms across her chest. "So exactly how did he come up with that kind of money and all of a sudden have this little *accident?*"

Marcel shrugged. "I heard he's coming along nicely. The last time I spoke to Judge Ramsey, he assured me that Cole is receiving excellent treatment at the prison hospital unit."

She slowly bobbed her head up and down. Although she didn't have any proof, she'd bet everything she had that Ken and Alex, along with the Baptiste men, including the one standing in front of her, were somehow involved. She smiled. "I think I'll take you up on the suggestion to spend some time getting to know my father before I take over the foundation. Thank you."

"How do you feel about finding out that Ken's your father?"

"Scared, overwhelmed, frightened. It's a big shock to learn that after all these years I have family. I'm just grateful I don't have to worry about Cole anymore."

He wrapped her in his embrace. "Cole is a closed chapter in your life. There's no need to worry about him. I'm the one who needs to be worried."

"Why?"

He chuckled. "Your father has issued a warning to me."

"What warning?"

"That I better do right by you."

"Really?"

He nodded. "Really."

257

She laughed. "And what did you say to him?"

"What any man in his right mind would say."

Caitlyn smiled. "What's that?"

"Yes, sir." He dangled the engagement ring in front of her face again. "So, will you marry me?"

"*Oui.*"

"*Merci.*" He swiped her lips with a kiss. "When?"

"The fifteenth day of December."

He frowned. "That's two months away."

Caitlyn nodded. "It's also my father's birthday.

Kenji and Max barked in unison.

Marcel smiled because he understood. With one arm still holding her to him, he held up his finger. "I need to take care of two things real quick."

Confused, she looked up at him. "What?"

He grabbed his cell phone and punched in a number. "Moni…yeah, yeah." He shook his head. "Listen…no, Moni, you can't talk to her. Just do what you do best and get the word out that she said yes." He shook his head again. "Look, Moni, she's not taking calls until noon tomorrow. Got it?"

Caitlyn laughed. "What's the second thing?"

"We need to drop these two members of the canine species who think they're people off somewhere." He looked down at Max and Kenji.

Max growled. Kenji whimpered.

"Why?"

"I don't plan to share you with them or anyone tonight."

Caitlyn looked down at the two puppies. "Guess I'll see you guys in the morning."

"Don't count on it."

EPILOGUE

Marcel suggested to Caitlyn that instead of them going back and forth between her apartment and his estate, that she move in with him until their wedding. She said no on the basis that it was against tradition. He countered and politely reminded her he wanted his *bébé* sleeping under his roof every night, and if she could find a way for that to happen without her sleeping there, he'd give her idea full consideration.

She moved in the same day.

The reality of impending fatherhood finally hit Marcel about two o'clock one morning and he snatched back the covers from Caitlyn's body and cradled a protective hand over her stomach. "God, my *bébés* are in there." An early ultrasound had revealed not one, but two strong, tiny heartbeats, just as Mama Z had predicted.

The days that followed made impending parenthood even more believable when Caitlyn would awake with morning sickness. They stumbled upon the fact that plain oatmeal helped with her bouts of nausea, and Marcel made sure he had a bowl sitting on the nightstand by the time she woke every morning.

"Marcel Xavier Baptiste. Turn her loose. Ya don had her long enough." Mama Z stood in the middle of the foyer with her hands against her hips. Mama Z, along with Aimee, Moni and Vic, had burst through the door of Marcel and Caitlyn's estate like a SWAT team arriving at the scene of a crime.

"Come on, people. We've got a wedding happening at five o'clock around here." Brie rushed around with her entire staff following in her wake. She had Caitlyn's wedding gown draped on one arm and her accessories on the other.

At the top of the staircase, Caitlyn and Marcel stood together laughing at the scene unfolding below. She lifted his chin and looked straight into his eyes. "Remember, when I'm with you…no fear."

"No doubt," he whispered.

She smiled and whispered back, "No shame. Nothing but love…"

Marcel caressed her cheek. "Nothing but love." He kissed her tenderly and patted her stomach before he descended the staircase.

He planted a kiss on his grandmother's rounded cheek, bowed, and tossed her a bad-boy grin. "She's all yours now."

Moni rubbed her belly and looked around at everyone. "What have they been doing all morning? I don't see why Caitlyn isn't downstairs already. She knew we'd be here—"

"Moni, shut up." Vic turned and tossed an annoyed look. "Go sit down somewhere. You're already a week overdue, and I don't have time to be delivering a baby…not today. She was probably doing the same thing that got you both in the condition you're in now." She looked up at

Caitlyn and issued another warning. "You need to stop playing honeymooner, Caitlyn Renee Thompson. Let's go."

Moni remained in her seat as ordered. Aimee took charge of Taylor and Tyler, Caitlyn's flower girls, while Vic raced around, giving directions to the wedding planners. It wasn't long after their arrival that the estate was transformed into a winter wonderland, and the heady aroma of over ten thousand imported white roses sweetened the air.

Marcel and Caitlyn's wedding day proceeded without a hitch of the fifteenth day of December. At five o'clock sharp, Caitlyn descended the staircase on the arm of her father, wearing a sleek, long-sleeved white gown designed by Valentino and accented by an antique diamond necklace and earrings, a wedding gift from the groom. A cluster of white rosebuds helped to fasten her lace-and-silk veil to her hair, which was beautifully arranged in a French twist. She carried a cascading bouquet of white roses that complemented the blossoms adorning her headpiece.

As she entered the living room, she spotted her foster mother, Ms. Ruby, sitting in one of the front chairs with Kenji and Max cuddled securely on her lap.

When she reached him at the front, Marcel almost reached out and kissed Caitlyn before the ceremony started.

He was handsome in a white double-breasted tailcoat. It was tailor made with a six-button front and a satin-notch lapel. He was wearing his wedding gift from his bride, a pair of sterling silver cufflinks.

On tiptoe, Caitlyn whispered in Marcel's ear. "I thought you said you were getting a sitter for Kenji and Max today."

Marcel whispered back. "I know, kitten. But aren't they family? They had to come, too."

With their fingers entwined, they heard the minister begin: "Dearly beloved, we are gathered here today…"

ABOUT THE AUTHOR

LaConnie Taylor-Jones, a native Memphian, is a health educator consultant, and holds advanced degrees in community public health and business administration. Married, she is the mother of four children and resides with her family in Antioch, California. She is an active member of the Contra Costa Alumnae Chapter of Delta Sigma Theta Sorority, Inc., the African-American Community Health Advisory Committee, Black Women Organized for Political Action and the San Francisco Area and Black Diamond chapters of Romance Writers of America.

More information on LaConnie and her upcoming novels can be found on her website www.laconnietaylor-jones.com. You can contact her by email at lovestories@comcast.net.

WHEN I'M WITH YOU

2007 Publication Schedule

January

Corporate Seduction
A.C. Arthur
ISBN-13: 978-1-58571-238-0
ISBN-10: 1-58571-238-8
$9.95

A Taste of Temptation
Reneé Alexis
ISBN-13: 978-1-58571-207-6
ISBN-10: 1-58571-207-8
$9.95

February

The Perfect Frame
Beverly Clark
ISBN-13: 978-1-58571-240-3
ISBN-10: 1-58571-240-X
$9.95

Ebony Angel
Deatri King-Bey
ISBN-13: 978-1-58571-239-7
ISBN-10: 1-58571-239-6
$9.95

March

Sweet Sensations
Gwendolyn Bolton
ISBN-13: 978-1-58571-206-9
ISBN-10: 1-58571-206-X
$9.95

Crush
Crystal Hubbard
ISBN-13: 978-1-58571-243-4
ISBN-10: 1-58571-243-4
$9.95

April

Secret Thunder
Annetta P. Lee
ISBN-13: 978-1-58571-204-5
ISBN-10: 1-58571-204-3
$9.95

Blood Seduction
J.M. Jeffries
ISBN-13: 978-1-58571-237-3
ISBN-10: 1-58571-237-X
$9.95

May

Lies Too Long
Pamela Ridley
ISBN-13: 978-1-58571-246-5
ISBN-10: 1-58571-246-9
$13.95

Two Sides to Every Story
Dyanne Davis
ISBN-13: 978-1-58571-248-9
ISBN-10: 1-58571-248-5
$9.95

June

One of These Days
Michele Sudler
ISBN-13: 978-1-58571-249-6
ISBN-10: 1-58571-249-3
$9.95

Who's That Lady?
Andrea Jackson
ISBN-13: 978-1-58571-190-1
ISBN-10: 1-58571-190-X
$9.95

2007 Publication Schedule (continued)

July

Heart of the Phoenix
A.C. Arthur
ISBN-13: 978-1-58571-242-7
ISBN-10: 1-58571-242-6
$9.95

Do Over
Celya Bowers
ISBN-13: 978-1-58571-241-0
ISBN-10: 1-58571-241-8
$9.95

It's Not Over Yet
J.J. Michael
ISBN-13: 978-1-58571-245-8
ISBN-10: 1-58571-245-0
$9.95

August

The Fires Within
Beverly Clark
ISBN-13: 978-1-58571-244-1
ISBN-10: 1-58571-244-2
$9.95

Stolen Kisses
Dominiqua Douglas
ISBN-13: 978-1-58571-247-2
ISBN-10: 1-58571-247-7
$9.95

September

Small Whispers
Annetta P. Lee
ISBN-13: 978-158571-251-9
ISBN-10: 1-58571-251-5
$6.99

Always You
Crystal Hubbard
ISBN-13: 978-158571-252-6
ISBN-10: 1-58571-252-3
$6.99

October

Not His Type
Chamein Canton
ISBN-13: 978-158571-253-3
ISBN-10: 1-58571-253-1
$6.99

Many Shades of Gray
Dyanne Davis
ISBN-13: 978-158571-254-0
ISBN-10: 1-58571-254-X
$6.99

November

When I'm With You
LaConnie Taylor-Jones
ISBN-13: 978-158571-250-2
ISBN-10: 1-58571-250-7
$6.99

The Mission
Pamela Leigh Starr
ISBN-13: 978-158571-255-7
ISBN-10: 1-58571-255-8
$6.99

December

One in A Million
Barbara Keaton
ISBN-13: 978-158571-257-1
ISBN-10: 1-58571-257-4
$6.99

The Foursome
Celya Bowers
ISBN-13: 978-158571-256-4
ISBN-10: 1-58571-256-6
$6.99

Other Genesis Press, Inc. Titles

A Dangerous Deception	J.M. Jeffries	$8.95
A Dangerous Love	J.M. Jeffries	$8.95
A Dangerous Obsession	J.M. Jeffries	$8.95
A Drummer's Beat to Mend	Kei Swanson	$9.95
A Happy Life	Charlotte Harris	$9.95
A Heart's Awakening	Veronica Parker	$9.95
A Lark on the Wing	Phyliss Hamilton	$9.95
A Love of Her Own	Cheris F. Hodges	$9.95
A Love to Cherish	Beverly Clark	$8.95
A Risk of Rain	Dar Tomlinson	$8.95
A Twist of Fate	Beverly Clark	$8.95
A Will to Love	Angie Daniels	$9.95
Acquisitions	Kimberley White	$8.95
Across	Carol Payne	$12.95
After the Vows	Leslie Esdaile	$10.95
(Summer Anthology)	T.T. Henderson	
	Jacqueline Thomas	
Again My Love	Kayla Perrin	$10.95
Against the Wind	Gwynne Forster	$8.95
All I Ask	Barbara Keaton	$8.95
Ambrosia	T.T. Henderson	$8.95
An Unfinished Love Affair	Barbara Keaton	$8.95
And Then Came You	Dorothy Elizabeth Love	$8.95
Angel's Paradise	Janice Angelique	$9.95
At Last	Lisa G. Riley	$8.95
Best of Friends	Natalie Dunbar	$8.95
Beyond the Rapture	Beverly Clark	$9.95
Blaze	Barbara Keaton	$9.95
Blood Lust	J. M. Jeffries	$9.95

Other Genesis Press, Inc. Titles (continued)

Bodyguard	Andrea Jackson	$9.95
Boss of Me	Diana Nyad	$8.95
Bound by Love	Beverly Clark	$8.95
Breeze	Robin Hampton Allen	$10.95
Broken	Dar Tomlinson	$24.95
By Design	Barbara Keaton	$8.95
Cajun Heat	Charlene Berry	$8.95
Careless Whispers	Rochelle Alers	$8.95
Cats & Other Tales	Marilyn Wagner	$8.95
Caught in a Trap	Andre Michelle	$8.95
Caught Up In the Rapture	Lisa G. Riley	$9.95
Cautious Heart	Cheris F Hodges	$8.95
Chances	Pamela Leigh Starr	$8.95
Cherish the Flame	Beverly Clark	$8.95
Class Reunion	Irma Jenkins/	
	John Brown	$12.95
Code Name: Diva	J.M. Jeffries	$9.95
Conquering Dr. Wexler's Heart	Kimberley White	$9.95
Crossing Paths, Tempting Memories	Dorothy Elizabeth Love	$9.95
Cypress Whisperings	Phyllis Hamilton	$8.95
Dark Embrace	Crystal Wilson Harris	$8.95
Dark Storm Rising	Chinelu Moore	$10.95
Daughter of the Wind	Joan Xian	$8.95
Deadly Sacrifice	Jack Kean	$22.95
Designer Passion	Dar Tomlinson	$8.95
Dreamtective	Liz Swados	$5.95
Ebony Butterfly II	Delilah Dawson	$14.95
Echoes of Yesterday	Beverly Clark	$9.95

Other Genesis Press, Inc. Titles (continued)

Eden's Garden	Elizabeth Rose	$8.95
Everlastin' Love	Gay G. Gunn	$8.95
Everlasting Moments	Dorothy Elizabeth Love	$8.95
Everything and More	Sinclair Lebeau	$8.95
Everything but Love	Natalie Dunbar	$8.95
Eve's Prescription	Edwina Martin Arnold	$8.95
Falling	Natalie Dunbar	$9.95
Fate	Pamela Leigh Starr	$8.95
Finding Isabella	A.J. Garrotto	$8.95
Forbidden Quest	Dar Tomlinson	$10.95
Forever Love	Wanda Y. Thomas	$8.95
From the Ashes	Kathleen Suzanne	$8.95
	Jeanne Sumerix	
Gentle Yearning	Rochelle Alers	$10.95
Glory of Love	Sinclair LeBeau	$10.95
Go Gentle into that Good Night	Malcom Boyd	$12.95
Goldengroove	Mary Beth Craft	$16.95
Groove, Bang, and Jive	Steve Cannon	$8.99
Hand in Glove	Andrea Jackson	$9.95
Hard to Love	Kimberley White	$9.95
Hart & Soul	Angie Daniels	$8.95
Heartbeat	Stephanie Bedwell-Grime	$8.95
Hearts Remember	M. Loui Quezada	$8.95
Hidden Memories	Robin Allen	$10.95
Higher Ground	Leah Latimer	$19.95
Hitler, the War, and the Pope	Ronald Rychiak	$26.95
How to Write a Romance	Kathryn Falk	$18.95
I Married a Reclining Chair	Lisa M. Fuhs	$8.95
Indigo After Dark Vol. I	Nia Dixon/Angelique	$10.95

Other Genesis Press, Inc. Titles (continued)

Indigo After Dark Vol. II	Dolores Bundy/ Cole Riley	$10.95
Indigo After Dark Vol. III	Montana Blue/ Coco Morena	$10.95
Indigo After Dark Vol. IV	Cassandra Colt/ Diana Richeaux	$14.95
Indigo After Dark Vol. V	Delilah Dawson	$14.95
Icie	Pamela Leigh Starr	$8.95
I'll Be Your Shelter	Giselle Carmichael	$8.95
I'll Paint a Sun	A.J. Garrotto	$9.95
Illusions	Pamela Leigh Starr	$8.95
Indiscretions	Donna Hill	$8.95
Intentional Mistakes	Michele Sudler	$9.95
Interlude	Donna Hill	$8.95
Intimate Intentions	Angie Daniels	$8.95
Jolie's Surrender	Edwina Martin-Arnold	$8.95
Kiss or Keep	Debra Phillips	$8.95
Lace	Giselle Carmichael	$9.95
Last Train to Memphis	Elsa Cook	$12.95
Lasting Valor	Ken Olsen	$24.95
Let Us Prey	Hunter Lundy	$25.95
Life Is Never As It Seems	J.J. Michael	$12.95
Lighter Shade of Brown	Vicki Andrews	$8.95
Love Always	Mildred E. Riley	$10.95
Love Doesn't Come Easy	Charlyne Dickerson	$8.95
Love Unveiled	Gloria Greene	$10.95
Love's Deception	Charlene Berry	$10.95
Love's Destiny	M. Loui Quezada	$8.95
Mae's Promise	Melody Walcott	$8.95

Other Genesis Press, Inc. Titles (continued)

Magnolia Sunset	Giselle Carmichael	$8.95
Matters of Life and Death	Lesego Malepe, Ph.D.	$15.95
Meant to Be	Jeanne Sumerix	$8.95
Midnight Clear (Anthology)	Leslie Esdaile	$10.95
	Gwynne Forster	
	Carmen Green	
	Monica Jackson	
Midnight Magic	Gwynne Forster	$8.95
Midnight Peril	Vicki Andrews	$10.95
Misconceptions	Pamela Leigh Starr	$9.95
Montgomery's Children	Richard Perry	$14.95
My Buffalo Soldier	Barbara B. K. Reeves	$8.95
Naked Soul	Gwynne Forster	$8.95
Next to Last Chance	Louisa Dixon	$24.95
No Apologies	Seressia Glass	$8.95
No Commitment Required	Seressia Glass	$8.95
No Regrets	Mildred E. Riley	$8.95
Nowhere to Run	Gay G. Gunn	$10.95
O Bed! O Breakfast!	Rob Kuehnle	$14.95
Object of His Desire	A. C. Arthur	$8.95
Office Policy	A. C. Arthur	$9.95
Once in a Blue Moon	Dorianne Cole	$9.95
One Day at a Time	Bella McFarland	$8.95
Outside Chance	Louisa Dixon	$24.95
Passion	T.T. Henderson	$10.95
Passion's Blood	Cherif Fortin	$22.95
Passion's Journey	Wanda Y. Thomas	$8.95
Past Promises	Jahmel West	$8.95
Path of Fire	T.T. Henderson	$8.95

Other Genesis Press, Inc. Titles (continued)

Path of Thorns	Annetta P. Lee	$9.95
Peace Be Still	Colette Haywood	$12.95
Picture Perfect	Reon Carter	$8.95
Playing for Keeps	Stephanie Salinas	$8.95
Pride & Joi	Gay G. Gunn	$15.95
Pride & Joi	Gay G. Gunn	$8.95
Promises to Keep	Alicia Wiggins	$8.95
Quiet Storm	Donna Hill	$10.95
Reckless Surrender	Rochelle Alers	$6.95
Red Polka Dot in a World of Plaid	Varian Johnson	$12.95
Reluctant Captive	Joyce Jackson	$8.95
Rendezvous with Fate	Jeanne Sumerix	$8.95
Revelations	Cheris F. Hodges	$8.95
Rivers of the Soul	Leslie Esdaile	$8.95
Rocky Mountain Romance	Kathleen Suzanne	$8.95
Rooms of the Heart	Donna Hill	$8.95
Rough on Rats and Tough on Cats	Chris Parker	$12.95
Secret Library Vol. 1	Nina Sheridan	$18.95
Secret Library Vol. 2	Cassandra Colt	$8.95
Shades of Brown	Denise Becker	$8.95
Shades of Desire	Monica White	$8.95
Shadows in the Moonlight	Jeanne Sumerix	$8.95
Sin	Crystal Rhodes	$8.95
So Amazing	Sinclair LeBeau	$8.95
Somebody's Someone	Sinclair LeBeau	$8.95
Someone to Love	Alicia Wiggins	$8.95
Song in the Park	Martin Brant	$15.95

Other Genesis Press, Inc. Titles (continued)

Soul Eyes	Wayne L. Wilson	$12.95
Soul to Soul	Donna Hill	$8.95
Southern Comfort	J.M. Jeffries	$8.95
Still the Storm	Sharon Robinson	$8.95
Still Waters Run Deep	Leslie Esdaile	$8.95
Stories to Excite You	Anna Forrest/Divine	$14.95
Subtle Secrets	Wanda Y. Thomas	$8.95
Suddenly You	Crystal Hubbard	$9.95
Sweet Repercussions	Kimberley White	$9.95
Sweet Tomorrows	Kimberly White	$8.95
Taken by You	Dorothy Elizabeth Love	$9.95
Tattooed Tears	T. T. Henderson	$8.95
The Color Line	Lizzette Grayson Carter	$9.95
The Color of Trouble	Dyanne Davis	$8.95
The Disappearance of Allison Jones	Kayla Perrin	$5.95
The Honey Dipper's Legacy	Pannell-Allen	$14.95
The Joker's Love Tune	Sidney Rickman	$15.95
The Little Pretender	Barbara Cartland	$10.95
The Love We Had	Natalie Dunbar	$8.95
The Man Who Could Fly	Bob & Milana Beamon	$18.95
The Missing Link	Charlyne Dickerson	$8.95
The Price of Love	Sinclair LeBeau	$8.95
The Smoking Life	Ilene Barth	$29.95
The Words of the Pitcher	Kei Swanson	$8.95
Three Wishes	Seressia Glass	$8.95
Ties That Bind	Kathleen Suzanne	$8.95
Tiger Woods	Libby Hughes	$5.95
Time is of the Essence	Angie Daniels	$9.95

Other Genesis Press, Inc. Titles (continued)

Timeless Devotion	Bella McFarland	$9.95
Tomorrow's Promise	Leslie Esdaile	$8.95
Truly Inseparable	Wanda Y. Thomas	$8.95
Unbreak My Heart	Dar Tomlinson	$8.95
Uncommon Prayer	Kenneth Swanson	$9.95
Unconditional	A.C. Arthur	$9.95
Unconditional Love	Alicia Wiggins	$8.95
Until Death Do Us Part	Susan Paul	$8.95
Vows of Passion	Bella McFarland	$9.95
Wedding Gown	Dyanne Davis	$8.95
What's Under Benjamin's Bed	Sandra Schaffer	$8.95
When Dreams Float	Dorothy Elizabeth Love	$8.95
Whispers in the Night	Dorothy Elizabeth Love	$8.95
Whispers in the Sand	LaFlorya Gauthier	$10.95
Wild Ravens	Altonya Washington	$9.95
Yesterday Is Gone	Beverly Clark	$10.95
Yesterday's Dreams, Tomorrow's Promises	Reon Laudat	$8.95
Your Precious Love	Sinclair LeBeau	$8.95

ESCAPE WITH INDIGO !!!!

Join Indigo Book Club©
It's simple, easy and secure.

Sign up and receive the new
releases
every month + Free shipping
and
20% off the cover price.

Go online to www.genesis-
press.com and click on Bookclub
or
call 1-888-INDIGO-1

Order Form

Mail to: Genesis Press, Inc.
P.O. Box 101
Columbus, MS 39703

Name _____
Address _____
City/State _____ Zip _____
Telephone _____

Ship to (if different from above)
Name _____
Address _____
City/State _____ Zip _____
Telephone _____

Credit Card Information

Credit Card # _____ ☐ Visa ☐ Mastercard

Expiration Date (mm/yy) _____ ☐ AmEx ☐ Discover

Qty.	Author	Title	Price	Total

Use this order

form, or call

1-888-INDIGO-1

Total for books _____
Shipping and handling:
  $5 first two books,
  $1 each additional book
Total S & H _____
Total amount enclosed _____

Mississippi residents add 7% sales tax

Visit www.genesis-press.com for latest releases and excerpts.

NOV 02 2007